THE
HUSBAND
HABIT

Also by Alisa Valdes-Rodriguez

Dirty Girls on Top

Haters

Make Him Look Good

Playing with Boys

The Dirty Girls Social Club

THE HUSBAND HABIT

Alisa Valdes-Rodriguez

ST. MARTIN'S PRESS ☙ NEW YORK

THE HUSBAND HABIT. Copyright © 2009 by Alisa Valdes-Rodriguez. All rights reserved. Printed in the United States of America. For information, address St. Martin's Press, 175 Fifth Avenue, New York, N.Y. 10010.

www.stmartins.com

Library of Congress Cataloging-in-Publication Data **(TK)**

ISBN-13: 978-0-312-53704-3
ISBN-10: 0-312-53704-2

First edition: July 2009

10 9 8 7 6 5 4 3 2 1

FOR

PATRICK AND ALEXANDER

ACKNOWLEDGMENTS

I would like to acknowledge SKA and FC for their help with all things military pilot, war, Middle East, and interrogator. I also wish to thank Topaz, the original Red Dog, for being a great friend.

Papa, potatoes, poultry,

prunes, and prism,

are all very good words for the lips.

—CHARLES DICKENS, *Little Dorrit*

THE
HUSBAND
HABIT

OFFAL MAN

April. Spring. Hope in the air. Vanessa Duran in the air, too. The plane's wheels touch down in darkness of night, and though our heroine is no *longer* superheroing through the blue-black sky, she has brought the Eternal Hope of Love down out of its chilly heights with her—along with her inexpensive carry-on bag and an expectant box of condoms.

Off she goes, a propitious spring to her step, into the cool and sterile quiet of the Philadelphia International Airport. She has come here for a man, but first she must locate a bathroom. Grooming issues are likely to have come up on the tedious, bumpy flight from New Mexico. Interminable, really. Interminable and cramped, with all that noise and all those constant thoughts of the plane falling to the earth, the sort of thoughts creative types are given to entertain in such moments. At any rate, rumpling is inevitable with hours spent crushed in a tiny seat against a cold oval window, with smoothing imperative at this point. Smoothing of fabric, skin, hair, disposition. Perhaps, Vanessa hopes, there will from this trip come a smoothing of her own turbulent love life.

Not tall, not short, she walks from the Jetway into a corridor that during the day must be under construction, but which now seems to be a mess of drywall and cement bags. Her heart falls a bit. She accepts the metaphor when it presents itself from the universe, her life having always somewhat echoed those details within it. Vanessa has little use for horoscopes, because life, and, in particular, her garden, offers her clues at every turn. This is no garden, she tells herself. No scent of earth and growing things here. In her excellent nose, the hard gray aroma of new cement.

She follows the more practical signs next, finds the one with the cutout figure of a woman in a skirt, meaning "women's room." She wears jeans. She wonders why bathrooms are still segregated. She wonders if there are actually women among us who wear triangular skirts of this type. She begins to think about the many false ways the world tries to make women different from men—the artificially smooth legs, the artificially pink cheeks, the artificially doe-eyed lashes. Her insides begin to rumple from this, so she suggests to herself, recalling the words of her sister, Larissa, that she stop overthinking everything and try to just *be*. And in just *being*, be *happy*. Larissa's advice—Larissa being older, wiser. Larissa, who is happy and would never fly cross-country to meet a man she'd found on the Internet. *Oooohm*. Deep, cleansing breath. Shoulders up and back, belly in, yoga back, yoga neck, long and graceful. That's better. It will all turn out just fine.

Vanessa, mind clear as a drink of water, steps into the bathroom, gets slapped in the forcibly peaceful face by the foul hand of fetidness. Like a woolly mammoth took a dump in here, and died promptly after. Metaphor, dear universe? She takes the symbolism and twists it through her body. Bad things coming. Cement. Excrement. Experiment. Disillusionment. Wonders what is meant. Wonders what she has gotten herself into. Wonders why hope, of all things, has, so far, smelled so rancid. Reminds herself to stop. *Stop*. Overthinking. Every. Little. Thing. *Jesus*. Walks across the curiously wet and rotted tiles of the bathroom floor, hopes the *eau du* dead mammoth will not stick to her shoes like toilet paper.

She stops at the long bathroom mirror over the bank of sinks, looks at her reflection. Horrified to find that the front of her rust-colored silk blouse is dotted with grease spots, as though some distracted fishwife had run into her with a fistful of offal as she fled the king. How did she get so stained? Then she remembers. It's her own fault, of course it is. Butter.

Curses to the homemade butter scone she had brought on the plane with her, a terrible choice for a woman in a silk shirt. Curses to her palate and its inability to tolerate the chalky mouth paste of airline peanuts. Curses to silk shirts, which she never wears and which she was talked into borrowing from her best friend, Hazel.

You might think that the name Hazel is enough to sway you away from any of said person's suggestions, but this particular Hazel is as pretty and fashionable as her name is not, and, well. Vanessa was in a low place, susceptible to suggestion. If it had been left up to her alone, she would have worn a T-shirt. The haircut, neither long nor short, and the dark brown dye job were also Hazel's idea, Hazel having long been opposed to Vanessa's lack of concern for the army of grays determined to colonize her head.

Vanessa is horrified, upon looking more closely at her reflection, to find that she has also sweated dark wet spots into the armpits of the silk shirt.

Offal, offal, fishwife, damp. Gah. She's like an independent movie about the ancient English countryside, on PBS.

She glances around, looking for a solution. Spies the wall-mounted hand dryer, positions her body twistingly beneath it, so that her armpits face the blast of air, like brave and slippery penguins against the Arctic wind. Only this wind is hot, which serves mostly to make her sweat *more*. Curses to nerves. Curses to humid cities. Curses to stinky bathrooms and low-hung hand dryers. Curses to love and all its variety of humiliations.

An old woman shuffles from the handicap stall to the sink in shoes like chunks of chocolate, ogles Vanessa up and down. Vanessa tries to look natural as she cooks her pits.

"Sweat," offers Vanessa, with a mock-exasperated roll of her eyes that she hopes will breed sisterhood across the generations. "Humid here in Philly!"

"Disgusting," creaks the crone.

Vanessa does not know whether this single word, spat at her with the venom of the ages, is intended for her, Vanessa, or for the concept of humidity, or for the city of brotherly love itself.

"Yes, well, have a good evening," replies Vanessa, as the hag shuffles out without washing her hands.

Pit stop complete, Vanessa sets off down the concourse in her awkward heels, something of a fake reptile skin to them. Hazel's shoes, of course. Vanessa feeling a fool. She doesn't wear heels as a rule.

No self-respecting *chef* wears heels. Not unless she wants to destroy her back, or unless, say, she is hoping to impress a strange man in a strange city—a man who, from his online dating site profile, appears to prefer overtly feminine women. Back in Albuquerque, looking at his delicious smile in the online photos, Vanessa thought she could feminize herself just a bit. A little lipstick never killed anyone, even if it does destroy the taste of whatever you drink or eat while wearing it. Gah, a million times *gah*. Ludicrous, this whole arrangement. She doesn't know how long she can keep this frilly illusion up. Maybe a week. She has no idea how other women do it. Maybe she'll adjust. Maybe she should just go home now, and tend to her garden and her dog. *No, no, no*, she tells herself. *Onward ho*. Where, she wonders, has she placed her dignity? Ah, well. She totters on.

Darrius Colfax is waiting for her in front of the crowd outside the restricted gate area from which she emerges. She gasps at the sight of him, just a little, fast inhale. He is six feet tall and has a ruggedly handsome face, dotted now with just a manly trace of stubble. His blue eyes are smallish, but sparkle with intelligence and humor beneath the serious yet playful brow. Right, she thinks. *That's* why women do it. Maybe she could keep the illusion up indefinitely.

Unlike so many less fortunate men his age, Darrius is blessed with a full head of hair, dark hair in his case, cut rather short but with enough length on top to look tousled and not at all militaristic. She mistrusts men who look like they belong in the military. It's the liberal in her, the pacifist, the child of New Mexico ex-hippies. She notices that he holds a book, which only serves to turn her on even more. It can be difficult, in a city like Albuquerque, to find single men who read for fun, and in public. Perhaps he has done it just for show, she thinks, before quickly banishing the thought from her mind. Think positively, she tells herself, and good things will come.

Darrius's well-formed mouth turns up on one side, into a grin, as if he is simultaneously pleased and amused by the sight of her, and he steps forward from the crowd, his shoulders broad but not overly so, and just a tiny hint of chest hair wisping in the V formed by his button-down shirt, beneath his excellent, masculine neck.

"Vanessa?" he mouths, from across the crowded room.

She nods, grins like a goof.

His answer is a smile, and arms held open for her. They have e-mailed for two months, sent instant messages in their downtime at work, she at the restaurant, he at his shipping-and-imports business.

She hurries to him in her ridiculous footwear, conscious of the sweat stains sprouting anew in her armpits. She hopes he doesn't notice. He takes her in his arms, and she falls against him, breathes him in as her hands feel the strength of his muscular back through the excellent fabric of the shirt. He smells good. This had worried her. It was, in fact, the only thing she really thought could, at this point, be a deal-breaker—if the man smelled bad, smell being a central sense for the professional chef. But there is no issue. If he were a wine, he would be a full-bodied, rustic red, a fine pinot noir, paired with a smoky duck breast.

In jeans, he is tanned and healthy-looking, like he's been chopping wood all afternoon or something, and when the lips part, his teeth sparkle with promise.

"Vanessa, Vanessa, Vanessa," he says in his sexy low rumble of a voice. He says her name as if he cannot believe she is finally here, kissing her neck, her chin, her lips, her cheeks. He speaks firmly, with control and conviction. A grown man. If she were a less independent woman, she would relax now. As it is, she remains ever watchful for the thing that will pop the bubble of her happiness.

He smiles at her when he's done, and again she sees a dazzling light of intelligence and humor in his eyes.

"Darrius," she whispers back, hissier than she'd like to sound, but he doesn't seem to notice. It's not easy to say "Darrius" without sounding like a snake with a lisp. And they kiss again. They stand like this, hugging and kissing like teenagers, and she notices a few among the crowd of people smiling at them in their happiness.

"Here," he says, grabbing her carry-on bag from her hands and tucking the book under his arm. She sneaks a look at the title. It is a Dickens novel, *Bleak House*. She swoons harder at this, of course. He is her soul mate, she is certain. She relaxes now, but just a little. In another incarnation, years ago, Vanessa was a Victorian-literature professor, back before she realized her true passion lay in cooking. Books are the second key to her heart, food and drink being the first. Darrius, the reading foodie. Gulp.

"How are you?" she asks him. "I forgot to ask you that."

"Aching for you now," he says, pulling her close again, with his free arm.

"So I pass the test?" she asks.

"Let's get to the hotel," he suggests. "I'll answer you there."

His black Mercedes is parked near the entrance to the parking garage, and he opens her door for her to get in before stuffing her bag in the trunk.

When he gets in, he hands her a bottle of port with a red ribbon around it. She stares in astonishment, for this is a brand and year she knows to cost upward of two thousand dollars a bottle. A port older than she is. A man with more to blow on a bottle of wine than she has in her checking account.

"Oh, Darrius," she cries, trying not to think of how this man might actually be able to finance the restaurant she has been wanting to open for years. "Thank you for this."

Darrius taps his temple, smiles that James Bond smile, and says, "The only catch is that you have to drink it with me tonight, my love."

She ignores his use of the corny phrase "my love," because it would be too devastating to begin hating him so soon.

The dark gray interior of the car is spotless, except for a photo of his two children that dangles from the rearview mirror. She has seen their photos before, in e-mail attachments. The teen boy is handsome like his father, though a bit fat, and the young girl is pretty in a mousy sort of way.

She stares at the children in the photo and wonders, again, if they will like her, because she has already stupidly allowed her mind to rush to that place where she imagines herself married to this man, stepmother to his children. In food, she is all about slow—grown slowly, cooked slowly, savored in the mouth. But in love, she has unfortunately been all about the sprint. That she is in her midthirties now does not help in the least. Tick, tick, tick. She would like children, and this man comes with them built-in.

Darrius settles in behind the wheel, leans to kiss her passionately once more before pulling out of the space. She watches as he produces a slick leather wallet, as he pays the parking attendant with crisp, clean cash. Vanessa's cash, when she has it, tends to be as rumpled and stained as her silk shirt, which she at the moment tries to conceal with arms folded across her chest. Larissa, Vanessa's sister, will be pleased to hear about how responsible and adult Darrius Colfax has turned out to be. Vanessa can hardly wait to tell her.

The lights of nighttime Philadelphia slide past outside the window, and Darrius, with a calm, loving expression on his face, takes her hand and kisses it gently. They talk, catch up, make each other laugh. Lovely. Already, Vanessa imagines moving to this city and, with Darrius's help, opening the restaurant. Lovely indeed.

Soon, Darrius turns the Mercedes into the valet area for the luxurious Rittenhouse Hotel. Vanessa looks at the bronze sculpture of the free-spirited woman sprouting up out from a fountain in the flowerbed to their left, and she takes a deep breath. Metaphor come to her here, now. Yes.

Darrius leaves the car with the valet, and together, looking every bit the normal couple in love, they begin to walk toward the revolving door of the stately old hotel.

In short order, however, they are stopped by the sound of a car horn bleating in close proximity, and the sickening crunch of metal on metal as a large white Lexus SUV comes barreling through the valet area and smashes with purpose into the back of Darrius's Mercedes, with the poor, surprised valet inside.

Vanessa gasps, which seems to be something she cannot stop doing on this trip, and watches as Darrius drops her hand (along with his jaw). The Lexus backs up, only to smash into his car again, leaving no doubt that the driver has intended this destruction.

Vanessa looks into Darrius's face, expecting him to look worried, or afraid, or stunned, any of the normal emotions (not that *she* is any great expert on normal emotions, she understands, but she can at least theorize about them). But he does not exhibit those feelings.

Rather, he looks angry, furious, really, in a way that reminds her of her own mother's tight-lipped rage—not that she is analyzing herself at this moment, though you are free to interpret her associations in any way you choose.

Darrius looks suddenly very cruel and cold. He makes direct eye contact with the obese but pretty woman behind the steering wheel of the Lexus. He seems to avoid the furious gaze of the chubby teenage boy seated next to her.

Vanessa recognizes the boy's face as being the same one that smiled at her from the rearview mirror all the way here from the airport.

In front of the hotel and on the sidewalk just beyond the sprouting statue of the liberated woman, people are screaming and shouting to one another to call the police. The valet has gotten out of the Mercedes and run to the side of the driveway with a couple of frantic glances over his shoulder at the commotion.

Smash, smash. The Lexus crashes again and again into the Mercedes.

"Darrius? What's going on?" Vanessa asks, as she watches the horrible Lexus come at the Mercedes again like an angry hornless bull.

"Oh, Jesus," says Darrius, slumping his shoulders just like the boy in the Lexus, shrinking into something less than confident. He covers his face with his hands.

Before she has time to say another word, the Lexus pulls back and rams the Mercedes yet again, jabbing it into the statue in front of the hotel and knocking the free-spirited woman off her feet. Of course. Metaphor, metaphor.

Vanessa sees her, the crazed woman behind the wheel, a guinea pig of a woman of middle age, with her hair cut into a short, un-layered blond bob that sits mushroomlike on top of her head and does little to conceal her jowls. She wears what appears to be a zippered sweatshirt in a light color over a T-shirt in a dark color. The guinea pig glares at Vanessa, shouts at her through the closed windows of her vehicle, her tiny little gerbil hands flying, furious, all over the place.

Vanessa looks at the pimply boy, and he smiles as if this were fun somehow. He flips Vanessa off. Snarls.

"What is this?" she asks Darrius again. "Do you *know* these people?"

He sighs, looking older now than he did at the airport, and weary. He holds up a hand to indicate that he wants Vanessa to stay where she is. He strides toward the Lexus, which has come to a halt. Darrius moves purposefully, and Vanessa notices, now, that he wears his pants much too high on the waist. Oh, yes, she saw it earlier, but overlooked it. Now? Impossible to ignore.

The woman and the boy get out of the SUV to confront him. She is short, plump as a hen, angry as a badger. Yelling begins. Crying. A sickening mess of emotion, spilled out all over the front of the hotel. Security guards seem too scared of them to do anything other than watch, waiting, Vanessa presumes, for the police to arrive.

After a few minutes of gesticulations and shoving, yelling and crying, Darrius returns to Vanessa on the sidewalk, red-faced and fuming with those high, high pants. The boy and the woman barrel toward them.

"Get back!" he tells them.

But the guinea pig and the boy barrel on, directly toward Vanessa. The woman is rolling up her sleeves now, ready to—to what? To fight Vanessa? Dear God. Images of Hester Prynne and a village hurling stones come to Vanessa's mind, and then the disquieting image of Vanessa's own body rotting in the long weedy grass of a Pennsylvania roadside.

"Opal," says Darrius to the crazed woman. "Pipe *down*, Opal."

Opal? Vanessa remembers this as the name of Darrius's ex. A horrible name. Of course. Like offal. Stains. Grease stains. Fishwife.

She turns to ask him, "Your ex-wife? How did she know we were here?"

"She follows me," says Darrius with great weariness. "Spies on me."

"*Ex*-wife?" shouts the woman, shaking her head and growing pinker and greasier in the face, smiling her big top teeth like a lunatic bunny rabbit. "What do you mean *ex*-wife? No, no, no, honey. I'm not an *ex*-wife. Is *that* what he told you?" She cackles out a horrific laugh.

Darrius looks at Vanessa, anger all over his puffy face, as if this were somehow her own fault now. "Vanessa," he says, suddenly patronizing. As though this were a simple matter of the women being unreasonable.

Vanessa looks at the woman and the boy, both of them smiling strangely.

"You think you're the only one, right?" cries Opal. "What a stupid little girl you are. You're not his only one. He has one of you in California, and one of you in upstate New York. He has a girl in every port, this one. You are disposable. But he has only one *wife*. Only one *true love*."

Vanessa clutches the bottle of port, reprises the cliché in her mind: *A port in every girl?*

"Shut up, Opal," Darrius tells her. "Go home. Quit causing a scene, you freakin' psychopath."

Opal raises her pudgy hand to punch Vanessa. Winds up and around like a tubby cartoon baseball pitcher. Vanessa sees the flash of gold, and the diamond. Wedding ring.

Vanessa turns, and she runs into the building. She whirls through the revolving door, Opal's voice drowned out for a moment. Darrius and his family chase after her, like some crazed group on a hunting trip, Vanessa in the starring role as the unfortunate deer.

They all make it into the lobby as Vanessa sprints as best she can in the blasted, uncharacteristic heels, beneath the chandelier toward the front desk. Darrius catches up to Vanessa just as three security guards arrive to restrain Opal. The boy screams at them to leave his mom alone. His *mom*. Dear God, Vanessa thinks. Someone might actually have a worse mother than she herself.

Silver linings.

"I'm the only one he loves!" Opal crows after Vanessa, startling everyone in the lobby and even seeming to shock the drunks at the hotel bar.

An unnatural silence falls over the cavernous room.

"Vanessa," Darrius says, trying to hold Vanessa by the elbow. Ignoring his screeching wife. "Stop. Let me explain this."

"Let me guess. You're not divorced. You're not normal. You're not the man of my dreams." She shrugs as though this were nothing, sarcasm always having been her best defense of choice.

He smiles pitifully. "When I met you, I thought I would be, but things got better and then worse, and here we are. I'm sorry. It doesn't change how I feel about you. She doesn't mind, really."

Vanessa turns toward Opal, and sees her staring at them through the glass of the doors as the guards haul her outside to a police car. The boy gets out of the grip of one of the guards, and pushes fast through the door.

"I *hate* you!" cries the boy to Vanessa, as the guards pursue him again, grab him, and start to pull him back outside. "How can you try to break up a happy family? You have no morals!"

Everyone stares at Vanessa now. She looks around the room, at the astonished, mildly frightened faces. It is so quiet in here, like a tomb.

"I can explain," Darrius says quietly.

She wiggles out of Darrius's grip. Disgusted that this man's son is being handled brutally by police, and he is here, still trying to seduce her.

"Get away from me," she says. She turns away from Darrius, and walks toward the counter as calmly as she can with everyone's eyes still on her.

To her great relief, Darrius does not try to follow her this time.

Vanessa approaches the registration counter, where the tidy young female workers, with their tight ponytails, navy blazers, and hoop earrings, try to look like they haven't seen the entire incident.

"I didn't know," Vanessa tells them with a fragile smile she hopes conveys her innocence. "This is the first I heard he was still married. I met him online. He said he was single. Last time I do that."

One of the women nods and looks at Vanessa with pity. "Room for one, then?" she asks.

"Yes, please. The shameless homewrecker special, if you've got it."

The woman cracks a grin.

"How many nights?"

"Just one night. I'll get a flight home in the morning."

"Smoking or nonsmoking?"

"Nonsmoking," says Vanessa, admiring the young woman's professionalism.

She smiles, takes Vanessa's card, and asks her for her name. It takes Vanessa a moment to remember it. She is not Vanessa Colfax, wife of a filthy rich, literate, wine-loving businessman from Philadelphia.

"Vanessa Duran," she says with a sigh.

"Can I have some identification please?" the woman asks.

Vanessa hands over her driver's license. The woman hands it back, after looking at Vanessa closely, to compare her currently disappointed visage to that of the hopeful, fresh-faced driver in the photo.

"Thank you," she says.

As Vanessa signs the paperwork, the woman programs her key card and mutters, without looking up at Vanessa, "Men totally suck." When she finally looks up, she seems sympathetic.

Vanessa locks eyes with her and smiles gratefully.

"You wouldn't believe how many married men come in here with women who aren't their wives," she tells Vanessa with a roll of her eyes.

"Oh, I have an idea," says Vanessa.

And she does.

As Vanessa heads toward the bank of elevators, she laughs out loud (through her humiliated tears) because this is not the first time she's fallen for a married man who forgot to tell her about his wife.

It is the second.

You, she thinks to herself as she steps into the blissful privacy of the elevator, *are developing* quite *the husband habit*.

She is better off, she thinks, with the garden and the dog.

A SURPRISE BOUNTY

OF ARUGULA

Early August, a Monday. Darrius? Forgotten in these months, pushed down into the well of unspeakable things, vanquished. Vanessa has moved on, and here she is, meditative and in the garden, where she feels she belongs. Where she is peaceful. The silk shirt forgotten, and the heels returned to Hazel. Normalcy reclaimed.

The lush, green North Valley of Albuquerque, midafternoon. Above, hot, clear white sun. The sweet scent of Rio Grande cottonwood fluff in the air, the river of the same name two blocks away, brown and muddy but moving fast from rain up north. And here, a pale pink adobe cottage that squats and sags beneath the gnarled old arms of a towering stand of cottonwood trees.

Albuquerque, with a metro area population of about 830,000,

is a sunny, spacious high desert city of striking contrasts. At 5,280 feet above sea level and occupying 181 square miles—a space roughly the same size as Mumbai, India—Albuquerque is a massive grid of mostly one-story adobe buildings. Bordered in the east by the massive purple flat-topped Sandia mountain range and in the west by ancient volcanoes and mesa scrubland, the city was founded by Spanish explorers in the seventeenth century. It is bisected east to west by Route 66, and north to south by the Rio Grande River, and can be lush and green or dry and riddled with cactus, breathtakingly beautiful or sickeningly hideous, depending upon where you go. From any point in the city you can usually see many others, thanks to the grid sloping through the valley at about a five-degree angle. Having grown up with this incredible sense of space and freedom, being able to see for miles and miles in every direction at all times, Vanessa has felt claustrophobic anywhere else.

Vanessa's home is found in the verdant green slash known as the North Valley, close to the river, with a view of the majestic purple Sandias to the east. Like most neighborhoods in the city, the North Valley is economically and ethnically diverse. It is considered one of the most affluent parts of town, but that doesn't mean it's exclusive. There are shacks among the mansions. Many of Vanessa's neighbors with money make it by working for Sandia National Laboratories, one of the nation's top weapons research institutions and a main economic motor for the city. Others work for the University of New Mexico, or in the arts or, more recently, in the exploding film industry. Thanks to tax incentives, the entire state of

New Mexico has, in recent years, come to be known as Hollywood Southwest, and it is not unusual to find film crews set up in the North Valley, with its vineyards and wineries easily filling in for Tuscany.

On days like this, Albuquerque's new glitz and glamour are off-set by those ancient and unchanging things about it. Today, it is obviously the city that time forgot, which is good when you are talking about things like rivers and mountains and gardens and maybe not so good when you're talking about things like roach-clip earrings and man-perms (done for irony only in the Nob Hill district, deadly serious everywhere else). Albuquerque. More than anything, Vanessa finds Albuquerque to be a tolerant, accepting city—probably too much so when you consider that no trend or music hit ever dies here, no matter how antiquated, annoying, or deserving it is of death. Disco? Sure. We got that, with a side of Barry Manilow and Pat Benatar. Mullet haircuts for women? Abso-diddly-lutely. You say you're a member of a has-been hair-metal band with a taste for spandex for men (mandex?)? Dude, we got your number, and all your fans, waitin' at the casino on the edge of town. Such a strange city, one part Hollywood chic and Austin-like hip but two parts small children with rattail haircuts riding ATVs in the Wal-Mart parking lot. Ah, well. You take the good with the bad, bend like bamboo (or like a peacock feather on a roach clip, depending upon your style or lack thereof). Above all else, it is Vanessa's home, the largest city in the state—a state where her mother's family has lived for seven generations, and where she hopes to make her mark with haute cuisine in a world of stubbornly hot (as in chile, not trendy) eats.

The house is tucked off a forgotten dirt road at the front of half a forgotten acre of land, the walls baked in the hot, hard breeze that, when it comes, silences the cicadas and worries the red dog on the porch, enough that she lifts one eyelid, but not enough to raise her whole head. A dark gray storm plumps itself like a contented hare along the northern edge of the sky, somewhere over Santa Fe. No threat, not yet, but soon. Rain comes like a miracle every afternoon this time of year. All things made clean.

Inside, Vanessa's home is cluttered and clever with books and papers, colorful with paintings, some hung, some leaned, and some stacked, just 1,100 square feet of house, more than half of it dedicated to a spotless country sprawl of kitchen made when she knocked first one wall, then two down with the urgency of creation. Top-notch appliances, the most recent addition a sixty-inch restaurant-quality range—six burners up top, with two full-size convection ovens below. She has also splurged on the best cookware money can buy. Old paint peels upon the walls, ancient cabinets creak at the hinges. She has her priorities. She gets only what she needs.

There is a small living room with no television, a small bedroom with towers of Victorian novels (including *Mansfield Park* by Jane Austen, *Jane Eyre* by Charlotte Brontë, *Middlemarch* by George Eliot, and *Tess of the d'Urbervilles* by Thomas Hardy) on the nightstand, a bathroom with a claw-foot tub, homemade bath oils, and a shy daddy longlegs spider she has named Julia, for the most famous woman chef of all time. She did not buy this place for the architecture, or the insects. She bought it for the wild, isolated expanse of land, and the promise of all that could be coaxed from it. She did it, as she has done most things, with a dream of flavor, texture, scent, and sensation.

Tumbling behind the house, and oozing around its sides, a garden. It draws life to it. Blue orchard bees, roadrunners, fussy wrens, rabbits, butterflies, prairie dogs, hummingbirds suspended at the openings of tubular flowers, and, at night, there are coyotes. All the neighborhood cats flop on the flagstones here, sunning themselves in the open spaces between the spill of rosemary and chamomile ground cover, watching for birds at the burbling fountain and well-stocked feeders. Vanessa's garden. No. There is something wrong in calling it merely that, a garden. It is her sanctuary, this tangle of greens, explosions of purples, yellows, reds, silvery chimes in a dozen timbres, flags and pinwheels, rioting clumps of herbs sprinkled about, compost marinating in barrels here and there, winding paths and no straight lines, food tossed with flowers, benches and bird feeders, lavender folded gently with lilac, a canopy of fruit above, with four kinds of apples stirred into the apricots, cherries, pears, cornstalks rattling sentry at the painted old turquoise gate, grapevines drizzled over the mud walls that were once the color of the house and are now ripe with leaf and berry.

Today, as most days, in this symphonic chaos Vanessa is the

conductor, thoughtfully strolling the garden in her cargo shorts and simple tank top, the rubber gardening clogs abandoned on the path because it is the feel of earth—wet, dry, damp, whatever, between the toes—that she has come for.

She kneels at the pumpkin patch, frowning, and considers trimming back the arrogant vines that have snaked out among the mint in the night. Nothing grows quite so fast, or threatens to overtake so much, with so little thought to others, as pumpkins. Well, maybe gray hair. Or tract-home subdivisions on the West Side. But that's about it. Any other day, she might have pruned the thick, prickly vine, and protected the more delicate plants. But today she is planning dinner for Bryan, and she has decided that she loves him enough to tell him so, which changes everything. She is in love. Renewed. Hopeful in the late summer. You don't just give up because a woman tries to kill you in Philadelphia, after all.

Vanessa moves on, the pumpkin vine spared another day. Her chestnut hair, back to its normal self, cascades past her strong shoulders, glints in the sun, loose spirals, a few touches of gray that do not make her look older somehow. She wears no makeup. If she were to paint a self-portrait, it would be of hands, covered in flour; or expertly trimming the backbone from a small, tender *poussin*; or in repose, wrapped cozily about a clay mug of dark Turkish coffee and turning the pages of a beloved novel. They are strong hands, with short nails, capable hands that do not fear dirt, because Vanessa knows that from dirt comes life, and from life comes flavor. Curses to trying to seem clean. She is what she is. And, thankfully, Bryan seems to like her this way. He is not rich, no, not fancy. He is a food artist. Just as she is. She's surprised she had not noticed him there, the friend of her friends, interested in her all these months, and she never took the cues until now, until she was ready.

She checks this and that, and then, as she rounds the corner toward the area where the rhubarb has come and gone, her hazel eyes open wide at the sight of a bright green burst of arugula pushing up out of the earth, all confidence and peppery aggression. She had forgotten it would be here. But of course it's here, she thinks. Arugula reseeds itself, unique among herbs and lettuces, and it will reappear, just like rhubarb, returning year after year. She kneels to get a closer look at it. Healthy enough. Only a few spots of bug nibble. She breathes deeply, enchanted by the incomparable taste of new earth on the back of the tongue as she inhales.

She can't believe she'd forgotten the arugula.

She knows where each thing was planted, how to find it, when it will be ready, ripe. She knows it all so well she could come here in the dark of night, if you had need for fresh basil, a ripe heirloom tomato, or, even, an eggplant—except she has never known what to do with eggplant. It is the only food that has never cried out for her hands to change it into something magical. She has found a place for many other things, more complicated things, things that might make another person's face crinkle in revulsion: veal tongue, sheep testicles, brains, raw quail eggs. But it is eggplant, part Styrofoam, part masking tape, eggplant that confounds, eggplant, the one thing she has never conquered. She grows it here, in several varieties, because she is optimistic by nature and believes everyone and everything should get a second chance, or a third.

Vanessa takes the arugula expertly in her hand, and breaks off a corner of leaf to taste it. Bitter, pungent, spicy, peppery. It might go well with the salad she had planned for Bryan's meal this evening. No, wait. Pesto. She will make a fresh arugula pesto, and change the menu altogether. You have to be prepared to change, if need be, to be flexible if something delicious and unexpected comes along. Unless it is an ice cream truck, which, in this city, is usually just a money-laundering front for drug lords. Some surprises you ignore. But not arugula.

She takes her shears and cuts the arugula leaves from the ground, drops them into the wicker basket at her feet, along with the sage and sorrel. She will not yank it by the root, so it may continue to grow. Arugula, she thinks, with a self-satisfied smile. Now that was a pleasant surprise.

Vanessa returns to the house, her menu for the evening having shifted with the discovery of the unexpected. She sets the basket on the blond granite of the kitchen island, and searches the pantry for fine Italian bread flour, and pine nuts. She's in luck. Plenty of flour, enough pine nuts, though she'll need more soon. So expensive. Next, eggs. She checks the supply in the refrigerator, picked from the hen coop at the very back of the garden that morning. Enough eggs. Pecorino cheese. A beautiful Italian olive oil. She's in business.

Out come the glass mixing bowls, the heavy marble rolling pin,

the mortar and pestle. Where practical, Vanessa avoids food pro-
cessors in favor of slower methods, because it is the connection of
energies, hers and the food's, that makes a dish sing. The under-
cabinet iPod comes on, and she presses past the varied mixes to
find something that will put her in the mood to roll homemade
pasta, working the dough thinner than a dime, backbreaking labor.
An Italian pop singer. That will do it. She will play the same song,
over and over, as she mixes, work herself into the trance where
inspiration lies. Pasta is not easy to make, yet she makes it easily
and often. There is no better match for homegrown-arugula pesto
than homemade pasta. She captures her hair in an elastic band,
pushes the window over the sink open to the breeze, cleans the
counter well, washes her hands like a surgeon, to the elbow, and
sets to work.

Once the pasta is drying on racks, and the pesto ingredients
arranged on their corner of the counter, she begins to think about
the rest of the meal. She has a couple of pieces of excellent halibut
that her friend at the fish shop called her about this morning. But
fish feels like too much for this night. Something light, Bryan told
her. A tomato salad with balsamic vinegar, the pasta, the pesto, a
hunk of crusty bread, excellent butter, and she is quite sure she's
come up with the perfect meal for a summer evening.

He is a chef, just like she is, though his specialty is pastry and
hers is, as they say in the business, new American cuisine, or California cuisine. Still, she doesn't want to overwhelm, or seem as if

she has tried too hard. The wine? Classic sauvignon blanc. They've got some interesting ones coming out of New Zealand lately. She has a bottle in the wine pantry, and puts it in the fridge to chill.

Next, it is time to shower. And dress. Nothing fancy, because Bryan is the male version of Vanessa, all about what's real and good. She will look the same to him in the morning as she did at dinner, no smoke, no mirrors, no silk, no heels. Jeans, a tank that she knows shows off her collarbones, a silver necklace. Sandals. She puts mousse in her hair, scrunches it, moisturizes her face with something unscented from the natural-foods store, and she is ready. Perfume and cooking do not go together.

Back to the kitchen, fifteen minutes until Bryan arrives. Bryan, with his mocha brown eyes and nutmeg hair, quirky sense of humor, always able to make her laugh. Bryan so real, where Darrius was so phony. Bryan, the perfect match for her. She'll find money for her own restaurant on her own, someday. Maybe, she thinks, she and Bryan can go into business together.

She sets the salted water to boil with a few drops of the olive oil, and will wait until he gets here to throw the pasta into the pot. Cuts tomatoes, red, orange, and yellow, mixes the dressing with a dark balsamic so excellent and mellow you could eat it over ice cream, sets the table. Checks the wine. Lights the candles. Then snuffs them out again. Trying too hard. Picks different music, something Bryan will like. A soulful adult alternative singer, male, from England. That's Bryan's cup of tea. Strummed acoustic guitar, easy drums, Stevie Wonder channeled via Essex.

Seven o'clock comes, but Bryan does not. He does not come at eight, or eight thirty, either. She has turned off the singer just as he's begun to sing of heartbreak, and called Bryan's cell phone to make sure nothing happened to him on his drive to Albuquerque from Santa Fe, what with the storm and all. He does not answer. By nine, the rain has come to her house, and she is no longer in the mood for music. The food is cold, and she feels as though the very trees in the yard weep for her.

Without eating, and without clearing the table, she goes to her bedroom and phones her sister. Larissa is four years older than she is, and though they did not play together much as children, they are very close now. Vanessa tells her that Bryan did not show up. Larissa, always one for good advice, says, "Wait a little more, and if you don't hear anything, forget about him."

"But what if he's hurt?" Vanessa asks, but Larissa, who does not share her sister's mistrust of instant news, like on television and online (though the morning paper is fine, and *Harper's* even better), is watching the news, and has Internet, and quickly confirms that there have been no fatal accidents on Interstate 25 this evening.

"You don't think he's . . . like the others?" Vanessa begins, but she cannot finish the thought.

It is much too difficult to imagine that she is quite *that* unlucky.

Larissa interrupts her anyway, changes the subject because Larissa is the sort who believes that what you put into the universe, what you give words to, is what will come back to you. Soon they say their good-byes, with arrangements made for Larissa to come by for lunch the next day. Words will be spoken better after a rest. So says Larissa, and in matters of logic and romance, Larissa, happily married, with kids, is usually right.

Vanessa shrugs into her nightgown, the roomy white cotton one, climbs up into her high, soft bed, and tries to read Charlotte Brontë again. Tries not to let this bother her. People make mistakes. Perhaps Bryan simply forgot. Perhaps he did not, and he is at a strip club. You just don't really ever know, and that's the part that mucks it all up, isn't it?

The rain hammers the flat roof, blows up against the window screens, dripping a bit onto the swollen wooden sills and nearby pale pine floor, a price she is willing to pay for the intoxicatingly fresh air. She can hear the water dumping to the gravel from the downspout just outside, and imagines the nearby marigolds and zinnia giggling for joy at the flood of minerals from the sky. Deep breath, so good.

People think the scent of rain is ozone, or water, but Vanessa, deeply interested in the science of scent and taste, knows that it is actually, ironically, sweet-smelling filamentous bacteria, actinomycetes, that cause the smell of desert rain when they get stirred into the air by the falling drops of water. So many delicious, rotten things, she thinks. Actinomycetes, mushrooms, cheese, wine.

Men.

Red Dog sighs beneath the bed, her favorite place to sleep when it rains, her special little cave.

At eleven thirty, he calls.

Vanessa has been reading the same passage of *Jane Eyre* again and again, the galaxy of letters spinning meaningless against her eyes as she wonders if she should phone the police to report him missing. He tells her he's sorry, explains that he's been at the hospital.

"Are you okay?" She sits up with worry, can hear that he has been crying.

"I'm fine," he sniffles, more like a man with a cold than a man who is crying.

"Do you need me to come? What hospital is it?"

"No! Don't come!" he shouts. Then, he repeats it, softly. "No. Don't come. Please."

Silence for a moment.

Then, he breaks down, and tells her it is not him in the hospital. He's not ill. He's not the one in the coma from overdosing on prescription painkillers.

"It's my . . . wife," he states. "She's found out about us, and she's tried to off herself. I'm the worst man alive. Poor little Oliver. What will he do if she dies?"

Vanessa freezes, a statue of herself, and tries to speak, but says nothing. She had not known there was a wife. Or a little Oliver.

"I should have told you," he says simply, as though he were speaking of nothing more than being late for a meeting. "I thought it was over, but, well, things are complicated."

She remains mute. Her lips move, a pursing that is not able to formulate a word. Can't. Tries, but the words are caught there, just below the sternum. A crushing weight of fear, and then a twist of recognition.

If it were the first time, it would be tragic. If it were the second time, it would be odd. But now, the third time—in a row!—it is almost funny, except that it is not funny at all.

Has she drawn this to her the way the garden draws birds? Is there something about her that attracts married men? Is she a subconscious junkie, with a husband habit?

Not again, she thinks. *This is not happening again.*

Only it is.

"Are you there?" he asks. "Hello? Vanessa? Vanessa? Look, I can explain."

Vanessa hangs up, and drops the phone to the bed next to her. *Arugula*, she thinks, with a damning scowl. She blames the arugula. The bitter thing that keeps coming back, even when you did not think it would, when you forgot about it, when you had moved past it.

She should have seen it coming.

His words echo in her mind. *Are you there? Hello? Vanessa? Vanessa?*

Yes, she thinks with dismay, as she flops back against the wall of goose-down pillows. *I am here.*

Again.

She rises now, fury in her eyes, to set the universe right before it is too late. Puts her clothes back on, and the clogs, and heads out into the rain with her shears in hand. She walks with purpose along the paths, dark and wet, her brave silhouette illuminated by a flash of lightning against the sky, like something from a Hitchcock film.

Vanessa finds what she is looking for, and falls to her hands and knees to begin her work. It is *growing*, she thinks, even now. She slices and cleaves at the stalking umbilical of vine, until at last she has cut back the arrogant malignancy of wandering pumpkin, just before the stroke of midnight.

Curses to fairy-tale endings.

Screw Cinderella.

A SISTERLY CONSOMMÉ

Tuesday, work later for Vanessa, but for now, lunch with her sister. She needs to talk, to listen, to remember that there was life before Bryan, and that there will be life after Bryan. Not that her life revolves around the idea of a *man* in it, of course not. But it would be nice to find a male human that wasn't, say, *married*. Or pathologically dishonest. Or permed. Surely there must be one or two out there?

Larissa sits at the blond granite island, hippie-chic in her floral dress and earrings, with her designer eyeglasses and dark black eyeliner, elbows propped, chin in hand, watching Vanessa pour the chilled mirepoix into the bright red stockpot. Larissa was always the girlier girl, with her love of makeup and waxing and hair products, and, of course, her curvy, feminine frame. Even after having two children, Larissa still wears the same size four that she wore in high school, just as she still turns her head to the side in that cute, disarming way. She also wears her curly hair long, with layers, and styles it in a way that is wild and beautiful.

Beyond the window, in the garden, Larissa's daughters, three and six and bearing the wild toasted-cinnamon curls of their mother, play, looking every bit like Larissa and Vanessa in photos from when they were young—only happier and not coiled tightly, waiting for the next outburst from their mother.

"So I found out I'm leaving for Morocco in a couple of weeks," Larissa announces, over the gentle melody of Japanese new-jazz piano from the iPod. Comforting to know there are women whose lives carry on without drama. Comforting to think of Morocco, too. Mention of the North African country instantly conjures taste memories for Vanessa—pomegranates, dates, mint, and olives.

Vanessa makes an appropriately surprised and interested face, says supportive things to her sister the academic, who is always jetting off to collect data in one place or another. Adds the head, tail, and other scraps of the excellent haddock to the pot, some leftover shrimp and oyster shells, a bit of gingerroot, lemongrass, and the beaten egg whites, her hands moving as if on their own, two birds in a dance of creation.

The phone rings. Caller ID says it is Bryan. Vanessa frowns, disconnects the phone from the wall, and looks at her sister to continue speaking.

"Him?" asks Larissa.

"Of course."

"He's got some nerve." Larissa pauses, as she often does before casting a damning judgment upon Vanessa. Deep breath, and then, there it is: "But I wonder if you don't subconsciously *encourage* him somehow. I mean, he should have given up by now. Do you think you've established firm boundaries with him?"

Vanessa is not interested in discussing her shortcomings right now, or her subconscious, or any of those other timeless chestnuts Larissa enjoys rolling around in. She waves the ghost of Bryan away like a fly she will not let ruin the soup. Changes the subject.

"You were saying? Morocco? What are you doing there this time?"

Larissa shrugs and keeps talking as she pops a bit of fresh almond biscotti in her mouth, downplays her question being unanswered, moves on with a look on her face that conveys her certainty that she was right and Vanessa's answer would not have mattered anyway.

"You know. I wasn't supposed to go until spring, but my visa got approved, and I have all the clearances set up."

"That's great, Lar. I bet Fergus and the girls will miss you." Vanessa adjusts the blue flame to a simmer level, wipes her hands on the towel tucked into the waistband of her jeans.

"Oh! Didn't I tell you? They're coming, too." Larissa washes the cookie down with a gulp of honeyed mint iced tea. She smiles gently toward the window, where the sound of the girls laughing burbles up. "Amina and Shada are gonna be my little research assistants."

Vanessa frowns, and before she can stop herself deadpans, "They'll look so *cute* in little tiny veils, all wrapped up in second-class status."

Larissa smirks to express both her appreciation of the joke and her annoyance with it.

"Doesn't Fergus teach this semester?" asks Vanessa.

"Sabbatical," Larissa reminds her. "It's a good thing, too, because the poly sci department is a mess of infighting right now, and he pretty much has to come with me anyway, because women alone in Oujda—you know. I won't get very far there."

"Not even on the world's fastest camel," quips Vanessa.

"Hey. They *do* have cars."

"Just be careful." Vanessa shudders. "You could leave the girls with me."

"I'll be fine." Larissa looks around the house, shakes her head as if the very *thought* of leaving her girls with her eccentric, single sister scares her. "Anyway, you're at bigger risk of dying in a grease fire than I am of being hurt in Morocco. It's not as bad as you think."

Larissa now talks a bit about her doctoral research, on the changing role of food preparation in the lives of rural women of the Algerian diaspora in Morocco over the past fifty years or so.

Years ago, Larissa was the first to show Vanessa the old French cookbook a neighbor gave her, when they were girls. Back then,

Larissa fantasized about growing up to throw dinner parties for fancy friends. Vanessa, as usual, followed her sister's interests— only, as it turned out, Larissa could not cook very well. And here they are. The food sisters, one who cooks and one who can't. And, as they say, those who can't *do*, teach. When she finishes the Ph.D., Larissa will be a culinary anthropologist.

"I just have one little favor to ask of you," says Larissa. "I need you to check on Mom for me while I'm away."

Vanessa's back stiffens. She frowns.

Larissa eyes soften in sympathy, but a pompous sort of sympathy that also implies that Vanessa is being unreasonable, which she is *not*.

Larissa says, "I know it's hard for you. I'll ask her not to talk about your love life. Or your cooking."

"I don't know, Larissa. I'd rather not. Surely there's someone else who can do it."

"She's gotten better," Larissa assures her, but Vanessa doesn't believe it for a second. Unless their mother has stopped drinking and belittling the people who love her, there is little chance anything about her is different. "Please?"

Larissa waits for an answer from Vanessa, but does not get one.

"Please?" she begs again. "For me?"

"Oh, don't you mean for 'the smart one'?" asks Vanessa with an ancient bitterness scarcely concealed with sarcasm. The old pain washes up as fresh as it was then. And the rage of invisibility. A rage Vanessa has never quite known what to do with. A rage she has tried to cook out of her, but it remains, raw and bloody, attracting flies.

"Oh, Vanessa. Mom hasn't called me that in years. She knows better now. Everyone does." Larissa smiles in self-deprecation. "Clearly, you turned out pretty well."

Vanessa creases her brow. "Why doesn't Dad help her? He's mobile."

"He's useless in the kitchen, you know that."

"So is Mom."

Larissa smiles. "Well, he's *more* useless. Plus, Mom needs help with more than that. There's the shopping and cleaning."

"Dad can't do that either?"

"He's not good at it."

"By *choice*," says Vanessa. "He pretends to be helpless. You know that."

"We all have our strengths," shrugs Larissa. "Mom does the house stuff, and Dad does the computer programming."

"Well, my strength lies in avoiding Mom and Dad unless it's a holiday," answers Vanessa. "I think it has served me well so far."

Larissa sets her iced-tea tumbler down with purpose, looks Vanessa dead in the eye. "Listen," she says, ever the teacher's pet, still trying to get their mother's approval. "Mom might not be perfect, and she might have done some stupid things, but she's our *mother*. None of us are perfect, Vanessa. Not even you."

"Please. I'm the last person to think I'm perfect."

"Anger doesn't help anything. Maybe if you have kids of your own someday, you'll understand how hard it is to be a parent."

Vanessa slams the long wooden spoon on the counter next to the cooktop with a loud snap. Turns with an amused fury in her eyes to look at her sister. "What is that supposed to mean? '*If* you have your own kids'?"

Larissa seems to look for something in the bottom of her tea glass. "Nothing. I'm sorry. I shouldn't have said that."

"You don't have to have kids to be a real woman," says Vanessa.

"I know. I misspoke. It's just, Mom's back is really bad since the accident, and Dad, you know. He's *Dad*. I swear, I think he has Asperger's or something. He's like a robot. Have you ever noticed how hard it is for him to make eye contact?"

"That's because he's drunk, Larissa."

"That's an awful thing to say."

"The truth often is."

"You have to see Mom for what she is now—a sad old woman who doesn't get any support from her husband. Plus, I think going to see them will keep you out of trouble until I get back."

"Trouble?" Vanessa gets a chill from her sister's well-meaning judgment. "What do you mean by that?"

Larissa's eyes soften. "Vanessa. I love you. I can't stand to see these guys hurt you over and over. I want to suggest something to you. No more dating for you for a while."

"Like I'd want to, after Bryan." *And not your business if I do,* Vanessa thinks.

Larissa looks at her doubtfully.

"Fine. I *won't*." Vanessa promises, though she is not entirely sure that she's being truthful.

"So that's a promise? No rebound dating."

"Sure, what the hell." Vanessa realizes how unconvincing she sounds. "No rebound. No hoop-shooting. No scoring. No game. Nada."

"Seriously, Vanessa. This isn't a joke. I want you to promise me, right here and now, that you'll stop dating until you've worked out why you keep ending up in the same situation."

"Sure," says Vanessa, without enthusiasm.

"No, I want you to mean it. It's not that I think you deserve to be punished or anything like that. It's just . . . I think you should learn to be alone before you can trust yourself to pick the right companion. Don't just fall for the first guy who comes along."

"Yeah, yeah, okay," says Vanessa, wondering what it must be like to give someone such pointed advice. "Must be nice to be perfect."

"I'm not perfect, that's not what this is about," says Larissa.

"That's what it's always about."

"It's about you learning to protect yourself."

Vanessa considers this, and it makes sense. Maybe it would be smart, to avoid men for a while. "Fine," she tells her sister. "I'll take a break. It can't hurt."

"Promise me."

"Promise you what?"

"Promise you won't date again until I've met the guy, and we've talked about it. You need, I'd say, at least six months off."

"Sure. Fine. No problem."

"Okay, good. I should warn you, before you start going up there, there's this *guy* living next door to Mom now."

"What guy?"

"I forget his name, but he's some army-looking guy with big arms and a crew cut and a nice tush."

Vanessa smiles through her annoyance. "Oh, and you just *assume* I'm going to jump into bed with him because he's a male, right?"

"He looks aggressive or something," says Larissa. "Like it's been awhile since he was around women."

Vanessa, furious now. "Oh, goody. On prison leave."

"I'm just saying, just look out for him."

"It might surprise you," says Vanessa, "to know that I'm actually interested in being some guy's everything, not some guy's furlough lay."

"He can be charming," says Larissa. "In that military, Boy Scout 'yes, ma'am' way. Mom can't *stand* him."

"He can't be half bad, then," says Vanessa.

"*That's* what I was worried about. You'd go after this guy just to make Mom angry. It's time to grow up, Vanessa. Sometimes Mom is right. You have to understand that."

"Okay, okay."

"Just promise you won't do anything stupid with him."

"What? Why would you even say that? Do you really think so little of me? No, wait. Don't answer that. Really, don't."

"I just— When I saw him, he made me worry for you."

"Maybe when you saw him, *you* wanted him," suggests Vanessa.

"Hardly." Larissa's blush belies her words.

"Well," says Vanessa. "The perfect solution to this is that you get someone else to watch Mom. That way we're both happy."

Larissa's face falls with disappointment. "Forget I mentioned the guy, okay?"

"Yeah, okay." Vanessa's voice is gloomy.

"I'm sorry," says Larissa, her face melting with compassion and empathy. "I know it's hard for you right now. What's wrong with me today? You loved him, didn't you? What was this last one's name again?"

"Bryan. Yes. I did. I loved him. But I really don't feel like talking about it."

Larissa stares hard at Vanessa, with concern in her eyes. "I hate to have to leave you like this. It feels irresponsible."

"Leave me like *what?*" asks Vanessa.

"Single and devastated."

"I'm not devastated."

"Yes, you are. You need me."

I can take care of myself. Vanessa shakes her head. "I'm a big girl. How long do you plan to be gone?"

"Just a month. Well, five weeks, actually."

"A whole *five weeks* of Mom?" whines Vanessa. "I can do the no-dating thing, but I don't think I can stand Mom that long. I'm sorry. Seriously. She's a total nightmare. Please don't do this to me. Don't."

"Maybe it'll do you good to get out of your routine a little bit," offers Larissa, cheerily.

"No, actually. I'm good with my routine."

"Vanessa, c'mon. I'm asking you for help here."

Vanessa looks out the kitchen window and tries to focus on the delicious, well-seasoned *now*, not the tepid, boozy, crippling past. Sky, garden, trees, home. Paradise. Larissa, looking back at her, imploring, kind and wise, a survivor, too, but somehow nicer for it, more rooted, her strength monumental.

Vanessa takes a deep breath, smiles as best she can. Larissa, the big-shot academic, bounces in her seat, momentarily becoming the little girl she used to be.

"Is that a yes?"

Vanessa nods.

"Thank you!"

"But it's *not* for her," Vanessa clarifies. She takes her sister's hand. "I'm not doing it for her. Okay? I'm doing it for you."

A piercing shriek comes from the garden, and a cry for mommy. Red Dog begins to bark by the back door. Larissa bolts from the room, slightly annoyed and not nearly as worked up as she ought to be, in Vanessa's opinion. But maybe this happens a lot. Maybe, she deadpans to herself, once she has kids of her own—*if* she has kids of her own—she'll understand. Ha, ha.

Vanessa continues her patient stirring, one ear cocked to the garden in case she is needed. It is only ten o'clock. They will not eat until noon. Consommé, simple and clear as it seems when you sip it, takes time to do right. Anything worth eating, or doing, takes time.

Vanessa adds the chilled fish stock and lemon juice. Lowers the heat. Makes sure the simmer feels right to her, in her solar plexus, the place cooking comes from, like channeling. She cooks by instinct. It means few others can replicate her recipes, even when she writes them down, because there is the intangible element of gut feeling. She rarely measures things precisely, preferring the feel of the weight against her palm, or the sense of things in the pan.

She could never be a pastry chef, because they must be so exact in their calculations. Not surprising, she thinks, that Bryan, the head pastry chef for the famed Fuchsia Adobe restaurant, concealed so much from her, and she did not notice. Pastry chefs are very careful and controlled.

Creators of new American cuisine, like Vanessa, do it by feel.

The screen door slaps shut, and there's Larissa, carrying Amina, the youngest girl, as Shada stomps at her side, insisting that she did not do it, whatever *it* is.

"Band-Aids?" Larissa asks Vanessa, patient, so amazingly patient in the face of all this noise and pressure. So much to admire in this woman who is her sister, she thinks. So much patience for people.

"Is she all right?" asks Vanessa, in a panic. Larissa is calm and smiles with a gentle roll of the eyes, to assure her it's okay, that this happens all the time, even though Amina howls like a banshee and insists Shada *did* do it, whatever *it* is.

"Nothing a Band-Aid won't cure," says Larissa, with the sweetly reassuring, strained smile of an empathic, but maybe a little tired, mother.

"In the bathroom. Medicine cabinet."

While her sister plays doctor, Vanessa stands over the fish brew, admiring how the crust (some call it a raft) forms and floats across the top. Chemistry. Things combined, and under the right conditions, becoming other things. The stirring will stop now, and become more of a basting. And waiting, for the simmer, the separation, the sieve, the patient pressing through with a rubber spatula, and, in this case, the chill time. As they wait, Vanessa will assemble the dumplings. Crab and pork, scallions and sesame seeds. Whip up the dipping sauce. What else? Green salad. More cold tea. Bubbly water with juice for the girls.

Larissa returns from the bathroom, still cradling a pouting Amina in her arms. Shada follows at a distance, and settles, in dark and grumbling disposition, on the sofa in the living room, arms folded across her chest with the injustice of it all.

"What makes an ouchie go away?" asks Amina, holding up her

arm with the Band-Aid on it. Old tears drying on her face, but no new ones flowing.

"Just time, sweetness," says Larissa.

"But it hurts now," whines Amina.

Larissa locks eyes with her sister, and Vanessa understands the look to mean that whatever Larissa is about to say is intended for her, too. Larissa comes across to people as the sensitive one, and Vanessa the tough one, but the sisters both know it is actually the other way around. Vanessa holds on to pain, jars it, cans it, bottles it, hordes it, seasons her life with it.

"Time heals all wounds. We just have to be patient, and gentle with ourselves, and not think about it too much." Larissa tries to smile as she shoots another glance to Vanessa.

Vanessa watches her sister kiss little Amina on the forehead, and even as the child pops her thumb into her mouth and seems to feel better, Vanessa's own eyes fill with tears. Pints of them. She turns to the soup so no one will see, careful not to drip into the pot.

So that's what good mothers do, she thinks, with a half-joking shrug. They *hug* their kids when they get hurt, and kiss them without the smell of industrial-strength wine and the dregs of an ashtray.

Fascinating.

A RIO GRANDE HARISSA

Wednesday, midmorning. Vanessa locks up her silver mountain bike behind Hawk's restaurant, hawk. Yep, that's what it is called: hawk. The place is named after the owner himself. Of course it is: HAWK, in lowercase black letters on a white oval sign hung prettily on the outside of the old warehouse building just south of downtown, elegant, uncluttered, and understated. But still his own name. Don't let the modest size of the font fool you. Hawk loves Hawk—the person, the legend—madly, and gourmands of Albuquerque love him for it.

Vanessa is grateful to Hawk, in her own increasingly frustrated way—after all, it is he who believed in her from the first interview and audition, he who trusts her enough to give her control over the menu when he travels. Hawk travels a lot, to promote his books and cooking videos and to take his assortment of bleach-blond model girlfriends to exclusive resorty-type places with cabana boys and mud baths. But she dislikes the hell out of him for his arrogance. You might say it's a love-hate relationship, except that Hawk knows only of the love. He has no room in his self-image for hate. He *can* hate, of course, and often he does—his preferred victims being other male TV celebrity chefs who, he insists, can't cook to save their lives. But Hawk, filled with self-love, cannot imagine himself hated by anyone, which is all the better for Vanessa because she believes she has finally reached the point where the hatred overshadows the love, the way a sack of flour might overshadow a speck of pepper.

No chef in this state is as famous as Hawk. Vanessa finds it hard to understand the almost psychotic love affair the city has with the man, especially considering how little creating the man actually does anymore, and how very much is left, quietly and anonymously, to Vanessa herself, whose name is all but unknown because Hawk would really rather not share the love, preferring to smear it all across himself like cocoa butter. Vanessa does not try to figure it out anymore; she knows there is no predicting the mores and tastes of the public, and she knows the value of showmanship, at which Hawk excels. That is likely the root of his popularity.

Hawk is a boisterous presence, huge and hulking, funny in his own weird way, the opposite of shy even though his eyes were planted a bit too close together. Perhaps because of it. He has the overbearing personality of those who must compensate for their school years for some reason.

The public loves Hawk. They love his pointy shaved head and motionless eyes the color of cold seawater. They love his many earrings and skull tattoos, and the biker bandanna knotted too tightly over his prominent brow. They love his hulking shoulders and thick neck without regard to the bushels of steroids that created them, or their disproportion to his scrawny calves and nearly girlish feet. They love his Belgian accent and Hasselhoff-style salon tan. They love that he is straight and dates famous models from Los Angeles and New York. They love, perhaps more than anything else, that he once had his own show on a national cable television network, the ultimate Albuquerque signal of having arrived. When the local paper revealed that Hawk collected kitschy saltshakers, they loved kitschy saltshakers. They love that he is taller than average and drives a Porsche 911 Carrera Cabriolet with a ridiculously huge spoiler and a vanity plate that reads, unsurprisingly, DA HAWK.

None of this impresses Vanessa. There was a time, she is sorry to say, when she was as awestruck by Hawk as anyone else. This was before she got to know him. Before he began to make a habit out of stealing her ideas and parading them around with a big stamp of *Hawk* on them, before she knew him for what he actually is, which is to say, a supreme culinary plagiarist.

Hawk lacks Vanessa's originality, because he lacks respect for people who cook without regard for classical training. During her time at the Scottsdale Culinary Institute in Arizona, Vanessa, by contrast, began to haunt ethnic neighborhoods for inspiration, and realized that most of the world's talented cooks were invisible to the people who edit the fancy food magazines and produce food shows. She began to spend time with the soft-spoken women behind the scenes in Vietnamese restaurants, and the women who patted out perfectly round tortillas in obscurity, and she started to get a clear understanding of the continued underestimation of women in this business.

Vanessa also understands, now that she knows Hawk personally and he trusts her enough to water his plants for him when he's out of town, how severely he and others overestimate his celebrated self. He certainly has culinary strengths—he is well-versed in classic French techniques, and he has familiarity with Spanish and Italian repertoire. But she knows that there are massive blank spots on Hawk's palate, too, blanks the size of forgotten continents and with the weight of history upon them, including her own beloved New Mexico, and this is where she comes in, and he knows it.

The rest of New Mexico is not so fortunate. The rest of New Mexico still believes Hawk to be some sort of genius; they act like those people hoping for an autograph outside the *Today* show studios in Hawk's beloved New York—that he was most recently from there lending him instant credibility to the perpetually insecure Western state. No city in America, Vanessa thinks, has such undeservedly low self-esteem as Albuquerque, which is similar to New Orleans in possessing its own culture and traditions, and which wishes to be thought of like Denver or Dallas, but which cowers in shame at being forever mired in the bland middle with Tulsa and Tucson.

Luxury cars will fill the lot soon, at lunch, and again later, for the private dinner party, because hawk is the place to be seen, by those who are to be seen by. When Vanessa was growing up in the city, there *were* no "it" places, unless you counted The Frontier, a restaurant shaped like a barn and filled with the world's largest collection of hideous John Wayne portraiture. The city has changed significantly since then.

Lines of people often snake around the entry, out the door, sometimes down the block, and Hawk generally leaves Vanessa in charge of the kitchen so that he can stroll across the wide, dark wood planks of his floors in his trendy European shoes, smile at the faces of his admirers, who sit on the white modern chairs at the quirky white modern tables, beneath hanging white paper lanterns in their odd geometric shapes, agape that so famous a chef has chosen to set up shop here, in lowly 'Burque.

She is early because she does not own a car, out of principle, and must shower in-house after her half-hour bike ride to work, then put on her white uniform with the white hat, stored here and laundered with the napkins and kitchen towels. She emerges, clean and ready, scrubbed and hungry, and greets the staff.

Lately, they have begun to grumble about staging a coup. Overthrowing Hawk. Vanessa has had nothing to do with this—well, at least in the sense that she was not the first to mention the idea. Rather, the brewing insurrection is led by a bold and outspoken waitress and medical student named Hazel. Yep, the same Hazel who oversaw the doomed makeover for Philadelphia. Pretty young Hazel, soon-to-be-married Hazel. Hazel, Vanessa's best friend, other than her own sister.

Today is another day of Hawk's absence. He is at the Mayo Clinic in Arizona, having a mole checked on his back. The man has many habits other than ripping off his employees, like smoking, drinking to excess, being sexually promiscuous, collecting fast cars and pushing them to their limits on the open road, and sunning himself lizardlike and leathery for hours upon hours at the side of his lap pool. Vanessa takes little comfort in the knowledge that his behaviors will ultimately lead to much suffering, pain, and an early demise. She dislikes the man, but she would never wish death upon him. He seems plenty good enough at that himself.

In Hawk's absence today, the kitchen burbles with laughter. The staff jokes in the sterile, bright space, with its crypt-cold counters, hospital-grade sinks, ovens, grills, and cooktops. Music plays, and they move to the beat. Hawk prefers silence when he is here, and says music in a kitchen can ruin the roux. Like he'd *know*.

Vanessa begins her day. Menus are discussed, plans and lists made. Sacks and slabs of things are lifted and hauled from the supply room or freezers to the kitchen, with the help of others. She is strong from the lifting and enjoys the feel of her muscles working. It is an honest living, this, creative but filled with motion and gravity, the way most work was before the industrial revolution. Lists are checked, supplies monitored, preparations made. People are given assignments. There is so much administration to this. Math, chemistry. Magic most splendid and sensory.

Lunch will be the usual, with two specials, one created by Vanessa, the other by Hawk. The private dinner he has left to her, because of his unexpected medical absence. In honor of Larissa, Vanessa has dreamed up a Moroccan-inspired theme, the mint and cucumber of it seeming perfect for this last hot phase of the summer, some old dishes that she has made, but a new one that has come to her only last night, and which she spent the morning perfecting.

"A New Mexican harissa, for my sister, Larissa," she tells the staff in the planning "meeting," held in a semicircle in the kitchen. Hazel, arriving in time for the meetings so that she can memorize the specials and the wine pairings, beams at Vanessa as she describes the dish—a Moroccan take on Caribbean *picadillo*, made with lamb and served over Israeli couscous instead of rice.

"Beautiful idea," Hazel says. "I love how you incorporate the personal into the food."

They have had this discussion before, over wine on Vanessa's back patio. Hazel, who majored in women's studies at the university for her undergraduate degree, and who hopes to go into women's health as a doctor, thinks women chefs tend to make statements in their food about the people and places they love, while male chefs seem to make statements about . . . well, about themselves. Vanessa is fairly sure she agrees.

A newer hire, Isaac, a male prep cook who seems to harbor ambitions of greatness and has a habit of dressing and talking like

Hawk, suggests that Vanessa should check with "the Hawk" before doing anything too radically different. Vanessa smiles at him with a polite shrug. She wonders what will come of Isaac, knowing now that in Hawk's kitchen there is only room for one egotist. Ultimately, Hawk and Isaac will butt shaven heads. Hopefully, she'll be long gone by then, though she'd pay for tickets to that showdown, frankly. It would be tremendously gratifying, regardless of who lost, as both men deserve a sound beating.

Hazel answers for Vanessa. "Hawk wouldn't know a harissa if it bit him on the pimply ass."

Laughter. Totally unfair laughter, really. Of course Hawk would know a harissa. *The New York Times* recently stated it was the new chipotle. Harissa has gone somewhat mainstream, and Hawk is of the class of local who reads the *Times* in search of validation for everything from the books he buys (but does not read) to the shirts he wears (though much too tightly).

"I appreciate your concern for Hawk," Vanessa tells Isaac, trying her hand at diplomacy. "But he has left me in charge today. He'll be fine with it."

"And if he isn't?" asks Isaac, bold, too bold. Humorless defiance in his eyes.

"If he isn't, then it's my butt on the line, not yours," says Vanessa. "Now, let's get to work. Rush is coming. Time waits for no man."

"Or woman," adds Hazel.

"Or space alien," says Vanessa.

"Not so," counters Hazel. "Space and time are related. A space alien could conceivably stop time, with the right apparatus."

And so it goes. They work. They banter. The lunch rush comes in a whirl of activity in the room, and the music continues. During a lull, Hazel chats with Vanessa about her weekend, and her wedding plans. Oh, goody, thinks Vanessa uncharitably. Another friend is about to be married, and she herself continues to be the unwilling other woman.

Hazel asks about Bryan, and Vanessa tells her the truth—that he was a lying sack of crap with a depressive and unstable wife. Hazel suggests they hang out sometime in the week to talk more about it, and then asks Vanessa if she would consider cooking for Hazel's bachelorette party, which, she assures her, "is going to be more about good food and conversation than G-strings and bow ties, because I'm a geek and not a player."

"Which is why we're friends," is Vanessa's quick reply.

"Geeks of a feather," says Hazel.

"Of course I'll do it. Happy to." And she is. Already her mind is flying across the possibilities.

The workday continues. Vanessa has brought her iPod and plugged it into the sound system in the kitchen, chooses a Moroccan woman pop singer, upbeat, to get them in the mood. The line cooks dance through the chopping, the dishwashers do hip-bumps and smile through their unenviable tasks. All of them seem to have the guilty sense of freedom that comes with ditching school. The music and the energy are almost enough to make her forget her immediate past and the pastry chef who drearied it up a bit with his mendacity.

Lunch ends, a success. Compliments pour in for Hawk, borne on the furious lips of Hazel, who almost cannot contain herself anymore. Everyone smiles with strange satisfaction in knowing Hawk gets more praise when he's gone than when he's in the kitchen. Everyone except Isaac, that is.

"Superstar," Hazel whispers to Vanessa as she takes a tray of tiny, pretzel-shaped honey cakes and espresso to the dining room. "You put the phony bastard to shame."

"Thanks," smiles Vanessa.

"Who's a phony bastard?" asks Isaac, though he knows exactly whom they're talking about.

Hazel blows air from her mouth and rolls her eyes. "Oh, I'm sorry. Was I talking to you? I hadn't realized I was."

"Hawk won't like how you're talking about him," says Isaac. "I suggest you have more respect for da master."

Hazel looks from Isaac to Vanessa. "I agree," she says. "We should all have more respect for the master. The real master."

"Not here," says Vanessa to Hazel. "Not now. This isn't the time. Later."

"Raise your hands if you're sick of Hawk taking credit for Vanessa's ideas!" cries Hazel, finally seeming to lose it. Everyone raises their hands. Everyone except Isaac.

"Disgraceful," says Isaac.

"Yes, you are, little man," snaps Hazel. "Vanessa, we have to bust this joint. I'm serious."

"Eventually," says Vanessa under her breath. "Not now. Stop it."

"You'll be free! You'll be a star."

"Let's just get through lunch," suggests Vanessa. "We'll talk about all this later. Okay? These things take money, remember?"

Hazel storms out of the kitchen with another order on her arm, and Isaac gives Vanessa the sort of look cyclists give motorists when they come a wee bit too close.

"Just relax," she tells him. "It's all good."

The lunch crew leaves, the night crew arrives. The kitchen is scrubbed and made new again, and they begin anew with the meeting, the checklists, the preparation. In her chest, Vanessa's heart swims with adrenaline. It is a performance, what comes for her tonight, her chance to shine, twirl, show them what she's made of. She is the composer, singer, conductor, dancer, actress, and poet. All in one. And so it begins. Harissa for Larissa, Rio Grande style.

The Moroccan singer is on again, ancient strains of the stringed oud mixing with drum and bass loops, and the garlic sheds its skin provocatively across the cutting boards, a promise of good things coming. Red and green chiles from New Mexico, rather than North Africa, soaked first in hot water, Moroccan spice echoed with our Southwestern heat, their chile with ours, all the world in one spoonful, and this is her credo tonight. New American cuisine? New World cuisine. She will not be boxed in. Don't we all eat? Don't we all feel? Don't we all love? Don't we all hurt? There are only so many tastes. The coriander now, the caraway, the cumin, and just a touch of anise, her own New Mexico regional addition, dropping into the massive food processor from her hands like rain from the sky, just the right amount. Olive oil added, and the mixture is ground into a paste. Rio Grande harissa comes to life, perfect unity.

Curses to men who steal your power.

Dinnertime comes and the guests arrive, invited by the organization that hosts the massive Albuquerque International Balloon Fiesta in town every fall. Exotic minty and fruity cocktails flow like water. If the board members, including many wealthy business types from around the world, like the dinner, they have told Hawk, they will give him the exclusive catering contract for the opening gala, which, it is rumored, will be attended by none other than the president of the United States. Silently, Vanessa prays her boss will be delayed so that he won't come and alter her recipes all by adding his famed "Hawk Frites," a fancy, conceited phrase for French fries.

Hawk comes huffing into the kitchen just as the finishing touches come to the openers, and all is ready to go. Mercifully, he has been delayed long enough to have very little influence on the meal, though he seems annoyed that they have chosen to go with Vanessa's ideas rather than sticking to the tried-and-true Hawkian recipes that, he says with Schwarzeneggerian verve, "drives da peoples wild."

"I tried to tell them, boss," says Isaac, all sniveling sidekick and Igorian deference.

"Taste before you judge," suggests Vanessa.

To Hawk's credit, he does. He knows her talent is not minor, even if he does not say so often. Or ever, for that matter. There is garlic soup, a roasted red pepper salad with yogurt dressing, and the crowning glory of the night: the lamb and apricot *picadillo*, cooked in capers and red wine, with dates and pine nuts and just a hint of local green chile, atop large Israeli couscous swimming in a fiery, garlicky harissa cream sauce, and surrounded with raw, sweetened cucumbers, garnished liberally with fresh chopped mint leaves.

Hawk samples it, raises an eyebrow in appreciation, but does not speak a word to her. Rather, he tells them all, "The Hawk approves," ties his head in a tight red bandanna, and waltzes out to deliver the plates himself.

"You lucked out," Isaac tells her.

Hazel, listening in, cringes and locks eyes with Vanessa.

"It's okay," says Vanessa.

Hazel grabs her by the hand, and drags her into the dining room. "Time for the intervention," she says. "Just watch."

The adrenaline in Vanessa's heart freezes over now, as she stands at the edge of the dining room. Back when he stole her first idea, then her second, her third, and so on, Hazel confronted Hawk about it, and, mysteriously, Vanessa and Hazel both got raises.

"He's used your ideas in his books," hisses Hazel. "How can you stand it?"

"I can't," says Vanessa.

High ceilings, cavernous, a minimalist airiness, with enormous black-and-white photos of New Mexico desert scenes on the red-brick walls. Trendy, for New Mexico. A jazz trio swings through miserable old standards in the corner, the music all wrong, so wrong for this meal. And there is Hawk, standing over a table with the most important of the guests, the Balloon Fiesta board members, Hazel tells her. Hawk's hand amiably on the shoulder of a white-haired man in Day-Glo cowboy boots who sits at the head.

"That guy right there?" whispers Hazel. "Loaded. I used to know him back when I worked at the bar. Billionaire."

The rich man says something, about him, Hawk, and Hawk does his best to appear modest, resulting in a mildly arrogant face, and the guests clap for him. Hazel drags Vanessa close enough to hear Hawk bragging to them of "his" inspiration for the meal. It is a lie, something about a caravan, a safari, the filming of that 1990s movie *The English Patient*.

"Oh my God!" whispers Hazel. "Are you hearing this?"

Vanessa nods, and of her own volition now moves forward, and sideways, until she is in Hawk's line of sight, and clears her throat, her hands clasped behind her back, her chin unusually high. Hawk looks up, and the smile disappears from the upper half of his face.

"Ah, Vanessa! My darling!" cries Hawk, all fatherly affection and cheer. "So good of you to visit."

He introduces her to them as "his" "little" sous chef, but does not tell them the meal was entirely her doing. There is something of a threat to his eyes as he looks at her, as if to demand: Don't embarrass me. *To hell with you*, she thinks.

"What a lucky girl you are, to study under the master," says the man at the head of the table. He points his fork at his empty plate. "Take notes on this one, it's a classic. Global cuisine with a New Mexico flavor. Classic Hawk."

"She is such a horse work," says Hawk. Vanessa can only assume he has meant to say "workhorse," which is not exactly flattering, either. "The Hawk think his horse work deserves another big raise."

He winks at her and she smiles with a polite bow, turns to the furious-eyed Hazel. His communication: You two keep it quiet, or else.

Vanessa retreats to the kitchen, surly now, hardly able to breathe, with Hazel wound tight, furious at her side.

"If you don't say something, I will," Hazel threatens.

Vanessa answers in a whisper, "I will. Just not right now. We have to do this right."

Everyone else in the kitchen tries to ignore them, except for Isaac, who stares openly and with great hostility, as he chops an onion.

"Let's talk about this later," says Vanessa. She shoots a glance at the other workers. "Okay?"

Hazel takes a deep breath. "Okay," she says, and her eyes soften.

Hazel hugs Vanessa, then returns to the dining room. Vanessa refocuses on her work, until it is time to go home, and fights the lump of emotion in her chest and throat.

"You girls better be careful," Isaac tells her.

"Yeah?" she asks. "How about you mind your own business?"

Isaac stares, open-mouthed, shocked by this. Vanessa has always been pleasant to him at work, even when it required superhuman strength. But there's just too much going on now. It's just too difficult, all of it.

"You don't speak to the Isaac that way," says Isaac, grandly.

"Yes, I do," she tells him. "Go to hell, the Isaac."

Vanessa finishes her work for the night, and when Hawk pats her on the back, she snaps: "Don't touch me."

"What?" asks Hawk, stunned just as Isaac was earlier. It is truly as if he has no idea why such a lucky young woman would be so terribly angry.

"I *said* don't touch me," she tells him. "I'll see you later."

She moves away, and heads out the door into the night.

A MAN LIKE A GOOD BACON

A Friday, two weeks later, and Larissa has flown off to North Africa and left her red Subaru with Vanessa. The Subaru, for its part, is a poor substitute for a sister. It sits in the gravel-and-dirt driveway as though confused, attracting butterflies and ladybugs who hope it is the planet's biggest, juiciest flower. The car answers in metallic disdain: *What am I doing here in the blazing sun, enduring bird droppings? Where is my concrete floor, my garage overhead? Where are the children who sprinkle my backseats with cracker crumbs? Who is this ambitious, single woman who never drives and always picks the bicycle?*

For *her* part, Vanessa looks out at the car from her living-room window, Mrs. Elizabeth Gaskell's *Wives and Daughters* in hand, page

201, Molly's naive and tempestuous relationship with her step-mother doing nothing to ease Vanessa's anxiety about the day. About the inevitable visit to her mother. Gah.

The sight of the car makes her feel weighted down, flightless, encumbered as a fruitcake. She wishes it away because it obstructs her view of the wildflowers, and because of where it demands she take herself. It's not that she cannot drive. It's that driving is fast, and life, savored well, ought to be slow, even its fast moments taken not too seriously if at all possible.

Vanessa, in the days before cooking school in Arizona, when she worked as an English professor at a small college in Minnesota, was a very good driver, even in snow, but just because one is good at something does not necessarily mean that it is a thing that ought to be done frequently, or at all. Vanessa, like most people, is quite good at picking her nose, a skill much-needed by those who live in the very dry high desert of New Mexico. This does not, however, give her reason to do so in public.

But enough of this remembering and explaining to herself, justi-fying and dreading, navel-gazing and nose-picking. The Gaskell slams shut on Molly just as she's wondered if she accidentally spoke of metaphysics without intending to. Physics, metaphysics, none of it to be dallied with for its own sake, best left to simply unfold un-der observation by humans but never in their care. It is nearly eleven in the morning, and Vanessa has promised her mother she would be there by noon, with a prepared lunch and ingredients for a dinner in hand.

"I guess you plan to poison me with your fancy food," her mother had asserted, with her famously ripe and teasing tone. Words delivered in a friendly enough fashion, but meant to destroy. Think Doris Day, with fangs.

"You'll like it. Egg salad. With a bit of a surprise." Vanessa had tried to sound cheery, tried to remind herself of Larissa's words about their mother as sad and old.

"Isn't it *always* a surprise with you?" was the fake-pleasant, secretly sarcastic reply.

Ah, yes, the perpetual surprise of Vanessa's ineptitude. How many times had she heard it from her mother? Her inability to choose a career and stick to it, her inability to choose men who'd stay with her, her inability, back in grade school, to do a simple cartwheel. So many inabilities, so surprising, all of them.

Papers gust from the desk to the floor in a burst of wind coming from the windows. The wicked witch blown into town, Vanessa thinks. She pulls the window shut and steels herself to the task at hand, reminds herself it is for Larissa.

Red Dog flops down from her post on the sofa, follows Vanessa to the kitchen in a gentle tinkle of tags, watches with a moderate wag as her master pulls the window closed over the sink, still hopeful they will take a walk to the river to chase ducks, lizards, white-winged doves, and shiny-eyed twitches of squirrel.

"No such luck, my love," Vanessa says. She finds a crispy bit of cooked bacon in the refrigerator (you never know when a crumble or two might come in handy) and breaks off a piece for the disappointed creature. Bacon makes Vanessa think of Dickens. Someone in Dickens is always doing something to bacon (or, as they called it, a rasher)—frying it, boiling it, plating it, eating it with bread and beer. Food sounds so good drawn beneath Dickens's pen. Even the simple crusts in the mouth of poor little David Copperfield, alone in all the world and taken advantage of terribly, sound scrumptious when you read them. Same, too, for the bit of meat and bread given to Pip by Estella on the overrun doorstep of Miss Havisham.

But then, it is difficult to make a bad bacon, the fatty pork being nearly as good underdone as it is burned, and in those unfortunate states being quite nearly as good as if it were cooked to perfection. Vanessa decides she needs a man like a bacon, good in every turn of mood.

Red Dog takes the crunchy cold delicacy to the living room to eat it off her favorite spot on the hook rug. Food tastes better there to Red Dog. No one but Red Dog knows why, and, experimental though Vanessa may be in matters of food, she is not inclined to eat off the rug to find out. She does have boundaries. Occasionally. Though apparently not today—thank you, Larissa.

Now, for the food. This day's meals will safely come directly from the large yellow *Gourmet Cookbook* Vanessa's mother got her for a recent birthday. It was a gift that doubled as an insult.

"If you have to make something fancy for us, how about you make it out of here," her mother said at the time, the "us" meaning Vanessa's parents. "None of this crazy foreign food." As though

France, the nation the book fixates upon, were local. Ignorance heaped upon ignorance.

"Gah," says Vanessa as she opens the massive book and tries not to dwell on her mother's negativity. *Negativity breeds negativity*, Larissa had told her before leaving for Morocco.

Positive thoughts, that is all Vanessa wants now, to draw positive things to her, like a good man, though, thus far, she has been true to her sister's orders not to date anyone until she has stopped thinking of Bryan. Not even a man like a good bacon, should one mysteriously appear at the garden gate with a wine and cheese in hand, and wouldn't that be lovely if it did happen?

"Gah," she repeats, and settles down to business.

First, the sandwiches. Tarragon-Shallot Egg Salad Sandwiches, to be exact, page 185. No deviation allowed, because in this way, when her mother insults the food, Vanessa will take comfort in the fact that it is someone else's recipe drawing her mother's ire. Eggs, mayonnaise (and not homemade, but the jar kind Mom likes best), shallots, tarragon (dried, from the store, fresh being too "stringy"). The next ingredient is the hardest. Vinegar. The recipe calls for white wine vinegar, or tarragon white wine vinegar, and it just so happens that Vanessa has some of the latter in her cupboard, homemade. One of the many useful things she learned at the institute was how to make one's own vinegar.

She did not know, until those precious days at the institute, that all vinegars can be made from the same acidic bacterial substance, added to liquids to ferment them. She has worked hard to perfect her cloudy fog of vinegar base, known in the cooking trade as the Mother of Vinegars, and has proudly experimented with it in many different ways. Dozens of excellent handmade offspring of Mother Vinegar line her shelves.

For the recipe's tarragon vinegar, she will use her own, even though she made it with champagne instead of flat wine, and added essence of rose petal. *Mom will never know*, she tells herself. How could she? Just a sad old woman, Larissa had told her, and that is what she must remember now. A sad old woman who long ago burned her palate to ashes, chain-smoking.

To cook by, she chooses something by the French composer Hector Berlioz, the appropriately bipolar and drunkenly unpredictable fifth movement of his *Symphonie Fantastique*. She chops, mixes, samples, then spreads the salad on kaiser rolls with shredded Boston lettuce. *Mom should like that*, she thinks, but quickly reminds herself not to hope for such a thing. There is also a simple green salad, assembled and put into a plastic travel container. The vinaigrette, made from scratch with red wine vinegar and olive oil, is loaded into a spill-proof clear glass travel bottle, and packed into the medium cardboard box with the sandwiches and the ingredients for dinner—two pounds of fresh scallops packed in ice, olive oil, garlic, tomatoes, fresh thyme, and oregano. Everything to make a satisfying scallops Provençal, something they can all enjoy. She knows better than to pack wine. Mom will surely have plenty of her own.

Vanessa starts the drive to her mother's, slowly so there are no

spills, careful as a first-time mother with a newborn in the backseat. She listens to a talk show on Air America. Her parents live in
the Northeast Heights, a neighborhood whose name used to mean
something when she was growing up there, before the north and
east of Albuquerque exploded to include neighborhoods like the
very expensive High Desert and the chillingly born-again North
Albuquerque Acres, where children in Halloween costumes are
met not with candy, but cards decrying the Satanic holiday.

She arrives without incident. A yellowed white-brick ranch
house with a pitched shingled roof, in one of the residential pockets
near the Arroyo del Oso Golf Course. A neighborhood that used
to be the High Desert of its time, its time having been the early
1980s, back when bathtubs did not resemble small swimming pools
and closets were not the size of small bedrooms. Back when Americans had appropriate notions of proportion in both their housing
and upon their plates.

A neat square of green grass with a straight gray cement walkway cut through it, from sidewalk to porch. A large oak tree in the
middle of the lawn, not a leaf out of place. A driveway, a two-car
garage. All houses on the block, variations on this same sterile
theme, everything clean and safe and as it should be. On the outside, anyway.

She parks the Subaru at the curb, instantly notices that the
corned-beef red house next door has finally sold. It was on the market for more than five years. Dad would "joke" that no one wanted
to live next door to Mom; Mom would sling the same joke back at

Dad, in reverse, and on it went, with no one laughing and both meaning every word. She's not sure why they've stayed together all these years, but at the same time does not see how they could possibly live apart. She is quite sure the house next door did not sell because people could hear her parents fighting through the walls. It is, as it happens, the very same reason Vanessa moved away as soon as she turned eighteen.

In the driveway of the newly sold house basks a wide, muscular gray pickup truck, new and shiny and American. If it were a man, it would be bowlegged. A Washington State license plate, a yellow "support the troops" magnetic ribbon on the bumper next to the enormous decal of the American flag.

Vanessa shudders because she has found that most people sporting such decals do not understand that truly supporting troops means never sending them to die for a war based upon lies, greed, and oil. The truck's garage gapes, an open mouth with nothing interesting to say.

She steps onto the street, and the music comes flooding loud and garbled from the bowels of the red house's garage. An incomprehensible torrent of rock drums, thrash guitars stuck on a single note, a stuttering staccato of bass, and a monstrous male voice that can't seem to decide whether to sing or to vomit. When did singers start to do this?

She jimmies the cardboard box of food from the backseat, all without looking again at the clamorous neighbor house. No need to seem friendly to them, now is there? Arms heavy, posture circumspect, she hurries up the walkway, eyes averted, shoulders tensed. But it is not enough. The music volume comes down, and a throat clears, and then: "Howdy, there!" A boom of deep voice, much too friendly, off-putting in its confidence, altogether much too steeped in testosterone for her mood, post-Bryan.

Vanessa glances across to the gaping garage, against her will, and feels her lower belly tighten at the significant, perhaps even epic, sight of him. Fit, shirtless, in dark jean shorts and beige work boots. A manly nose, tan skin, he is about her own age, with hair in a tight, low crew cut that would probably be a dark blond if he wore it longer. Which he likely never would. This must be the man Larissa warned her about. As usual, Larissa's instincts were good. Vanessa finds this man very attractive, on a purely physical level. Larissa knew she would.

Clean shaven, some kind of a heavy silver tool in his hand, maybe an enormous wrench, a mess of what looks like scrap metal twisting beneath him on the ground. Top him in a helmet with horns, plant him at the helm of a longship, and he's a Viking, she thinks. A rapacious pillager. Him and his yellow ribbon and enormous gas guzzler. A big old patriotic relic of the Bush II era. She will nod a hello, because, manly and handsome or not, he's not worth the breath it takes to shout a greeting at the moment. He is a man like a canned ham, or maybe canned Spam, and hardly a man like a good bacon. Nope.

A ragged edge of sidewalk tugs at her sneaker, and Vanessa stumbles, clumsy, his Viking eyes upon her. The irony of the timing is not lost on her. Just when she needs to be toughest, she comes across as a foolish little girl. She catches herself, and pauses just long enough for the crew cut to decide he's the world's burliest Boy Scout.

"Oh, hey, here, lemme help you." He drops the tool with an urgent clatter, gallops toward her in his heavy, unlaced footwear, a stallion, all neck tendons and rectangular jaw. A human exclamation point. In the garage he leaves behind, a drum set and a weight bench, and posters of women in bikinis and fur hats. Holding frosty beers. Original. Perhaps they also have flat heads.

"No, I'm okay," she calls. She doesn't have it in her to be rude to him, exactly, because rudeness takes more energy than she is willing to expend, but she certainly does not wish to burn energy being friendly, either. Not when there is a very distinct possibility that he will want to talk about something that will make her uncomfortable, like hunting or war or Rush Limbaugh. He's probably one of those guys who, upon learning the new president was a Democrat, ran out and bought a bunch of guns.

He canters on, and then here he is, hands underneath the box, on top of hers. A smell of motor oil slickens the air, and sand, and hot skin. He has been exercising. His insistent pheromones, his sweet breath all over the egg salad. All over Vanessa. A smile a thousand degrees and rising, a cleft chin, tiny beads of sweat. She is dizzy with his scent.

"I got it, babe," he says. "You can let go."

She shudders and squints angrily at him. *Babe?* She is no one's babe. He does not understand the meaning of her squint, apparently, because he lobs back a smile big and broad as his shoulders, and more curling up of that invisible musk that has caught her so off guard. Insistent, determined, not letting go. Too rough with the box, so she hangs on because she is not about to hand over her food to anyone.

"Really, I'm okay," she repeats. "Really. I only *appear* to be helpless."

He hesitates, as if recalibrating his brain to take in the idea of a sarcastic woman—and liking it?—and she hears the glass of the dressing bottle bang up against something else, hard. *No!*

She looks into the box, and the sun glints through the vinaigrette, oil blond on top, vinegar dark down below. A metaphor she could do without. Nothing broken, thank goodness, but with his hands and pheromones all over everything, there seems to be a distinct possibility of breakage. All wrong. No matter how good he smells to her, she thinks, this is the way of things. Daughter of vinegar, son of (motor) oil. Food, talking to her again, warning. She turns her eyes up to the Viking, determined, this time, to get him to listen.

"Please let go," she snaps. "If I need your help, I'll ask. How's that?"

"Sor-ry." Words poached in the sarcasm of the haughty and humiliated. Backs off, hands up, impertinent. "Just trying to help."

He staggers back, appears to breathe through his mouth. Of course he does. The tiny walnut of a brain must be clogging the nasal canal. *No, Vanessa*, she thinks, *don't be so ignoble*. Surely he has his good points. Everyone does. Vanessa turns back toward her mom's tidy blue door.

Well, *almost* everyone.

"Didn't mean to make you uncomfortable," calls the crew cut.

Vanessa turns her head to look at him, hopes the stolid look on her face will stop him from bothering her further. It does not. He grins at her, playfully defiant, handsome, electrifyingly all wrong. Crow's-feet at the corners of his eyes, and full, pink lips, and large, sky blue eyes above cheeks flushed with health and exertion—and all of it above a most spectacular body. He must be six-two. Not that she noticed. Not that it matters. She has to put him out of her mind. Forget that she has seen him, and smelled him. Except that he was not the type you forgot easily. He was not the type to disappear into the wallpaper at a party. He was more the type to cap himself with a lamp shade before making a disgusting noise with his hand in his armpit.

"I'm Paul," he calls. "And you are?"

"Late," she says with what she hopes is a polite smile. "Excuse me."

He moves toward her again, keeping a polite distance, but losing none of his morbid fascination for her. He mouths the words of the song, beats air drums with imaginary sticks. Pleased with himself. Unfettered. A big dumb man with rhythm. She hurries, and he hurries next to her hurrying.

He talks to her again, unperturbed. "You friends with old Mary and Greg there?"

"Sort of. They're my parents." Vanessa tries to avoid looking at Paul's chest and belly. It is like avoiding a boulder avalanched down upon the interstate—you do it only because you know it's there and just might kill you. She would not be surprised to learn that his last name was Bunyan.

"Good people, Mary and Greg." The Viking pats his belly, grins at her in a way that is trying to be innocent but clearly isn't, finds a dark blue T-shirt tucked into the back of his waistband and, out of some misguided compassion for her, pulls it over his head and the rippling rugged mass below. Sensuous man, him, even if he *is* ignorant.

"Yeah, well, *my* mom is *Phyllis*," he adds, as if this should mean something to her. He jerks a big thumb to the mottled redbrick house and its toothless maw of garage.

Vanessa did not know there *was* a Phyllis. She wonders when they moved in, but won't give the Viking encouragement by inquiring about his Spammy life.

The Viking trots ahead of her with his boyish grin, to the front door, and pounds on it with a fist like a sledgehammer. Trying to be helpful, she supposes. Vanessa's back stiffens with the stress of facing both Viking and mother, in tandem, but for some reason unknown to her, and entirely annoying to her, she smiles at him. He leans against the wall, talks, as if they were old friends, as they wait for the knock to be answered.

"Yeah, me, you know. I'm just hanging around awhile. Until I get back on my feet. Lookin' for work."

Smooth, thinks Vanessa, with sarcasm. Unemployed, and bragging about it. Men can be so clueless sometimes, she thinks. The front of his shirt has letters she won't linger on long enough to read fully, lest he misinterpret her gaze for seduction, as many men are wont to do. The script is something about the Air Force, and honor, and country. Of course it is. That's where they end up, his kind, moths to the flame.

The door opens. There hunches Mary, her Grecian nose held high, grumpy in her peasant skirt and thrift-store sweater, her short Annie Lennox hair the same as it has been for decades, but the white roots showing more now than ever. She grips the wooden walking cane Vanessa did not imagine she would need for many more years. Drunk driver did this to her, and even that is not enough to make you pity her for more than an hour or so. In the fingers of one hand smolders a lit cigarette.

"Miss Mary, Miss Mary!" barks the Viking brightly. "Look at you! Good to see ya up and at 'em, ma'am. Way to go." Oddly, he holds a hand up as though he expects Mary to give him a high five. Vanessa half expects her mother to singe him with the lit end of her smoke.

"Paul." Mary eyes him warily and places both her hands solidly on top of her cane. If he were a pile of some putrid steaming mess squeezed fresh from the backside of Red Dog, he could not have earned a more disdainful countenance from her.

He looks to Vanessa for support, asks, "She always this fun to be around?"

"Oh, it gets even better," says Vanessa.

"Lucky you." He smiles at her with more sympathy than she expected. And what seems to be a bit more intelligence, too.

Mary drags from the cigarette, blows it toward Paul. "We'll see you later, Paul. Good-bye."

He steps back from the smoke but does not wave it away. "I'll leave you ladies to your visit," he says, shivering under Mary's glare. Looks at Vanessa and tips an invisible hat. "Good to meet you, whatever your name is. You ladies have a lovely day."

Off he trots, whistling and air-drumming with gargantuan cheer, back to the aperture from whence he erupted.

"Pain in the ass," Mary grumbles after him as she slams the door. Then she turns to her daughter. "Vanessa, you look nice, other than the hiking boots."

"Thanks, I think."

"And your hair is long." Mary smiles as if this were a good thing, but quickly launches into the next part of her statement. "But what have you done to it? Is it up or down? What is all this halfway nonsense here?"

Mary fingers Vanessa's hair as though it were a rotting bit of string beans in a bin. "You could be so pretty, with a little effort."

"Mother, please," says Vanessa, pulling away.

Mary huffs. "At any rate, I see you've met the young Hitler next door."

"Paul?"

"*Paul*," Mary gripes. "Nothing but trouble. I ought to call the police on all that noise he makes. All that bellowing and marching around. Well, come in already, before you spoil the egg salad standing there in all that *sun*."

She says "sun" as though it were something to be placed in the rubbish bin.

Mary sniffs the air as Vanessa steps past her into the dark house. *No*, thinks Vanessa. *Don't do that. Please don't do that. Don't sniff.* Vanessa had forgotten how desperately uncomfortable the sniffs made her. How wretchedly she hates the sniffing.

"Interesting. Doesn't smell like a *normal* egg salad," Mary snaps, to no one in particular, and certainly not expecting any sort of answer from Vanessa. Mary sniffs again, a great twitch of sniffery up and down her long, thin nose, all vibrations. "Smells like vinegar."

"That's because I think the dressing spilled a little in the car."

"We have dressing *here*, for Pete's sake," says Mary. "You do too *much*, Vanessa. You don't have to complicate things for my sake. You always complicate everything."

Vanessa's back stiffens. "Please don't start this again."

"What? It's true. You know I love you. I just say these things because I'm your mother and I love you."

"I wasn't *complicating* anything. I just wanted to make something special for you."

"And what did you come up with?"

"A salad with edible flowers. You'll like it."

The house smells of smoke mixed with laundry soap and bug spray, old processed cheese and mushy apples. Her mother smells of the syrupy dregs of cheap dessert wine, dime-store perfume, and stale butter croissant from a bag.

"Oh, isn't that nice," says Mary with a fake smile. "I did not realize sensible people *ate* flowers. Is that the trendy thing these days?"

"People have eaten flowers for centuries, Mom. Capers are flowers."

"Oh, have they? People have? I see. I thought it might be a food-snob sort of thing, but now I see that it is just a tradition. Thank you for informing me."

"Mom, please don't do this."

"Do what, Vanessa? Come in. Set that vinegar down. Let's not have it all over the house. Don't want the house smelling of snob salad."

Vanessa follows her mother into the kitchen.

"It's just egg salad, and I made it from the book you got me."

"Oh," says Mary. "Well, it's nice to know you still listen to me now and again, isn't it? But surely you won't mind if I make myself a little something else to eat, will you? If I don't like the daisy-and-marigold sandwiches?"

"Egg salad. The flowers are the tossed salad."

"All these *salads*," Mary complains with a tight smile. "How many salads does one lunch need? Honestly. Whatever happened to good old meat and potatoes? Everything they tell you is good for you, just watch, in ten years they'll tell you it's bad for you."

"How are you feeling, Mom?"

"Well, I'd be better if there weren't so much vinegar all over the place. Honestly, I don't know how you can stand it."

Vanessa entertains a brief thought of hurling the bottle of salad dressing at her mother, before stuffing the idea down into that place where everything else about her childhood resides, locked up tight in the compartment right in between the ones that read MARRIED MEN WHO LIED ABOUT IT and BOSSES WHO STEAL YOUR STUFF.

There is lunch to be made.

A SANDWICH MOST CHILDISH

After lunch, Mary frowns through a round of solitaire at the rocky Formica kitchen table, with a weathered deck of cards. The ceramic kitchen witch, affixed to the same wall for decades, dust upon her long gingham skirts, looks on with grand enthusiasm. The obscenely rounded face of the honey jar, shaped like a bee, smiles with unfounded anthropomorphic perversion, the honey stick straight out the back like a tail. Same thing has been on the table since she was a child. Nothing changes here, here being like a shrine to the 1980s, untouched.

A fluorescent light flinches out its uncertain glow in the ceiling box where flies go to die. Does nothing to help the olive green fridge, God knows how old, or the counters, Formica made to look like wood and peeling up now at the corners to reveal the particleboard beneath. Lighting for an insurance office, thinks Vanessa. Lighting for an unloved actuary's funeral.

Her parents could afford better, but they don't see the point in replacing a thing not broken. She cleans up what is left of the rose-petal egg salad, which only she ate, and the remains of the processed-ham-and-Velveeta sandwich on white bread from Wal-Mart, which Mary nibbled through tight lips, as both insult and lesson on the trivialities of edible flowers and the superiority of Mary's very refined taste to the tastes of all others, culinary school or no culinary school, taste being innate and unteachable and having to do with realism and common sense.

"Do you think Dad will eat these?" Vanessa asks of the leftover sandwiches. Trying to be pleasant, for Larissa's sake. Trying to remember that her mother's opinion is not like most people's, and that most people do, in fact, seem to really like Vanessa's cooking. She thinks briefly of Hazel, and wonders how *she* would handle Mary. That might be fun to watch. God, yes.

Mary glowers a moment before laughing uncharitably. "Your father will eat *anything*." She slaps down a card. "I wish I'd known that before I married him. Certainly could have saved me a lot of trouble."

"I'll take that as a yes." Vanessa's shoulders tense painfully. A look at the green digital numbers on the microwave clock. Two o'clock. Two more hours until her dad gets home. Four more until she gets to leave. Unbearable.

"Oh lord, my back," gasps Mary.

The act of laughing at her husband of forty years has bred spasms or something, and her hand is behind her in a flash. Her face twists with the pain, and small noises escape her as they might from a distressed mouse. Vanessa, confused, hurries to her aid, helps her limp from the kitchen to the family room, lays her flat, as she has asked, across the plaid old sofa, same one they've had for years.

Vanessa's hands do not recognize this woman's body. Such thin arms, bones and softened, moveable skin working together to feel something like a cold, plucked, raw turkey shin. The skin so loose and baggy now, frailty like perfume. Is this the hand that so often pinched and shoved? Love and fear and pity, all at once washing over her, unexpected yet familiar, like the boiling moment in the shower after someone else in the house has flushed the toilet.

Vanessa asks Mary if that's any better now. Mary can only pant, like a woman in labor, like an overheated bird. Awful, thinks Vanessa, much worse than she realized. But then, a broken back, all put back together with steel pins, is not easy to overcome, especially for a woman nearing seventy. It's a wonder she was not permanently paralyzed, her doctor said.

"Pills," Mary manages to croak.

Her oxidized, inexpensive finger rings flash and rattle in the direction of the sideboard across the room, in the formal dining area, where Irish lace doilies come to convalesce beneath a thin film of dust.

Vanessa sees an assortment of prescription bottles there, next to the decanters, carafes, and flasks. She hurries to get the pills, and a glass of water. Rushes back. Administers the promise of relief.

Mary's face, momentarily grateful, maybe a little embarrassed, two expressions Vanessa has never seen there. Vanessa kneeling at her side, bigger, stronger, necessary. The grown-up. A strange feeling. Too little air. The scent of old newspapers and used cigarette filters. Her mother fading before her eyes, and wasn't this supposed to happen far, far into the future, in her own old age?

"Can I get you anything else, Mom? A pillow?"

Yes, that, but Mary, hacking a cough now, also wants some Martini & Rossi. A glass. And the remote.

She turns slowly, very slowly, onto her side, in grunts and grimaces, to face the shiny new flat-screen television on its stand on top of the entertainment center across from the sofa. One of the few new things they have. The remote is fetched by Vanessa. Mary jabs at it, until she settles on a judge-and-court show, the reality kind where people yell at each other about loans of a hundred bucks.

Vanessa settles her mother's head beneath the rubbery foam bed pillow she's brought from Mom's bedroom. Mary mutters of the pain under her breath, curls her knees in toward her chest, embryonic, and her eyes shut tight, open again, shut tight, open. Vanessa stares at her. Helpless. Horrified. Stunned. "I'm all right," Mary says. "I don't want you staring at me like that."

"I'm sorry, Mom. I . . . I just don't know what to do. What can I do?"

"Dishes."

"You sure you're okay in here by yourself?"

"I spend most of my life by myself," she says.

"That's so sad, Mom."

"No, it's not. That's how I like it. Now, go on. I'm fine."

Vanessa returns to the relatively easy company of the witch and the bee, to wash the dishes. When she stops running the water, she hears a low, rhythmic sound so strange and unfamiliar she almost cannot tell what it is. Until she understands, and fear washes over her for the unfamiliarity of it. And a sickening sort of guilt.

Her mom, alone with Judge Judy, is crying.

SWEETNESS FROM

THE BOTTOM OF THE SEA

Her father comes home much as he has come home every workday for the nearly four decades he has worked for the university. Tired, quiet, thoughtful, in slacks and a white shirt, smelling of computer programs and secret inky experiments, in search of his armchair, the evening news, and a cold one. The yellow and white hair thinner now, of course, and the paunch rounder, but all in all, the same old same old.

He could have retired by now, but seems to enjoy what he does, what he does being totally incomprehensible to Vanessa. By the time he arrives, Mary has turned off the TV and returned to the kitchen, her pills and liquor affixed heartily to her receptors, and she is slurring her words a bit, laughing at nothing distinct, and, apparently, feeling fine. She has made a shopping list for Vanessa on a yellow legal pad, and is, at the moment, sloppily probing for information about what has happened to Bryan.

Mary liked Bryan, the one time she met him at Larissa's Fourth of July barbecue, because he worked at a respectable old Santa Fe restaurant, not a fancy, trendy Albuquerque restaurant like *some* people.

Vanessa is not telling Mary what happened to Bryan, because she does not believe her mother needs more bad news, or more ammunition for the canon of inadequacies. Not here. Not now. Not tonight.

"Nothing, really, we just didn't get along. It happens."

"That is sho true," slurs Mary. "It *doesh* happen." She hiccups. "But it sheems to happen sho much more to you, more than to anyone else I know. I do know you, don't I?" Mary laughs at her own joke and nearly topples over.

As Mary continues to slosh around in the English language, Greg wanders into the kitchen, plants a kiss on Vanessa's cheek. Always nicer than Mom. The reason Vanessa is not completely batty. Smells like Dad. Part sweat, part Old Spice deodorant. A fitting duet, considering that if one is working properly, then the other must not be. Underarms as dysfunctional as his marriage.

"Nice of you to help out, Nessy," he tells her. Digs for the Budweiser. Pops the top, slurps the foam. He kisses Mary, who is lost in thought and prescription drugs. She realizes he's kissed her only too late, and kisses back into the air, like a snapping turtle that's lost its balance.

"Vanessa couldn't keep a man again," Mary tells him as he tries to walk away. "Very sad. But I'm not surprised she was dumped. Are you surprised?" Mary turns her attention to Vanessa. "No one likes a know-it-all, dear."

"Sorry to hear that, love," says Dad to Vanessa, true sympathy in his eyes, even if they *do* look across the room rather than at his daughter.

"That's not true," protests Vanessa.

"Yes, I really *am* sorry," says Dad. "Any man would be lucky to have you."

"No, I mean I wasn't *dumped*. It's more complicated than that."

"It always is," says Dad. Starts gulping down the beer.

"Ishn't that the truth? Complicated. *Complicated*. Her love life's so, is *sho* terribly complicated. I can't keep up with it, honestly." Mary's head bobbles on her neck as she goes for her Martini & Rossi again.

Greg fixes the corner of the room with his eye. "That is *not* what I meant, Mary. I don't mean Vanessa's love life is complicated, I meant love itself, as a general concept, is complicated."

"Thanks, Dad."

"If you weren't dumped, you wouldn't be afraid to talk about it," blurts Mary, words wet and unsteady. "It's all right. We're here if you want to talk."

"Think what you wish, Mom."

"Well, if someone broke up with you, sweetheart, it's because something better's waiting out there," Dad tells the refrigerator. Pats Vanessa on the back. Mary rolls her eyes as if this were utter nonsense.

"There ish *never* something better," slurs Mary. She presses a finger to her lips, whispers wetly. "Little shecret about love, Vanessa. Shettling is the name of the game." Bobble, bobble. "Look at us. Besht I could have done? Is that what you think?" Mary cackles and smooths back her hair. "I used to be pretty, you know."

"Sure, back before electricity was invented," replies Greg, with a brief and self-conscious wink to Vanessa to defuse Mary's escalating anger.

"We've made a shopping list," Vanessa tells him, before Mary has a chance to answer Greg, which she does not seem inclined to do anyhow, her latest glass of wine having suddenly taken on a most interesting quality. "Anything you want?"

Dad looks at the ceiling, lists a few items: Kashi cereal, an organic raisin bran with kamut flakes, nonfat milk. He surprises Vanessa with his request for wheatgrass and green tea, and explains, "I plan to live forever. I saw on this show that this stuff makes you live forever. If I can outlive her"—he tilts his head toward Mary—"I figure I'll have a shot at being happy again before I die."

"Nonfat milk," huffs Mary. She drinks only full-fat milk, insisting again, in the repetitive way of drunks, that everything they say is bad for you is good for you.

Vanessa looks at her dad as though to ask him how he can stand it. Greg, for his part, saunters out of the room with a last glance at the wall. She hears the footrest of the recliner kick up, rusted-over coils protesting briefly before giving in once more with a small sigh. She hears the TV come back on, and the soothing tones of a newscaster.

Vanessa starts on dinner now, with Mary working a crossword puzzle, looking up now and then to make sure nothing's gone horribly, terribly wrong. Seared scallops are hard to get wrong. You pat them dry, dust with good, kosher salt and freshly ground pepper, pop them in the pan, in some fragrant olive oil. No more than four minutes. You keep them warm while you make the sauce, harder than it sounds now because Mary has an electric range. Vanessa ranks electric ranges somewhere just above blood clots on the list of things she would most like not to have.

Hot olive oil, garlic cooked in it until clear. Red tomatoes halved and seeded, diced. It is straight from the big yellow book, impossible to forget. Sleepwalking, for Vanessa. Thyme chopped and stirred into the mix. Fresh basil ripped to pieces. A nice crusty bread. Hum a remembered Edith Piaf melody, think of the French countryside. And, soon enough, you have scallops Provençal.

Vanessa searches her mother's wine collection, stashed on the top shelf of the pantry, settles on a nice American chardonnay. Just what the doctor ordered.

"Smells pretty good," says Mary, as though surprised, too high from meds and wine to stop herself. "Doesn't smell too fancy, anyway."

A table set carefully. Use the CorningWare and the paper nap-kins. They eat without much to say, at the kitchen table. Mom and Dad do chat amicably for a time, surprisingly. He asks about her health, she plays down the severity of her afternoon misery, asks about his work. That's something, thinks Vanessa.

Dad then asks Vanessa how things are going at hawk, something Mary has not bothered to do all day. A shrug. A mental image of the bald head of Hawk, pushed down to the scrap heap of memo-ries. Locked away.

She mops up the oily sauce with her bread. It is sweet from the scallops, as surely as if it had been delicately sugared. Amazing how so few ingredients, put together just right and at just the right time, can taste so good. Amazing how good she feels, with her mother chewing and swallowing with gusto, even if she does say the dish reminds her of something from the buffet at Sandia Casino, the only place she and Dad go for entertainment anymore.

Dad goes back for seconds. Inspired, Vanessa does, too, and helps herself to another glass of wine. Driving. Probably shouldn't. But does anyway, because isn't this a reason to celebrate? Isn't this progress, of sorts? Mary eating her dinner without complaint? Mom and Dad talking, like healthy people?

Dinner finished. Vanessa clears and cleans, and Mary begins to smoke, and Vanessa, more to escape the haze than out of generos-ity, asks if she can check on the backyard and small garden she herself planted years ago, when she was in high school.

"Suit yourself," says Mary with a shrug.

Vanessa wonders if she should go home instead. She thinks of Red Dog waiting for her by the door. Where is she? On the sofa, watching out the front window—that's what Red Dog does when left all alone. Vanessa thinks of the books on her nightstand, and the welcoming puffiness of her bed.

Then she thinks of the sound of her mother crying, when she thought no one could hear, and the way her mother actually *ate* the scallops, and the needy backyard. She thinks about how sometimes you have to become more mature than your own parents, for the sake of your sanity, and she has to admit, she has never felt more grown up than she has this day, caring for her immature mother. Maybe Larissa had a point. Maybe the only way to move past a thing is to move through it.

She decides to stay awhile.

OLD RUSH

AND STUNTED GREENS

Vanessa stands on the back porch of her parents' house and surveys the damage. A strange sense she is being watched. Butane thin and oily blue on the wind, from someone's barbecue.

Inside, her parents' voices rising as they start to argue, the nightly routine sadly still intact, predictable as Stonehenge and the seasons. Maybe they were on their best behavior because she was in the room with them.

She turns to the house, half expecting to see her younger self staring out from her old bedroom window, forlorn, begging for rescue, escape, the tattered copy of the classic cookbook in her hand, as she dreamed of families that had cocktail parties and fine dinners together. The book her window to a better life.

Thunder rumbles over Sandia Peak, the huge mountain much closer here than it is in the valley, so close you can see rocks and trees, the long thread of the Tramway wire to the top. More rumbling. Loud, with echoes up and down the canyons. But no rain yet. Maybe none tonight at all. The spaces of this part of the world so grand, so huge, you can watch thunderstorms in the distance and yet bask in the sun. How she loves this desert. Crickets starting their night song, and a view through the veil of poplar trees of the western horizon, a spectacular smear of colors as the sun rests on clouds over the volcanoes on the mesa to the west.

This is not so much a porch as a slab of cracked concrete, ten feet by ten feet, with a green corrugated plastic roof that was hastily nailed to some boards decades ago, the kind of thing you find lying in roadways in tornado-prone areas, after the storm. A table and chairs, plastic, cracked. A clay sun nailed to the wall, cracked as well. A store-bought fountain long since run dry, with a carved cherub at the top, which she found creepy when she was younger. Vanessa feels a pang of sadness and guilt, realizes Mary once thought this ugly thing quite elegant. There was a time when Mary actually tried to make this place a home.

A small, scraggly, and sloping square of backyard that used to seem so much bigger. Plain gray cement bricks for walls. The decomposition of once-admirable elements has been fairly relentless in the two years since Mom's injury. Somehow, Vanessa had been sure Larissa was on top of tending it, given that this is where the girls would run when the fighting got too loud in the house, their secret hiding place, their shelter beneath the big New Mexico sky. A sacred place, really. But then, maybe Larissa is just a tiny bit busy, and as bad with plants as she is with food, the sister with hands like hemlock.

The tomatoes Larissa planted slouch helplessly, tired, dry, uncertain, like skinny girls in a refugee camp, their orbs deflated, their leaves burned crisp. The best Larissa could do, no doubt. Vanessa wonders what the garden is trying to tell her now. What omen this is, what truth being spoken.

She tugs her mother's crusty canvas gardening gloves over her hands, and begins to answer the call to rescue. She will start with the tomatoes, and move to the bowed heads of the dried roses, the great parched grape arbor next, and, finally, she'll see what, if anything, can be done about the funereal flowerbeds. Everything ordered at right angles. Hard and sharp. Dry and dying. Bitter, the best days behind, and winter coming fast. Perfect squares, made by railroad ties that smell of tar. Death in the yard as surely as there is a sun in the sky.

A metallic sound comes painfully to her ears, as nails to a proverbial chalkboard, issued up from the backside of the corned-beef house. Vanessa moves just her eyes, to see. Sure enough, the Viking is there, in a pair of well-fitting jeans and another T-shirt, this one gray with a big American flag across the front. Oh, *goody*.

The dividing cinder-block walls, she thinks, are far too low between these houses. Maybe four feet. Not quite five. She can see his feet if she cranes her neck. Not sure why she's done this, however, and quite sure Larissa would not approve.

He wears big black sandals with thick rubber soles, the kind that you might use to go hiking or rafting, and he's moving the patio furniture on cement. A huge new barbecue grill smokes covetously, butane source identified. He looks over, and catches her watching him. She looks away, but it's too late—his eyes laugh at her in their simple way, and the big white teeth bared in boisterous greeting. He stands straight and tall, his shoulders broad and strong, with not a scrap of fat on the tight belly, and with a most beautiful curve to his tush. His legs are tan and strong as the rest of him. The sight of him sends a shiver through her.

"Yo, late, how's it goin'?" A booming baritone, a little stuffy in the nose. Far too happy under the tense circumstances of their acquaintance to be anything but witless. He's like a gigantic and persistent puppy—a big, butterscotch puppy with big feet, a wagging tail, and a happy face that will keep smiling at you even if you ignore it or push it away.

"It is not *that* late, just after six," she says, noticing now that his mother's curvaceous garden is in tip-top shape. Of course it is. Noticing that her own voice sounds like bossy Peppermint Patty, which is better than Lisa Simpson but not altogether good, considering.

"No," he says. "That's your name, right? *Late.* That's what you said." He winks at her, obnoxious, checks the smoking grill in such a way as to give full view of his resplendent backside.

"I have no idea what you're talking about." She turns back to the tomatoes, hoping that will be the end of this exchange. No such luck.

"Earlier today. I said, 'Hi, I'm Paul, and you are?' and you said, 'Late.' Remember?" He taps his temple with a big, clean finger. Patronizing.

The Viking's back door opens, and three men about Vanessa's age tumble out. Stooges. The one with unkempt red hair and glasses carries a portable speaker system for an iPod. The fat one with curly hair holds a big tray of something covered in aluminum foil. The skinny one with the long, feathered hair and even longer legs holds tight to two six-packs of bottled beer.

An older woman follows behind them, with shoulder-length blond hair styled in waves, jeans, a nice shirt made of natural fiber, the sort of sensible European shoes you might buy at an outdoors specialty shop. Youthful for her age, Vanessa thinks. She assumes this to be Phyllis, and Phyllis, for her part, holds an assortment of large barbecue implements as though they were fresh flowers, sets them carefully on the substantial iron-and-glass patio table, next to a pitcher of what looks like homemade lemonade, and large reusable plastic cups.

"Mom," Paul brays. "Come over here. This is Vanessa, the pretty neighbor lady I told you about."

He winks at Vanessa again, more to show he's kidding than to be perverse, and she wonders how she can manage to ignore these people now, how she can return to death upon the land. At mention of a pretty lady, the other men look askance at her, a stand of timid deer alerted to a fang-glorious predator, more terrified than intrigued, too meek to move. They pretend to arrange things on the table and grill. Still afraid of women, in their thirties. A strange bunch, this.

Paul and his mother wait at the low wall now, patient as peasants in a breadline, the woman smiling with the same big, healthy teeth as her son, but with something different, a distinct sadness encircling her eyes. And humor. A nice woman, and doesn't that complicate the evening?

"Phyllis Stebbit," she says, and extends her hand. Forces Vanessa to the wall to shake back.

"Vanessa," she replies.

"Duran, is it?" asks Phyllis, referring to Vanessa's last name, which is still the same as her parents' last name. Shoots a look to her son.

"Yep," says Vanessa, gesturing to the white house with a smile. "They liked me enough to let me use it, amazingly enough."

Paul lifts a brow and looks toward her left hand, ring finger, appears pleased to find nothing there.

"That's funny," he says.

"It's a pleasure to meet you," says Phyllis.

"Fellas, c'mere," Paul calls to the men, his eyes never leaving Vanessa's. "Don't be a bunch of ballerinas. Come meet the cute little neighbor lady."

He chuffs, doglike, aware, it seems, that Vanessa does not like being referred to as the cute little neighbor lady any more than she likes hearing a man call his friends ballet dancers as though it were an insult. A grizzly man's man who enjoys annoying others. Probably has a whoopee cushion hidden in the glove box of his gi-

gantic truck. Probably has nicknames for everyone he knows. Probably opens beer bottles with those teeth.

The feathered hair belongs to Hal Reemer, a name that does
nothing to remove him from the early eighties in which he is stuck.
The redhead is called Dan Garcia, and he is in possession of a dis-
concerting gap-toothed resemblance to the cartoon boy in *MAD*
magazine. The overweight one is Jacob Kaminsky, the only one of
the lot who looks as if he might be well-educated, or fit in with
Vanessa's group of friends. He strikes Vanessa as sympathetic, maybe
effeminate, and interesting, and as out of place as she is.

Awkward. Paul smiles. Phyllis helps out by asking if Vanessa
grew up in the house. She says she did, and Phyllis explains that her
husband passed away a year or so ago, and she wanted to move to
something a little smaller, without all the memories. Too much information.

"Did you go to high school here in town?" Paul asks.

"Yes. At Del Norte," she tells him.

"Eldorado," he says, pointing to himself and the guys.

"Ah," she says. In her day, that school was known for having rich
kids and pampered jock types. Who knows what it is home to
now?

"They always said chicks from Del Norte were good-looking,"
says Paul. "Right, guys?"

The men nod uncomfortably, and Vanessa, flooded with a momentary image of herself and her high school friends with too
much eyeliner and too-tight pants, does nothing to hide her disgust

with Paul's comment. Even Phyllis looks embarrassed for him now. To make matters worse, a slop of shouting issues up from the home of Mary and Greg. The usual escalation. Mary shouting, Greg shouting back. Vanessa cringes to realize the neighbors can hear this. Nowhere to hide now.

Phyllis looks at her sympathetically. "We're having a cookout to welcome Pauly back to town," she says. "Why don't you join us?"

"Oh, that's nice. Thank you. But I already ate, just a little while ago."

"Well, then, just come have some lemonade," Phyllis pushes.

"Oh. That is so nice. But I promised my mom I'd get some yard work done."

"Well, we'll leave you to that, then." Phyllis seems to sense Vanessa's discomfort, and grabs her son's arm to pull him away.

"I make a mean barbecue," Paul calls out to her. "If you change your mind. We're not the best company in the world, but we'll do in a pinch."

He glances at her parents' house as if to imply that the parents themselves were a pinch.

"I've got a ton of work to do over here." Vanessa's eyes sweep the yard. Paul follows her gaze with a critical eye, and doesn't try to gloss it over or be polite.

"*Yeah*, you do," he says with a chuckle. "Years of work. I'll bring you a plate in a while. You'll need your strength."

THE YAHOO GRILLS A WAHOO

Forty minutes later, Vanessa is elbow deep in weeds, dirt, improvements coming slowly, sobriety also coming slowly, and the sun has nearly set, the scent of piñon and juniper coming down from the mountains, faint, but there. Porch light on next door, and the caveman party going full blast. Bugs everywhere and she doesn't bother to brush them away. Green bottles of beer, the guys laughing and talking about the girls they used to think were hot, makes her wonder why she bothers trying to find mature, reliable men in the first place. Surely these ones are her age, or close to it, and yet they prattle on about women as if they were fifteen.

Paul plays air drums compulsively, stopping only to man the grill. A most delicious scent from that grill. Fish? Fruit? Fresh corn?

Unexpected. Vanessa sniffs the air in surprise. She expected rancid ground beef, pumped with artificial flavors and colors, doused in A1 Steak Sauce, stuck to white bread drenched in cheap mayonnaise.

Then, the Viking with a plastic plate in his hands, at the wall again, saying it's too dark to dig around in the spiders, and life too short to just work, work, work. An unexpected way with words, humor. Not what she expected.

"Take a break, c'mon. Don't be unfriendly, now."

A cold beer, too. Bait, redolent, unnamed umami—that savory fifth taste popularized in Japan—bait, and he reels her in from curiosity, but only for the food, as if he might have known. The aromas. She must find out what they are, to test her guessing abilities. That, for Vanessa, is about as fun as life gets.

She peers at the plate. Finds a white fish steak, fruited salsa, corn on the cob with—what is that?—*queso fresco* crumbled on it, maybe a dash of red chile powder. A scent of peanuts. Grilled pineapple slices. Delectable.

"What did you make there?" she asks, mouth watering already.

Paul grins sheepishly and shrugs. "Mom tells me you're a chef. Can't make any promises."

"How did she know I was a chef?" Vanessa's face in astonished stillness, Paul's expression soft and friendly to calm her worries.

"We're neighbors, silly. She's talked to your mom a couple times. You know how it is. Moms like to brag."

Not my mom, she thinks. "Well, whatever it is you made smells pretty good."

Paul tells her he's grilled wahoo, a Hawaiian fish he had a pal on the island send him on dry ice. Says he's addicted to the stuff. Says he learned to cook it when he was "stationed at Hickam."

"Army?" she asks as she removes the crusty gardening gloves.

A polite grin, shakes his head, but points a conciliatory finger her way. "Close. Air Force."

Asks her with zeal to try the fish—"I've never had a real chef eat my cooking before!"—but she can't hold the plate all that well with the gardening gloves pinned between her arms and her torso. She hesitates, not wanting to go inside her parents' house, where the fighting goes on like clockwork and where, no doubt, the sickly sweet port has begun to flow.

"Oh, crud," she says, feeling all thumbs and fumbles. "Hang on. I'm not all that good at eating standing up."

"Climb on over," he suggests. "Plenty of room at our table. Here, I'll help ya."

He sets the plate down on the wall, holds out a hand.

She hesitates, and does not like how light he makes her heart feel, how easy he is on the eyes and the brain. Maybe there's something to the whole Boy Scout–soldier thing, she thinks, something she has missed all these years chasing highbrow intellectual types, rich metrosexuals, and chefs.

"I promise we don't bite," he says with a smile.

Ordinarily she wouldn't hop a fence to hang out with virtual strangers, but the essence of wahoo has her attention, and over she goes, scraping her knee on the way and tumbling at the end like the thirty-something she is. Climbing is for kids. He catches her on the other side, his smell cleaner than earlier, but every bit as enticing.

"Thanks," she says. "I'm not usually this helpless."

"You said that earlier, too, and I don't doubt it," he tells her. "You seem plenty capable to me."

Such a nice smile, she thinks, as he walks with her across the pretty yard, filled with bird feeders and fountains, toward the patio. Coming from her mother's backyard to this is something like Alice going through the looking-glass, she thinks.

Phyllis sets a place for Vanessa at the glass-top patio table, elegant with candlelight and flowers, and Hal turns the music down.

Paul beams and leans forward in his seat as Vanessa puts a bit of the fish in her mouth. His smile increases in voltage when her eyes open wide, as if she were a woman who has just heard a pigeon recite the preamble to the U.S. Declaration of Independence.

The wahoo is, simply, delicious—not overdone as so many are apt to do with fish, especially on the grill, flaky, tender enough to practically melt on the tongue.

"Wow," she says. "This is excellent."

"You're just saying that," says Paul, with a blush to his cheeks that seems out of place with the image Vanessa has of him as a strapping tough guy. Humility. She so rarely comes across this emotion in the presence of a cook and his excellent food anymore, she's taken aback.

"No, I mean it."

"My Pauly's a good cook," says Phyllis. "When he was a child, he was the only boy on the block who wanted an Easy-Bake oven."

"Mom!" he cries, the redness in his cheeks augmenting. "Don't *tell* people about that!"

"I thought it was sweet," says Phyllis.

"So do I," Vanessa tells them. "Very cute."

"Paul always loved the food," says the fat friend, Jacob.

"Hey. But I'm no chef," Paul insists. "Not like the pretty neighbor lady here."

His broad smile reveals that he loves the fact that she liked his fish, and that his ego is clearly not threatened by the risk involved in letting a real chef taste his creation. His confidence, so clear in his comportment, derives from another source, she thinks.

She wonders what that source might be.

Phyllis asks Vanessa about her job, where she works, and she tells them a little bit, trying to simultaneously catalog whatever it is she is tasting. Peanut sauce, mango, pineapple, a tart marinade.

"Tamarind?" she asks him, takes another bite.

Paul's face lights up. "Wow! How the heck did you *know* that? That's not fair!" He's laughing. "Tamarind juice in the marinade! That's my big secret."

"I'm sorry," she offers.

He laughs some more. "I'm kidding, Vanessa. Yes, tamarind. I'm an open book. No secrets here."

Vanessa chews, looks at Paul more gently than she has yet. He really is very, very good-looking, with a symmetrical, clear face and a very open composure. Social. Bryan was more introverted and—surprise, surprise—secretive.

When Paul hands her the next bottle of perfectly cold beer, Fat Tire, she can't resist—partly because he's thought to bring it to her. How many men think to get you something you need? Not many, sadly. It's so right for the meal, the setting, the company, all of it a most pleasant surprise. What's the harm? Just one more. She doesn't drink much, usually, but today seemed particularly stressful, and this socializing with neighbors feels just right. She is aware, of course, that her parents have drinking problems, but she is quite sure this is not a problem she has inherited. She rarely drinks more than a glass of wine with a meal.

"So, Vanessa, do you have any hobbies?" asks Phyllis.

Not drinking excessively. Vanessa tries not to giggle. Hobbies? It has been so long since anyone asked her a question like this. Since high school, maybe. It seems a forced question, a stock question. She thinks Phyllis is out of practice entertaining her son's friends. She still acts like they're kids. Very sweet.

"Gardening," she says.

Phyllis eyes Mary's anemic garden next door, and Vanessa pipes up. "Hey, that's not mine. Today is the first time I've even seen it in years. I avoid this place when I can. I live in the valley. I'm just here to help my mom—her back got broken a while back and she's got some trouble still—while my sister's out of town."

"I think I've seen your sister." Phyllis smiles. "Couple little girls? Cute as pie?"

"That's her."

Phyllis nods. "She always looks so busy, I've never had the opportunity to visit with her. So, Vanessa. What else do you like to do?"

Vanessa feels put on the spot. "Hike, I guess," she says. "I love hiking. Anything out in nature. And reading. I'm pretty boring. Cooking's my job and my hobby. I'm not a real exciting person, like I don't jump out of planes or anything."

At the mention of jumping from planes, the group members all seem to shift in their seats uncomfortably, with sidelong looks at Paul. What did she say wrong? Vanessa hopes she has not unintentionally offended someone. *Air Force*. Isn't that what he said earlier, about Hawaii?

"It's good to do what you love, Vanessa, and that's never boring," says Paul, comfortable as he was before, but almost as if to reassure everyone that he's fine with whatever it was that she just stuck in her mouth along with her foot. "I hope to do that myself soon."

"What *do* you love nowadays, Paul?" his friend Jacob asks him, seeming eager to change the subject.

"Besides the ladies," adds Dan, also working hard to distract Paul.

"Hey," Paul shoots back to Dan. "I'm not like that."

"He's gay," deadpans Jacob.

"No!" cries Paul. "I didn't mean I'm like *that*, either. I just mean I'm not like I used to be."

Dan looks at Vanessa and explains, "He used to be quite the womanizer."

Paul tells Vanessa, "That's a *lie*. Don't listen to these dorks. They just never had a date, so any guy with one date now and then turns into a womanizer to them." He looks at Jacob next, and addresses his earlier question. "I'm into building things now, for karma, like yin-yang."

They all talk now, and on it goes, and Vanessa relaxes and is surprised to realize she actually quite likes these people—and Paul most of all. He is less of the gooey canned ham than she initially thought, less of a Boy Scout, more of a mysterious soup pot with the lid tightly on, just heating up a tiny bit, the aromas leaking out, little by little, for her to guess at. A compelling mystery.

The others are equally charming. The chubby Jacob is a musical director for a flamenco dance group in town. The stuck-in-the-eighties Hal is vague about what he does, but seems like a nice, lost soul. He used to be a drum major, back in high school, and was as popular, she assumes, as such a personage might be. Vanessa senses that might have been the last time he felt good about himself. Dan, the redhead, was a trombonist with a major U.S. symphony in a far-away state, quit that to come teach music on the Isleta Indian Reservation because, in his words, "poor kids get screwed every way from Tuesday and I couldn't justify my cushy life anymore." He had to buy instruments with his own money. Phyllis, it turns out, teaches history at the university, and is looking forward to retiring because, she says, "academia has gotten as closed-minded as everything else in the country." She rattles off her areas of specialty— including Victorian England, emphasis on women's history.

"That's amazing," says Vanessa. "I did my master's in comparative literature, focused on Victorian English works."

Phyllis tilts her head in pleasure at this news, and Paul winks at his mother. "Where did you study?"

"Yale," says Vanessa.

Phyllis looks at her son with shock. "What an interesting degree for a chef," she says.

"Well, I've always loved food, so my focus was on the role of food in the lives of characters in Victorian literature." Vanessa feels as though her mouth is a spigot that just turned on, and she wishes she would not tell so much. Must be the beer. What is she even doing here?

"Fascinating!" cries Phyllis. "I would love to read your thesis."

"Really?" Vanessa grins at her, stunned because no one has ever said such a thing, besides her sister and advisors.

"Of course, dear," says Phyllis.

"Trust me," Paul tells Vanessa with a teasing air. "This is *exactly* the kind of thing Mom digs. If it's got lace, and a harpsichord, and powdery old English ladies, she's golden."

A sound of something breaking next door, shouting. All eyes to the white house for a brief second, out of shock, then to Vanessa, in pity, and then anywhere but Vanessa, in kindness.

"I'm sorry about that," says Vanessa to Phyllis. "They're a complete nightmare. I hate it so much. Do you hear it a lot?"

Phyllis wrings her hands together and smiles in sympathy tinged with frustration. "More than I'd like, yes."

"You should call the cops on them," says Vanessa.

"Can't have been easy growing up there," says Phyllis.

Best to be direct, thinks Vanessa. She has never wanted to be one of those children of dysfunctional parents who covers up for them, pretends that everything is fine, because in her mind that amounts not only to lying, but to being a coconspirator against her own well-being.

"It built character," Vanessa tells them. "I honestly don't come around that much, because of it, but my mom's in pretty bad shape."

"I noticed her cane," says Paul. "I asked her about it, but she didn't feel like sharing." He winks at Vanessa playfully.

"No, she usually doesn't," says Vanessa with a laugh. It feels good to talk openly about her mother, without anger, and she cannot imagine that she has matured past it all enough to feel this way. And yet she has.

"So what happened?" asks Phyllis. "How did your mother break her back?"

Vanessa tells them about the drunk driver who sped through a red light at the intersection at San Mateo and Montgomery two years ago, smashing into Mary's 1992 Chevy sedan at seventy-two miles per hour, pinning her to the steering wheel. Everyone winces appropriately, and offers sympathy. As Vanessa talks, she eats, and soon has eaten everything on her plate.

"Look at you," says Phyllis to Vanessa. "You ate it all. Would you like some more?"

Vanessa smiles guiltily, with a small shrug that stays by her ears. "Please?"

Vanessa happily lets the subject of her parents go, and the noises from their home mercifully scale back. She listens to the others talk as Phyllis goes to get her seconds. Old stuff, talk of the days when the four guys were in marching band together. People they knew, what they're up to now.

"You wouldn't know it to look at him now, but Paul here used to be the fat one," says Jacob, with a pat to his own ample belly.

"And Jake used to be the muscleman," jokes Paul. "He was like the dude who kicks sand in your face at the beach."

"You guys traded places," suggests Dan.

"Oh! And he used to have a freakin' bowl cut," says Jacob, of Paul.

"It was *her* fault," Paul explains, pointing to his mom.

She answers, "I didn't see the point in spending money on a child's haircut when I could do it just fine on my own."

"But in *high* school, Mom? C'mon," Paul teases, but Vanessa can tell that there is some real residual hurt there.

"Maybe I should have been a little less thrifty," says Phyllis. "But you've made up for it now. Isn't my Pauly handsome?" She directs this last question to Vanessa.

Paul rescues her, by interrupting before she can answer. "Moms always think their kids are attractive."

"Not always," jokes Vanessa, with a thumb toward her parents' house.

"Oh, come on," says Paul. "Of course they think you're beautiful. You are."

"Vanessa is a very pretty girl," agrees Phyllis.

Paul's hand goes to his head, feels the fuzz there. He looks at Vanessa. "Think I should let it grow out a little?" he asks her.

She finds it surprising that he would ask her such a thing, after knowing her for so short a time. She tells him the truth, that he'd look good with a little longer hair, and he answers with, "I concur."

"*And* he was short," adds Dan. "Now you're all Mister Atlas."

"Yeah, man," says Hal. "What the heck happened to you? Steroids?"

"Negative," says Paul.

"Wow," says Vanessa, finally loosening up to joke with them like the old friends they feel like now. "Fat and short, with a bowl cut. All that, *and* an Easy-Bake oven?"

Paul grins at her, delighted that she can dish it out. "I guess you could say I'm a real American original."

Vanessa finds herself laughing out loud, as she tries to picture this powerful, handsome man short, fat, with a bowl cut. It's hard to do, but it certainly explains why he has a certain sweetness to him, in spite of being spectacular enough not to. Paul just sort of watches her, amused.

When Phyllis accidentally drops the lid of the grill too hard, the loud bang makes Paul jump, a look of panic on his face. Then, he seems to go into a trance. His face is frozen, his eyes distant. He's gone, just like that.

"He's doing it again," says Jacob, to the others.

Silence now, as the laughter of moments before melts into thin air. At first, Vanessa thinks this is some kind of joke, but she quickly realizes it is not.

Vanessa sets her beer down on the table as quietly as possible, scared for herself, for Paul. The friends look at him and one another, and wince as if they expected this, but don't know what to do. Phyllis leaves Vanessa's plate on the barbecue grill's prep area, hurries to Paul's side, wraps her arms around him, and holds him tight, kisses the top of his head, rocks him like a baby.

"It's okay, son," she says. "You're here, back home. You're safe, Pauly. Deep breath, sweetheart. Mommy's here. There, there. Shhh."

Paul seems numb, his eyes distant, focused on something none of them can see, for a minute or two. Twitching in his face, grimacing, as if he were daydreaming and the daydream were a hideous nightmare.

He looks like he realizes he has made a mistake, and seems embarrassed, but still flooded with adrenaline. Gets up, paces a moment, takes his seat again, doesn't make eye contact with anyone at first. He focuses his eyes on his fingers laced together in his lap.

"Sorry, guys," says Paul, finally. His voice is low, and the words spoken slowly. "It happens. Just . . . just bear with me. I'm . . . whew. I don't know. I don't know what I am."

Phyllis continues to fuss over him, smooths his hair as though he were a little boy on his way to church.

Jacob moves his chair next to Vanessa's, leans close to her, and says just four words.

"Paul was in Iraq."

Her eyes narrow in empathy at Paul, and she can only imagine what that means, the war. Has he been in battle? Do pilots go to battle? What could it have been? Did he bomb people? What could he possibly be remembering?

Paul shakes himself again, shudders, takes a deep breath, and smiles at them all, makes light of it, jokes around. He thanks his mom, but pushes her away anyhow with something about how she's going to put a bib on him pretty soon. The men laugh with him, but not Phyllis. Her own eyes have tears perched in them, ready to fall, though she tries not to show it. She looks at Vanessa, imploring, solitary in her fear, and quickly looks away.

Jacob makes eye contact with Paul and leans toward him. "You want to talk it out, bro?" he asks. "That's what we're here for."

"Talk about what, man?" asks Paul. "There's nothing to talk about, Jake."

"What just happened, where you went just now. You want to tell us? We understand."

Paul stares him down, eyes hard now, ice. His mood has shifted instantly. "You wouldn't understand," he says. "There's no point. There's no way you could understand."

"You could try me," Jacob suggests with a shrug. A good friend, Vanessa thinks. A great guy.

"You like the wahoo?" Paul asks Vanessa, though he already asked her this two times earlier. It seems like he wants to get away from Jacob's questions. "It's from Hawaii." Told her that, too.

"Excellent," she repeats, feeling very sorry for him as he tries so hard to seem normal.

"They're dark blue, wahoos," he continues. "More of a prize fish than commercial, because they live alone instead of in schools."

"Oh, Pauly," sighs Phyllis, softly, almost too softly to be heard. Her hands wring together. He ignores it.

He rattles on. "You catch 'em in tuna nets sometimes, by mistake, you know, like dolphins. They keep the wahoos, but they're supposed to throw the dolphins back."

Vanessa's hands with nowhere to go, her face stuck in a pose of pity that he notices, but is too polite to ask her to remove. She is now just one of the deer in Paul's headlights, watching the accident about to happen, or, rather, watching the memory of the one that already came, in scrolling scars across Paul's spirit.

"So," he says, as if he and Vanessa were old friends. "Tell me what you like these days, in the food world. What's floating Miss Vanessa Duran's boat?"

Claps his hands once, like a teacher, looks like he's taken a course on active-listening skills. Pops an old bit of pineapple from someone else's plate into his mouth as though he'd been eating it all along. He is trying, she thinks, much too hard.

"Hmm." *Be honest*, she thinks. *Act naturally.* "I'm over the moon about Australian shiraz." Face still frozen in that formidable grin.

Paul's eyes dance with a strange, glassy light as he says, "I think I've heard of that. Shiraz. It's a fish, right?"

Vanessa shakes herself out of her trance now, and remembers her sister's words. No rebound men. And especially not *this* one. No needy men. No injured men. No men who don't have what she's looking for, and Vanessa is most definitely looking for someone who knows what a shiraz is.

Do not, she tells herself, *allow yourself to get too close to this guy. He is flat dangerous, in so many different ways.*

"Not a fish," she says. She looks at her watch now, makes an excuse about getting home, not feeling well, being tired, having had a long day.

Paul suggests, quietly and discreetly, that she might have had a little too much beer to drive safely, offers to drive her home, a Boy Scout once more. She stands, not drunk, but she probably *is* too tipsy to drive—and she's very tired on top of that. No need for her to have her *own* back broken, now *is* there? No need to augment the many assembled tragedies of this evening with one of her own.

"I can get you in the morning, bring you back to your car," he says, adding, "I'd like to see you in the morning."

"That's very thoughtful. But I think I'll just stay with my mom and dad," she says. "Thanks, though."

Vanessa says her good-byes, and starts to pick her way across the yard toward the fence, to hop it again. Total darkness now, and winged, papery things clicking in the shrubbery like little flamenco dancers.

"I'm happy to show you the front door," suggests Phyllis, offering Vanessa a steadying elbow, to turn her back around like some sort of tugboat after a fish barge on a slow river. "Here, I'll take you."

"I hope to see you again sometime," says Paul. "It's been fun hanging out with a real chef."

Their eyes connect, and in his she can see so many things, so many interesting things, that she must turn from him.

Inside the house, away now from Paul, Phyllis apologizes for her son. "He's had a tough time of it all, as you can imagine. This is not the Pauly I remember."

"No need for apologies." Vanessa connects her eyes with the older woman's, and takes in the great depth of pain in them. "He was only doing his duty, right?"

"It was his dad's idea, years ago. Thought it would give him discipline. I never wanted him to do it, and then this war came," Phyllis confesses with a disgusted look on her face, as they near the front door. "I never thought my son would be in the military. There are many ways to do one's duty, ways that don't involve—" She stops now, bites her lower lip. "I'll leave that for another time. We've only just met. It's up to him to tell you, if he wants to."

"I'm not dating anyone, just so you know," blurts Vanessa, before realizing how badly it sounds.

Phyllis blinking at her, in abrupt surprise.

"No," clarifies Vanessa. "I mean, I don't *want* to, I can't. I won't. I'm taking a break. So you can tell him that. I'm not in the market for a man right now. He's a lovely man, but I am on a man hiatus for a while."

Phyllis stares at Vanessa plainly.

"Don't worry, Vanessa, what Pauly needs right now are *friends*." A weight of sadness again, a bitten lip. "He's always been the kind of guy who has female friends, and you won't find a friend more loyal than my son. He takes the idea of duty very seriously. And responsibility."

Vanessa opens the door. "Thank you for the nice time. It was fun to meet all of you. And I'm sorry about my parents."

"Families are never perfect, are they?" Phyllis asks, taking Vanessa's hand in hers for a little supportive squeeze. "They're lucky to have such a lovely daughter. I look forward to visiting hawk to try your menu."

Maybe because she's a little tipsy, and maybe because she is not sure her own mother would worry about her this way, had she gone to war and come back startled at the sound of falling barbecue grill lids, or maybe because her own mother has never offered to come to hawk at all, Vanessa reaches out with both arms to hug Paul's mother good night. Sober enough still to know it is an odd gesture, not expecting to be hugged back. Phyllis returns the embrace, however, and seems to hang on to Vanessa as a drowning woman might clutch at a lifeboat. The older woman does not seem to breathe, for a long moment, and then the gasp comes and she moves away, drying her eyes on the back of her hand.

"You have a wonderful garden," Vanessa tells her. "And your son is a very good cook. That can only mean one thing, you know."

Phyllis lifts her eyes to Vanessa's and asks, "What's that?"

"It means everything is going to be just fine. *That's* what it means. Gardens talk to us. And yours tells me it's all going to be okay."

Phyllis smiles at her, softly, and nods her head in agreement. "I remind myself every day of the words Kahlil Gibran wrote, about joy and sorrow being inseparable, and how when one sits alone with you, the other is asleep on your bed."

Vanessa tries to ignore the goose bumps rising along her arms.

"It really has been lovely to meet you, Phyllis," she says.

She does not, however, tell the older woman that she envies Paul, in as kind and generous a way as one can envy a man come home from a war, for having been blessed with a most perfectly cured bacon of a mother.

THE KANGARILLA ROAD

GAMBLE

It has been a week since Vanessa spent a mildly drunk night on her parents' stale sofa, which means Larissa will be back in a month. One week of miserable solicitude down, four to go. Vanessa rather thinks she might be able to pull off the whole Mom-watching thing after all.

It is now a clear, chilly September night, after work, a night with piñon smoke in the air and an orange halo around the full moon. Vanessa returns to her garden-drenched cottage in Hazel's Toyota sedan, with her bike dismembered like a frying chicken in the trunk. She was happy to have the offer of a ride in this chilly weather, and the company. The conversation for the past several minutes has been mostly about comparing Hawk and Isaac to male members, in an unfavorable way. The women are not sure which of these men they detest more these days.

The friends both have the day off tomorrow and plan to spend the rest of the night discussing menu options Vanessa has come up with for the bachelorette party, talking shop and men and whatever else there is to be discussed between girlfriends who work together but often find they cannot discuss work because they *are* at work, surrounded by the very people they'd like to discuss.

They also intend, after another day of Hawk being petted and praised by his adoring public for scrumptious creations borne of Vanessa's palate and brainpower, to discuss the various sorts of strategies and long-term plans Hazel has been concocting and they have put off discussing.

Vanessa has continued to visit her mother in these intervening days, and has seen Paul and Phyllis only briefly, surprised at her heavy disappointment at their absence or busy lives. She likes them quite a lot, the mother and son neighbors. Phyllis told her Paul has been busy looking for work in construction, and seemed sad as she said it, but Vanessa, sober, did not press for more. Like the mother did not want her son to be a laborer. Like he was cut out for so much more.

The one time she did see Paul in the front yard, long enough to chat briefly, he made Vanessa feel strangely sorry for him once again, by saying, "Hey, Vanessa. I have a question for you. Friend of mine who's real into food asked me this question the other day, about something called 'affinage,' and I was too proud to tell her I didn't know what that was, so I listened and pretended I knew what she was talking about. It's chips, right? Like high-quality potato chips. Right?"

Vanessa had not corrected him, as he'd seemed so proud of himself. Rather, she had blinked at him blankly for a moment or two, before awkwardly changing the subject. He did not seem to notice anything amiss, which made Vanessa feel like a better actress than she believed herself to be. Potato chips? She was so disgusted by his thinking affinage was potato chips. It absolutely meant he was not romantic material, but he could still be her friend. She planned to tell him the real meaning one of these days, but did not wish to seem like a know-it-all, as her mother put it, right away.

Hazel parks the black Toyota behind the red Subaru, and the women unload the bicycle and crunch across the gravel toward the house in the still, cool night. Red Dog is barking inside, as surely she has been doing since she first heard the unfamiliar car turn off the dirt road toward the cottage. Night birds flit past, and a snow globe of nocturnal insects blizzards around the porch light with little regard for the repeated searing of their wings and thready scraps of leg. Sometimes instinct is too strong, Vanessa muses. Insects fly toward the light, thinking it the moon and the stars. Sometimes evolution is too slow. Sometimes instinct makes you burn yourself in search of heaven.

A large package from an overnight delivery service waits on the front porch, between the screen door and the main door, but Vanessa is not expecting anything. She picks it up, examines the box briefly in the dim light, batting the moths and mosquitoes away, but cannot seem to make out a sender's name or address, shrugs. She gives up for now, sticks her key in the door.

"Calm down, girl," Vanessa tells Red Dog as she opens the door to find her companion suspended somewhere between elation at the return of Vanessa, and agitation at the appearance of Hazel, whose smell is not yet familiar enough to put the dog at ease. Red Dog jumps, as she often does, and whines, and wags her oar of a tail in a big, excited circle.

Hazel holds her hand to Red Dog's nose, and waits to be approved. The dog whimpers slightly, lifts an eyebrow at Vanessa, tappity-taps with her claws on the wooden floor, seeking reassurance, and gets it. Vanessa pets the dog roughly, kisses the top of her head, and then, finally, locks the door behind them.

She turns on the lights, and Hazel instantly makes herself at home by removing her shoes and collapsing in an exhausted heap on the sofa. Vanessa thinks only too late to warn her of the red and white dog hairs that cover the couch, no matter how frequently she attacks it with the sticky lint roller, and Hazel pretends, as good friends will, that the furry aspects of Vanessa's home don't bother her in the least.

Vanessa takes a seat on the sofa near her friend, and holds the package in her lap.

"Whatcha got there?" asks Hazel, opening one eye.

"I have no idea." Vanessa turns the box over twice, looking for a hint about its sender. It is heavy, and sounds like it might have something liquid inside.

"You think it's okay to open it?" asks Hazel, always one to think the worst.

"What, you think someone's going to send me anthrax?" asks Vanessa with a teasing smile.

"You never know." Hazel does not smile in return.

"Oh, c'mon," says Vanessa. "No one hates me *that* much."

"Isaac," suggests Hazel, referring to the ambitious young line cook. The women laugh. Lately, Isaac has been the butt of many of their jokes.

"Oh, please," says Vanessa, as she gets up to search in the secretary desk where she keeps her mailing supplies for a letter opener strong enough to deal with the heavy-duty tape of the package. "The worst he could do is mail me photos of himself weight-lifting."

"Eew!" shrieks Hazel.

"In the nude," concludes Vanessa, knowing this image will disgust her friend. What's the use of having a friend if you cannot horrify them now and then?

"I don't like that guy at *all*," Hazel tells her, again. For the millionth time. Vanessa chooses not to comment on it, and instead returns to the package and busies herself opening it.

Inside the box, and after a bit of work to get through the packing materials, she finds an elegantly curved black bottle of wine and another tightly wrapped package that the caution across the box warns contains dry ice.

"Huh," states Vanessa, taking a closer look at the bottle's subtle, small beige label with grayscale grape-leaf etching on it. Kangarilla Road winery, in Australia, a shiraz, a good year. Vanessa's eyes dance with pleasure, for this is one of her favorite wineries at the moment, and this is certainly one of their top wines.

"Beautiful," sighs Vanessa.

"Who sent it?" asks Hazel.

Vanessa turns the bottle in her hands. "I have no idea."

"Larissa, maybe?"

Vanessa knits her brow and shakes her head. "I highly doubt she can get online much, or that she's got access to this sort of thing in the Moroccan desert."

"Not Hawk," says Hazel, with doubt.

"Do I look like a blond supermodel to you?" asks Vanessa rhetorically.

"You're prettier."

"Well, be that as it may," Vanessa teases, "Hawk doesn't give gifts to his staff, only to his stable of toothpicks."

"What else is in there?" Hazel sits up now, curious.

Vanessa starts in on the dry-ice package next, and finds inside a delicate, superb Brebicet, a sheep's-milk soft cheese, from the French company Guilloteau.

"Nice," says Hazel, herself a bit of a gourmand, though only in tasting, never in creating.

"The perfect company for this wine," Vanessa says, her eyes narrowing at the limited possibilities of who might be out there with enough food sense to send such a thing.

"Bryan," she states flatly, her smile sliding to a frown.

"You *think?*" gasps Hazel. "Why would he *do* that?"

"Because he thinks the way to my heart is through my stomach."

"He's still after you?"

"I didn't think so, but now with this, I don't know."

Vanessa sets the cheese next to the wine on the rustic wooden coffee table, scowls at it. Hazel takes up the hull of the box and peers inside, reaches her hand in and extracts a pale blue envelope that looks to contain a card.

"You forgot something," she sings in a teasing way, as she hands it to Vanessa.

Vanessa takes one look at the neat printed script across the front and realizes this is not Bryan's unkempt, psychotic scrawl. Her frown grows deeper as she uses the letter opener to extract the card within, a card that features a famous painting, *Still Life with Oranges*, by Henri Matisse, blank inside except for the two sentences and the signature. She goes to the name first.

"Paul *Stebbit?*" she cries, utterly and completely surprised that he would know of Matisse, though certain he cannot possibly know Matisse is one of Vanessa's favorite painters of food and eating scenes, or that her garden, when she conceived of it, was meant to be an impressionist homage to the painter's portrayals of people enjoying one another's company over a table of food.

"Who?" asks Hazel.

"That rah-rah military guy who lives next door to my mom," says Vanessa, unable to hide her curious excitement at the fact that he has sent such things to her home.

"The Viking?" asks Hazel, incredulous.

"Yeah, the Viking."

"Can Vikings even *write*?" asks Hazel.

"Apparently."

"What does it say?" asks Hazel, as she leans in toward the card. "You, girl. Me, boy. You sit on my lap. Ooga ooga."

"That's cold," says Vanessa with a wicked smile.

"That's why we're friends," says Hazel.

Together, they read the card.

Dear Vanessa,

Enjoy the fish and chips. Hope you know I was just testin' ya.

Wanna know your score? See ya soon, pretty neighbor lady.

Paul Stebbit

Hazel blinks at Vanessa, who blinks back. Stumped.

"Huh," says Vanessa, falling against the back of the sofa and letting the card drop into her lap.

"*Testing* you?" asks Hazel. "What do you think he means by that?"

"I have no idea."

"Call him and ask," says Hazel.

"I don't know his number."

"Ask your mom."

"I can't call her this late. She'll flip out."

"She's always flipped out."

"True, but it's still too late. I'll ask him when I see him."

"Well, that makes you a lot more patient than me. You have to call me right away and let me know what he says."

"Okay."

They agree that it would be silly to let the Viking's wine and cheese go to waste, even with the enigmatic missive attached, and Vanessa goes to fetch a cheeseboard, some bland flatbreads, the syrah wineglasses, and a couple of small plates.

As they share the offerings, Hazel grills Vanessa about the Viking, and gets what little she knows of him out of her. Hazel concludes that he sounds hot, "even if he does use the word 'lady' without irony," and just wounded enough to be exciting.

"Wounded?" Vanessa responds.

"Oh, c'mon, Vanessa. You know we women love to rescue screwed-up men."

"Sad, but true." Vanessa frowns into her wine.

"There's nothing hotter than a messed-up soldier," concludes Hazel.

Vanessa shrugs. "I don't know. He's more like the kind of guy who's your best friend. He's not really my type, romantically."

"You mean he's single?" Hazel teases.

"You suck," says Vanessa.

"You know I'm kidding!" Hazel pushes Vanessa good-naturedly, and Vanessa pushes her back, and suggests that they change the subject to the bachelorette party.

Hazel, enlivened by the possibility of now talking about herself—and doesn't everyone feel that way sometimes?—gives her the parameters. It shall be a small dinner party, maybe eight people, a five-course dinner, something creative and heartfelt. Does Hazel have any idea what kind of cuisine she'd like Vanessa to focus on? Not really.

"I trust you to know what to do," Hazel tells her. "Just be yourself. Be as creative as you can."

Vanessa spends the next hour or so asking for details about Hazel and Smitty, how they met, where they were, places they might have gone or would like to go, what matters to them, on and on. She gets the sense from what Hazel says of him that Smitty is every bit the discontented dreamer Hazel is. They are both the kind of people who go to open houses every weekend, and fool themselves with each house they love that they will, in fact, one day live there. They both grew up poor, but were smartest in their respective classes. They have traveled together overseas once, to Smitty's native Ireland, and have very fond memories of the time spent there. Hazel has opened businesses that closed down, and was suckered into at least one pyramid scam with a group of women from her neighborhood. A dinner of dreams, Vanessa thinks, something ethereal, otherworldly, something exotic and charmed, misty and foggy as the British Isles, as dreams often can be.

Now, Hazel is waitressing to make it through medical school.

Smitty works as a dental assistant while studying for his bar, almost finished with law school. Hard workers, upwardly mobile, big dreams, and bigger hearts. Soon enough, Vanessa has a very good sense of the direction she will take with this special dinner for a dear friend, something of Northern New Mexico to reflect Hazel's ancestry, something of the Irish to reflect Smitty's, but something elegant to reflect back to them where they are going in their shared imagined future. When she communicates her thoughts to Hazel, her friend's eyes well up with tears.

"Perfect," she says. "It's just perfect. When are you going to go solo? Get out of hawk?"

"Tomorrow, if you have a couple million dollars to spare."

"So are you saying money is your only issue?"

Vanessa sips the shiraz, truly an excellent wine, with spice and mulberry to it. "That's what I'm saying."

"Well, in that case, no problem," says Hazel, who, to Vanessa's knowledge, has even less money than she herself does. "I'm on it."

Vanessa gives her friend a loving look, grateful for her enthusiasm and support, and says nothing to dissuade her dreaming. Vanessa has spent enough of her own life dreaming to know that sometimes, dreams are all people have. Sometimes, dreams are all that keep you going.

A RIPENING OF THE CHERRY

The following day, Vanessa says a silent prayer as she drives up to her mother's house with Red Dog in the backseat, more Buddhist than anything else, just a mantra, a hope spoken softly on her lips, that he will be there. The shiraz Viking, with his lemon-lime scent. That she will be able to thank him for the wine, and ask him about the test, and whether she passed or failed.

Prayer answered. His garage door is open once more, and there he is, with that same heap of scrap metal, and the tool, and other tools, only now the metal has begun to take shape, and the shape it takes looks an awful lot like it wants to be a motorcycle. Just the sort of thing you would never want to make on your own, thinks Vanessa, unless you were a crazy person, or incredibly competent. Maybe Paul is both. That eternal anticipation of sweet, of tart, that comes with the first bite moving toward the mouth. Late summer. The mystery of Paul deepening like the color on a ripening cherry. Curses to Larissa and the pledge of nondating. Curses to blue states and red states, to divisions. Politics aren't everything. Animal attraction, now there's something a chef can sink her teeth into. Not that she's thinking about it. Except that she is.

As she pulls the red Subaru to the curb, she sees him glance up at her from where he crouches, at work on the garage floor. He smiles, a smudge of grease across his cheek. Old jeans, a ripped-up old white T-shirt, tight enough to show the sculpted body beneath, the big beige work boots, and, as she gets out and snaps the leash to Red Dog's collar, the music comes to her ears. Rock, as before. A predictable man of mystery, she thinks with a laugh. An incomplete enigma.

"Vanessa!" He's up off the floor, unfurling his magnificent body, on his feet, eyes shielded from the sun with one of those big hands. His hair has grown out a little more, and she realizes almost two weeks have gone by since she has been helping her mother, and she hasn't fallen apart yet, or gone insane. Paul's hair has a bit more brown to it than she'd thought. And maybe a sprinkling of gray. Still mostly blond, but dirty blond. Perfect against his tanned skin, atop his large, strong neck. Not that she notices, except that she does. Yes, she does.

Vanessa waves back, and holds on to the leash tightly as Red Dog pulls toward Paul, all smiles and wags. *That's odd*, thinks Vanessa. Usually Red Dog doesn't like men, has been that way ever since Vanessa adopted her as an adult mutt at the city shelter three years ago. She barks at men, snarls, cringes, and Vanessa is fairly sure that men, or a male, beat her in her past. But toward Paul she is over-joyed, as if they were old friends. Dogs, with their instincts. Vanessa trips up Paul's driveway in her running shoes and jeans, behind the enthusiastic canine.

"Who's this you got here?" Paul asks, squatting down instinc-tively to be less towering in the presence of Red Dog. He grins at her, and when she comes to whiff him and wag at him, he lets her sniff him, handles her with compassion and happiness, a man at home with dogs and in love with them.

"This is Red Dog," says Vanessa.

"What a pretty girl you are," Paul tells Red Dog, who clearly agrees and would like him to continue the praise. Paul rubs her un-der the chin, the best place to make a dog feel important. "Yes you are, yes you are, aren't ya, girl?"

Red Dog looks up at Vanessa and whines with happiness, as if to say, *I like this one, Mommy. Can we keep him?*

"She's my hiking partner today," Vanessa explains. "After I get Mom situated, I thought I'd take in some of the clear mountain air up here."

"Hiking! All right," he says.

"So, uhm," she says now, hand on her hip, eyes cast down to

where Paul continues to squat with the dog. "Testing me? What does that *mean*, exactly?"

His face brightens as he scratches Red Dog behind the ears. "Hey! You got the package?"

"I did. Thank you very much."

"Did you like it?" Paul stands up again now, and when Red Dog hops onto her hind legs, putting her forepaws on his waist, he lets her and doesn't seem annoyed at all. In fact, he wraps an arm around her like she was an old friend. He keeps eye contact with Vanessa, smiling devilishly, enjoying the tease, whatever it is.

She asks, "How did you get my address? Just curious."

"You mad?"

"No, just wondering."

"Did you forget I live next door to your mom?"

"No. I just didn't think she'd be that friendly."

"It's amazing what Mary does when you bring her a good bottle of wine," he says with a wink. Red Dog jumps down now, satisfied, and begins to sniff around.

"It doesn't have to be good, actually," says Vanessa.

Paul laughs. "Well, I went all out. I was on a mission. Mary was cool."

"That's because you've learned her secret spot."

"Secret spot?"

"I'll demonstrate." Vanessa kneels down now, and clicks her tongue for Red Dog to come to her. Then she rubs the dog in that certain spot on her side, near her right hind leg; the tail starts to thump as the dog squirms with pleasure.

"Ah," says Paul. "The secret spot."

"Dogs and moms have 'em," says Vanessa.

Paul arches his eyebrow and looks like he wants to say something, and Vanessa realizes the look in his eye is not entirely G-rated. But, to his credit, he stops short of the obvious flirtation she has volleyed to him, albeit unwittingly. She stands up, dusts the dog hair from her hands and runs them self-consciously through her hair, which hangs loose today.

"So what was that all about, the test? I don't get it."

"Okay, Vanessa, it's like this," he says, cocking his head kindly, like a teacher. "I was in the military, right?"

"Right."

"And I got some special training because I speak Arabic, and——"

She cuts him off. "You speak Arabic?"

"Yeah. And Spanish and German."

"Are you serious?"

"Yeah. I studied languages in college, and they thought I was good enough at it to keep training me on it."

"Wow. That's a lot of languages." Vanessa works hard to keep her jaw from dropping. She knew he had surprises to him, but this is a bit much.

"I like to talk," he says with a shrug and a wink. "So the more languages you know, the more people you can bore."

She folds her arms. Intrigued. Annoyed. More intrigued than annoyed. "I still don't see what that has to do with testing me."

"Patience, patience," he teases, bending down and petting the dog again. "I was just getting to that. It's like this, see. When you learn to interrogate people, you learn to—"

Again, she cuts him off, baleful. "You're an *interrogator*? For the *military*?" She shudders, unable to think of a job she would be less likely to do, or be more likely to fear.

"Yeah, but don't look at me like that. You can still like me. I wasn't one of *those* interrogators, okay? Some of us had scruples. Some of us had ethics."

She says nothing as images of tortured prisoners from Abu Ghraib flash across her mind, the man with the black hood, wires affixed to his limbs as he stood on a box, the naked prisoner bending over his private parts in the face of snarling dogs.

"Vanessa," he says. "I'm serious. I didn't get into all that."

"Okay."

"So there's this technique where you can learn a lot about a person by pretending not to know what you *know they* know, right? A window into how they handle what they perceive to be your ignorance in their area of expertise."

Vanessa has to think about what he's just said, very carefully. She nods for him to go on once it sinks in. She cannot imagine that anyone could be so in control of their behavior as to mislead another person to that degree. Quite a skill for a man to have. A man she should run away from, as fast as she can. So why isn't she moving? So why is he getting more and more attractive to her? Curses to being smart and easily bored. Curses to men who smell great.

"Like, if someone is a munitions expert, and you know that, and you want to see if they really know their stuff, you pretend like you don't know anything about what they know about, only you act like you know everything." He pauses. "You become the arrogant, ignorant bastard."

"And you did this to me *why?*" she asks, dumbfounded.

"Well, it's kind of like my way of seeing if you're good people."

"Good people."

"Not snobby."

"I'm sorry?" she balks. *Did he actually just use that word?* she wonders. Her mother's word. "Did I come off as 'snobby' to you?" Offended now by this whole thing, the whole game of it, the sense of having been manipulated. The assault. The preconceptions. Judgment. Ready, perhaps, to walk away from him, after all.

He grins, and if he is aware of how deeply he has offended her it does not show. "No, it's not *you*. Not you specifically. It's all me, see. I do it to everyone."

Vanessa glowers at him.

"Please don't look at me like that," he says.

"I'm just really surprised."

"I didn't mean anything bad by it. I just wanted to see if you were really as nice as you seemed, and I thought a good way to do that would be to act like I was really dumb about food, and then see how you, someone who lives for food, treated me."

"That's not normal."

"I never said I was normal, Vanessa."

She can't think of a comeback, so she just nods, like people do when they don't understand the language.

"You can tell a lot about people by the way they treat you when they think you're a nobody. If they're nice to you when you're nobody to them, they're legitimate. If they're not, they aren't worth your time."

Vanessa stares at him, a sick feeling in her belly, and can't think of anything to say. He looks deflated by her reaction.

"Hey, I'm sorry," he tells her, tries to put his hand on her shoulder. She backs away.

"That is probably the single creepiest thing anyone has ever told me," she says. Arms folded, brows furrowed.

"I'm sorry. I really didn't think it would upset you this much."

"You acted like you didn't know what I was talking about, just so you could see how I *reacted*?"

"Pretty much."

"That's so underhanded."

"Well, I didn't plan to do it forever. I just wanted to get your goat a little, and . . ." He waits a minute, seems to carefully consider what will come next. Locks his eyes on hers. "To see if what I was feeling about you was worth following through on."

What? "That's awful." Wait a minute. What he was *feeling* about her? She's not sure where to put her hands, her eyes, her thoughts.

"Yeah. I guess it sounds kinda bad," he says, as if thinking about it from her point of view for the first time. He puts on a salesman face suddenly. Clasps his hands, opens them again, nothing to hide. Says, "But you have to think about it this way. It saves a lot of time and energy. What I mean is, okay. Listen. I went into the military right out of high school—Air Force Academy, actually—and I've been in there all this time, just retired after twenty years surrounded by military types. I'm a little rusty at relating to normal people."

"I'd have to agree with that."

"Well, if it helps, you passed with flying colors."

"It doesn't help. In fact, I think it makes it worse." She shudders.

"You're a genuinely nice person," he tells her. "Which means that it's okay for me to be attracted to you. Which I am. Just so you know."

At this last bit of information, accompanied as it is by Paul's wide, goofy grin, Vanessa feels her belly react with butterflies, against her logic and will. She knows herself well enough by now to realize, too, that her face is probably flaming red. She wonders what it must be like to be so in control of your universe that you can analyze and manipulate people to this degree.

"I don't know what to say," she tells him.

"Not the usual come-on," he suggests.

"No, not really."

He grins again, pleased with himself. "Good. Hey, my mom told me about your hiatus from guys, and I totally respect that."

He holds a hand out to her in a gesture that appears to mock the idea of friendship at one level, but seems earnest, too. "So we'll be just friends. Okay? Friends?"

Vanessa is horrified to remember she has told his mother she is not dating anyone anymore. Why must she have done that?

And yet, Paul seems sincere. He is a little strange, but it doesn't seem like he meant to harm her. She hesitates. "Only if you don't 'test' me anymore. I'm not big on friends who test me all the time."

He winks at her. "Oh, I won't test you all the time. Just sometimes."

Vanessa reaches out, shakes his hand, and Red Dog nuzzles them both as if to say, *Good people, good, good people.* Vanessa looks at her dog and thinks, *Yeah, but what do you know?*

"Well, now that you know I'm not a culinary neophyte, how about some company on that hike today? I've been hoping to get up there ever since I got back, but I've been so busy looking for work and building this damn bike." He gestures toward the scrap heap.

"I don't know." Vanessa is still a little uncomfortable with him, even if he does use words like "neophyte," and correctly.

"Aw, c'mon. It's safer to hike in pairs."

"With normal people, sure," she says. "I just don't want you to put me through some sort of military survival course or something."

Red Dog wags up at Vanessa. *C'mon, Mommy, I like him!* How can she refuse to give Red Dog what she wants?

Paul laughs and shakes his head. "I think I just got off on the very wrong foot with you, didn't I?"

"Maybe."

He affects a puppy-dog face now. "Please? Just a hike. I won't test ya. No survivalist stuff. Promise."

Red Dog wags and wags. Vanessa folds her arms more tightly, but nods. "I guess you can come. But only because my *dog* likes you."

"Great!" he roars. He ignores her attempt to be somber and pouty. "I promise to behave."

He tells her he's going to get changed for the expedition, and she tells him it will be a few minutes until she's ready to go because she has to appease her mother first.

"A little wine, I'm telling you, and she's a different lady," says Paul. Cynical and accepting at once. Huh. "Miss Mary likes her wine."

"Hers, and everyone else's, too."

"Can't have been easy, Vanessa," he says, suddenly serious.

"What can't?"

He looks at her now with great respect, the humor fading from his eyes. "Growing up with that. Must've been tough."

"You don't really know us well enough to say something like that, do you?"

He shrugs in consideration and dismissal of her comment. "I hear them yellin' at each other all day and night. You make assumptions."

Naked, open empathy on his face now. Admiration, maybe pity, but whatever it is, he sees her. She knows this as surely as she knows how sometimes a vermouth is improved by the bitterness of wormwood. Knows he is sincere as surely as she knows that she is a vermouth, improved over time, incorporating the bitterness as best she can into something complex and desirable. He sees this.

"Get cleaned up," she says, turns her eyes from him, fighting the urge to get sappy, to tear up, because, no, it wasn't easy. Part of her wonders if he's just manipulating her again. "I'll see you back here in twenty minutes."

Embarrassed, and for some reason fighting back tears she did not expect to come, Vanessa turns toward her mother's house, dragging a reluctant Red Dog every step of the way. The dog doesn't want to go in the house. She wants to stay with Paul. Vanessa has never known Red Dog to be wrong about a person, or a place.

This dog, she thinks, *knows what she's doing*.

A CRACK OF HARD NUT

Vanessa opens her mother's front door some minutes later, pushing the underhanded complaints of Mary—and the passive-aggressive demands—from her mind, focusing on the now and not the then, and there he stands, Boy Scout, Viking, this big golden puppy of a man, with that dopey smile that seems, in the hot brightness of the afternoon, to have lost some of its blind buoyancy. Him, but matured internally in a span of minutes, and she wonders if he is the proverbial onion, layers beneath this, many more, and a core few see. More calm to the two of them together now, the ease of having a shared meal, and at least one confession, behind them. She can sense his essence plumping up, like a dried bit of fruit in warm water, that musk of lemons and poppy seeds, fresh milk and new-cut grass. A man has never smelled as good as this. Not Darrius. Not Bryan. Not the married man who came before them. And maybe she has been looking toward the wrong sort of man. Maybe it is the Boy Scouts and soldiers who uphold your honor. The ones who tell you the truth, even when they are lying to test you.

"You look great," he tells her, embracing Red Dog as she bolts into his arms. Vanessa doesn't know what to say. *Thanks, soldier, and you smell like fresh rain and Japanese lemon drops?* Lucky for her, he keeps on talking to her and the dog.

"So you girls have a favorite trail?"

"I—we like the Pino Trail. Up off Elena Gallegos. It's quiet, and the views are amazing."

He pops up, a jack-in-the-box, energetic and raring to go. "Great. You drivin'?"

"I *could*." Vanessa sounds less enthused than she hoped she would. She had hoped it would come across as confidence, but her rocky relationship with driving is obvious to the casual observer, and likely a glaring red sign to a seasoned interrogator.

"We can take my truck," he offers, quickly. A quick read of people, their needs, their thoughts. When she fails to respond right away, he responds with a shrug of deference, "Or your car. I'm good either way." He looks at Red Dog, and adds, "Whatever the pretty girl and her pretty pup want."

"It's actually my sister's car," Vanessa corrects him. "I don't have a car."

Again, that face of surprise mixed with pleasure. "You some kind of nature girl?" he asks. "Or just underpaid?"

Both, she thinks.

"It's by choice. I used to have a car." *Just like I used to be a professor. Just like I used to think I would one day have children with Bryan, or marry Darrius.* Vanessa is not happy to think about how much of her life to this point has involved letting go of who she thought she was, in search of the woman she would like to be.

"Intriguing." He looks at her fondly.

"Archaic," she says self-deprecatingly.

"Nah. Intriguing. So why no car?"

"Well, I think about stuff like carbon footprints. People act like it's crazy now, but it's real, what we're doing to the planet."

They walk toward his truck, without having said they would or should, and he asks, with pleasant confidence, "So does the carbon not count when you drive your sister's car? Like when you eat alone, the calories don't count, right?"

"Are you testing me again?"

"Nope. No testing. Teasing this time."

"Yes, it counts," laughs Vanessa. "Touché. But I only use it when Larissa's not in town, to help Mom."

"And how is Miss Mary today?"

"Quite contrary."

"Sorry," he says.

"Yeah, well, I gave up hoping for a change a long time ago. It's more of a thing about accepting it now. And keeping away as much as I can."

He seems to consider adding more, and decides against it. "So, if you don't mind me asking, how do you get around? Bus?"

"Bike."

"Even grocery shopping? In the winter?"

"Bike," she repeats. "And a good backpack. Sometimes the bus."

"That would explain the legs," he says. "Not that I noticed."

Vanessa stops and blinks at him for a moment. Should she respond? No. Best to change the subject.

"So you want to drive?" An obvious question, and answer, given that they are at his truck already. "I'm happy to, if not. I *can* do it. I just don't like to."

He opens the passenger-side door, and gives her a calm smile. "I promise I'll stop talking about your *legs*. No worries. Momentary slip." Puts his fingers to his temples. Closes his eyes as one in deep concentration. "Friends. Friends. Friends. We're just friends, me and this beautiful lady. Friends."

"Yep. Just friends," she says as she climbs in.

The cab is as clean and sweet-smelling as the man who inhabits it. He climbs in next, in one great burst of masculine energy, starts the engine, revving once or twice in a way that makes Vanessa roll her eyes. Of course he revs. He's a revver.

"I bet this is the worst thing for carbon footprints," he says, giving voice to her thinking again. "I bet you think I'm like the Sasquatch of carbon footprints."

"King Kong, maybe," she says, and he laughs at her, puts his arm on the seat back, swings his head over his shoulder, and backs the truck deftly and quickly down the driveway—a very good driver, a man who does not hesitate and knows exactly where his body is in the space around him. "But I try not to judge people too hard. I mean, what I do? Cooking? It's not all that environmentally friendly, some of the stuff I like to eat, like fish. We should stop fishing the ocean, but then we wouldn't have tuna steaks. I don't judge you."

"A nonjudgmental environmentalist," he muses as he spins the wheel to get the truck pointed forward in the street. "I like that. That's good."

"We exist," she says.

Paul fiddles with the stereo, and out comes a female singer with a calm voice, acoustic, soothing. Vanessa's face registers the surprise and pleasure. She expected headbanging rock, the usual.

"Let me guess," he says, without taking his eyes from the road. "You didn't expect that."

"Did you put it in just because you knew you'd have company?" she teases. "Another test?"

A big boom of a laugh. "Check you out," he says, eyes turned now, but only for a moment, to look at her in mock offense. "Here." He hands her his iPod, connected to the stereo system. "Scroll," he says. "You'll see. I'm not that predictable. And I told you, I'm done with the tests, unless you keep harping on it. Then I'll test you just 'cuz you're pissing me off."

She scrolls. And finds a mix as eclectic as any she has seen. Says nothing, because compliments do not come easily to her when the recipient is essentially a stranger. Doesn't have to say a word, because he seems to know what she's thinking anyway. Interrogator.

"Back in Iraq, guys always ribbed me about the Sarah McLachlan," he says. "The Joni Mitchell."

"I bet."

"No, Vanessa. *Listen* to me. You have no idea what jackasses guys in the military can be."

"Right," she deadpans. "They have that reputation for being so open-minded and good with their feelings."

He laughs, sincerely, and looks at her with excitement in his eyes. She gets the sense from his face that he has not spent time with many women like her.

"But, see. I am to Air Force as you are to environmentalism." He looks at her, a joke dancing in his eyes.

"Ah," she says. "You're the exception to the rule, then? You're the sensitive trained mass-killer?"

He shoots her a look of great pain, so brief she almost doesn't catch it, before pushing forward in the conversation.

"Dude. Seriously. Those boys almost lynched me for drinking lattes." Another booming bass note of laughter, as he remembers the "boys," whoever they are. "Dumb guys, I'm tellin' ya." He says this with great affection, but the edge of hurt is still there, in his eyes, just at the corners.

On they drive and drive, through the streets of this city. It is a grid, Albuquerque, in a huge, sloping mountain valley, the high desert. They go east, climb to the foothill edge of the city. Up here you look west and get a sweeping view of the entirety of the rest of it, lines crossing, a city poured thin and baked low against this ground, a mediocre collection of buildings set down in one of the most beautiful places on earth.

In the foothills now, on a narrow twist of road, sagebrush and juniper at their sides, massive houses here and there, with walls of window to it all. A magical place. A well-kept secret, as the rest of the nation makes their assumptions that this is like Phoenix, when, in fact, it is more like the collective idea of Denver than Denver itself.

He parks, facing west, and stares out at the expanse of land, the scribble of muddy river doodling miles and miles below.

"It's grown so much I hardly recognize it," he offers.

"When did you leave?"

"Right after high school. Back in eighty-eight."

She does the math. He is older than she is, by six, seven years, but looks young for his age. Must be thirty-eight, thirty-nine. Looks like he's barely thirty. She should tell him this, but that would be a compliment and, well. She doesn't want to encourage him to talk about her legs again. Not that she minds. It's more that if he did, she's pretty sure she wouldn't be able to resist whatever might follow, and she needs to resist, if for no other reason than to prove her sister wrong about her.

Doors open, and they step out. Others are here, maybe a dozen cars, a couple of skinny guys in biking gear, mountain bikes on racks. *They probably think we're a couple*, she thinks. *Just as long as* he *doesn't.*

Vanessa clips the leash to Red Dog's collar, knowing full well that once they're up the trail a bit she will release the dog to its nature and destiny. It is cruel to keep dogs on leashes when they don't really need them. Red Dog is never happier than when the leash is taken off, in the mountains, where rabbits and doves wait to be ferreted out from beneath sagebrush.

The narrow dirt trail leads off from the lot, among the scrub brush and cholla cactus, and away they go. Paul walking at her side, Red Dog smiling back at him every so often. Vanessa is walking at a good pace, and he easily matching it, the walk steep from the start, the feel of working muscle good for her mind.

"Beautiful day," he says, and she agrees. Popover pastry clouds to the north, as usual, but overhead nothing but pure cobalt, the temperature somewhere around eighty, maybe a little hotter. September.

Vanessa releases Red Dog, who instantly dashes off trail and toward a bush. A bird bursts from it, flies up and past them in a flash of blue, and as Red Dog barks at it, Paul casually names it.

"Gray-breasted jay," he says.

When the white wing doves flutter above, two of them, mates

for life, he knows them as well. And when they pass buffalo grasses, he knows the type, has facts about them to share. Same for the paddle cacti and the flowering agave. Vanessa is surprised a military pilot would have such terrestrial interests.

"Mom's big on the gardening," he says, answering her unspoken question with that grin that is part politician, part emotional wall. "She used to take us out here when we were kids, and teach us the names of things."

"Us?" Vanessa asks, as she loses sight of Red Dog now, the creature sprinting off over a hill. She'll probably get a cactus needle in her paw at some point in the hike; she always does. But it will have been worth the pain. Vanessa checks her pocket for the tweezers she always carries, for thorn removal from Red Dog.

"Me and my brother," he says.

Vanessa asks about the brother, and learns that he is a scientist, computer science, does very well, lives in Silicon Valley, married to a redhead, with kids, a couple years older than Paul. He does not, as have so many men Vanessa has spent time with, use her curiosity about him as a reason to talk on and on for the rest of the day about himself. Rather, he uses the moment to turn it around, and ask her about her sister. She tells him about Larissa, and he notes that they both have older siblings with families.

On they walk, through small canyons, and on, up the side of the mountain, the air growing thinner and the path narrower. He lets her go first when there is no longer room to stand side by side. Half an hour into the hike, he stops her, and points out the piñon trees.

"Best nuts in the world," he says, and she cannot disagree.

Paul is sliding off the path on purpose next, off trail now, circling the trees, searching, pulling down a cone when he finds one that appeals to him. Pocketknife in hand, he settles on a large boulder, in the sun, pats the spot on the rock next to him for her to come.

"Those are nearly impossible to extract," she warns him, but he only grins at her and pats the spot again, offers her a sip of water from his silver canteen once she joins him.

Vanessa watches as he opens the cone expertly, as he takes the tiny nuts out in their rock-hard wooden shells. She seriously doubts he'll succeed at getting the nuts out. And yet he does. He pops them out like it was nothing. Offers up a perfect little nut to Vanessa, who thanks him and eats it, the meat of it tender against her molars, with just the faintest scent of pine.

"When I was a kid, we'd drive out toward Las Vegas, New Mexico, in the fall, and you'd see all these families from the nearby villages, their cars parked on the side of the road, and they were all out collecting pine nuts to sell for extra cash, off national forest land," he says.

"Really?" He hands her another nut and she places it in her mouth. "Is that legal?"

"People have been eating from these forests for centuries. Laws don't mean much when you have your whole family tree looking down on you from heaven about it."

Heaven, she thinks. *He's religious.* Vanessa is not religious, even for all her superstition, and has never been able to imagine herself with a religious man. They'd fight all the time. This would never work. Not that she's taking it there, except that she has been considering what it might be like to kiss those lips of his.

Paul keeps talking. "We'd go join them sometimes, just to get some nuts to take out to the cabin."

"The cabin?"

"My folks had a cabin when I was growing up." He watches her eat, seems to want to drop the subject of the cabin.

"It's good," she says of the nut.

"Watch out," he says, with that slightly defensive smile to his eyes. "The Pueblos have this legend, right? Where a beautiful maiden eats a pine nut that a god gives her, and she ends up pregnant with Moctezuma."

"You're hardly a *god*," she says, thinking, as she says it, that the statement is only half true. Paul, hair growing out, tan in the sun, muscular as a professional athlete, food in hand, serene and informed about the desert, four languages at ease in his head, with an understanding of wine and cheese, is, well—if not godlike, he is certainly a tad more interesting than she once thought. *Once* being only weeks ago.

"I surprised you again." He looks at her, still as if ready to laugh at her. Proud of himself, a little mocking. Pops a nut into his own mouth next. She likes the way he chews, his lips firm and soft around the movement.

"You don't surprise me," she lies. Red Dog comes bounding out of the low forest to grin at them, wag at them, and then she's off again, free and happy.

"Okay." He says this without hiding that he does not believe it. Overjoyed, really, to have her underestimate him. She supposes he is the type of man who thrives upon proving people wrong; a fighter. And in this, she recognizes a kindred spirit.

He cracks another few nuts for her, and truly, they are delicious, so simple a thing, so tiny a thing, but eaten fresh from the tree, here in the mountains, a *wonderful* thing.

His eyes dance with laughter again, and he says, "Almost as good as that shiraz fish, huh?"

"You are *such* a dork," she says.

He's laughing to himself. "You're a good egg," he tells her. "You put up with me even when you thought I was an idiot." His smile loses some of the defensive quality now, and he really looks at her, the wall coming down a bit. A tiny bit. Just that. No more.

"Who says I've changed my mind? Maybe I still think you're an idiot, right?" she asks him, but he only laughs harder.

"Good," he says. "I like a woman who can give it back."

Moments later, they are back on the trail, and he is asking her all sorts of questions about growing up, college, hobbies, friends. And, finally, the big question.

"So what happened with your last boyfriend, anyway?"

"Uhm, I'm sorry?" she asks.

"The one who scared you off men for a while."

"Oh, that."

"Yeah, *that*. Him."

"Bryan," she spits in disgust.

"*Damn* him," offers Paul, only half joking. Vanessa can't help but laugh. She feels so at ease with Paul, it's unnatural. Unnerving. She second-guesses her comfort, wonders if she's not falling for the wrong guy again. It seems a habit of hers, falling for the wrong guy. It's like shopping hungry. She stops herself now, reminds herself of pain, of failure, of Larissa's wise words. *Learn to be alone before you can trust yourself to pick the right companion. Don't just fall for the first guy who comes along.*

And that is exactly what Paul is. The first guy who came along. *No fall*, she reminds herself. No shopping for men. A six-month hiatus from dating, at minimum. And, she thinks, what better way to seal the friends-only fate of their relationship than to tell Paul about her sordid romantic history, her endless parade of married men? That should scare him off, she thinks. The more unstable he finds her, the better off she will be.

She tells Paul all about the situation with Bryan, in more putrid and dripping detail than she had intended to give, but he is truly a very good listener once he wipes the tease from his eye. He asks the right questions, and gets the answers to pour out. She pants a bit from the effort of the hike, a trickle of sweat on her brow, but it all feels very good, to tell a complete stranger about her life, to have the fresh air in her lungs, to walk behind so significant a backside as his, to imagine touching it, to stop herself from imagining at all, to have that luxury. To be that strong, at last, and maybe that's what she needed, all the pain of the past loves, to give her the courage to be alone for a while.

And then she's done. It has been spoken, Bryan and the others, the wisdom of Larissa, the way her sister sees things in her that she herself is too close to notice, how grateful she is to have a sister to bounce these things off of. The big secret revealed: the habit of other women's husbands, despicable, sordid, abnormal.

"So you've given up on men, because of *that?*" he asks, failing, she thinks, to understand the gravity of what she has just shared. She is a rotten fruit he still seems to find fresh. "Do you think that's even *smart*, Vanessa?"

"Yes."

"I have to disagree."

"I haven't given up forever, just for a while."

"Because your *sister* told you to." Doubt in his voice, mockery, and kindness, or compassion. Some combination she is not accustomed to finding in anyone she knows.

"Sort of. Yes. No," she says, all in a run. "I mean, I need to be alone for a while. I really do. I haven't really ever done that."

He says, "You don't strike me as a needy kind of girl. You seem pretty damn independent to me."

"I like it, so far," she says.

"What? Being alone?"

"Yeah."

He laughs. "No, you *don't*."

And he's right. Terribly right.

"Yes, I do," she insists.

"Keep telling yourself that, Vanessa. There's millions and millions of years of evolution fightin' against you."

"You mean you're not a creationist?" she asks, half joking and hoping to sway the subject away from herself now that it has grown into her being defensive.

"You figured me for a religious nutjob?" he asks with a shake of his head. "Of course you did."

"Well, it kinda goes with the whole flag and yellow ribbon thing."

His expression dismisses her, and he says, "I can't remember who said this, but I subscribe more to something like 'I don't believe anything at all, I'm even too cynical to be an atheist.'"

"Wow," says Vanessa.

"See enough of the world, you get like that. I don't know what the hell's out there, all I know is I've seen more people hurt each other for their gods than any god worth his salt would probably want. So it isn't *God* I doubt as much as it is people's ability to know what God is. Maybe God's in the science of stuff."

"Maybe God is Carl Sagan," she offers.

"Oh yeah," he says. "That's hilarious. Yeah, billions and billions. That dude. I liked that show, when I was a kid. *Cosmos*."

Vanessa feels her heart jump. She had him pegged for a born-again.

"Stop looking so surprised by me," he says. "It's getting boring already. It used to be charming. Not so much anymore."

She decides this is a good time to change the subject again, and asks about why he came back here.

"It's a long story, and I don't really feel like telling it right now and ruining everyone's day," he says.

"Everyone? It's just me and you."

"And Red Dog," he corrects her. "Who, as it happens, seems to be having a great time. Me, you, Red Dog. That's everyone."

"No fair," she tells him. "I just told you everything. You gotta give me *something*."

They keep walking, and he says nothing for a time. Then, he finds another stand of piñon trees, and another rock, and they sit and drink water and he shells.

"Okay. I'll give you this much. I fly fighter planes. Or I did. I'm retired now." Gives her a smile to show that he is done, the way a child might after doing a little improvised tap dance. Ta-da!

"You seem a little young for retirement."

"Well, I went to the academy at eighteen, and that makes twenty years I've been in the service."

"Okay. So you're a retired fighter pilot who speaks a bunch of languages."

"And cooks," he says.

"Well, *sort* of."

He laughs again. "You're a funny girl. A funny, funny girl. Miss Vanessa."

"That's what they tell me. So finish your story."

"You don't give up easy."

"Nope."

A silence as he seems to weigh how much to give her. Then:
"They sent me to Iraq years ago, and I was ready to go because the
whole thing with 9/11 really pissed me off."

"But Iraq had nothing to do with that."

"I realize that *now*."

"Okay, sorry."

"You gonna let me finish my story? Because I'm happy to not
talk about it. I'm happy to let you tell it for me, if you want."

"No, go ahead. I won't interrupt you again."

"Okay. So I did some things I'm not proud of, and then I got old
enough to retire, and I did, but I would have left anyway. Lucky for
me I didn't have to, and I still have benefits. And now, here I am,
looking for work."

"Sounds so simple."

"It's not."

"I figured."

"Not even a little bit simple." He eats a couple of nuts and gazes
at the western horizon.

"It rarely is."

"War." He looks at her, as though she might not understand
what he's been talking about.

"I know."

"No, you *don't*."

"You're right. Tell me about it."

"Nah. That's about all I'm at liberty to say about it right now."

"You under orders not to talk, or something?"

He grins bitterly. "No. I just don't want to talk about it. Surely you can respect that."

She catches sight of his face in profile, and the wall is gone, the laugh is gone, and in their place a haunted sort of expression, frightening in its intensity and grief. A ghost pushing through from the inside, the man pushing it back again.

She tries to backtrack. "You having any luck with that job search?"

"Nah," he says. "I want to find something in construction. I know this will sound weird to you, but I want to be a construction worker for a while."

"Not weird. You seem like the type of creepy guy to loiter on corners whistling at women all day."

He chuckles and shakes his head at her. "Now, *now*, Vanessa. That's not very nice."

"Sorry. Maybe you need to devise a better test. You see? I'm not really as nice as you think I am."

"Nah, you got me all wrong. I'm more of a kissy-lips kind of harasser. Not a whistler. I can't even whistle. Never figured out how to do that."

She laughs, enjoying the easy banter with him. Tells him she seriously does not think working in construction is weird, but, rather, sort of noble. "I work with my hands," she says. "There's something very satisfying about it, in a preindustrial kind of way."

He affects a face she interprets as being designed to mock her own surprise when he says something intelligent. "Look at you, Miss Fancy History-talker."

"No, you know what I mean? It's honest work. I think we evolved for it."

"You mean you're not a creationist?" he asks her.

"Okay, okay. I'm sorry."

He laughs. Seems to consider her point about work for a moment, and find some kind of newfound respect in it for her. He looks at her admiringly. "So that makes two groups you're the exception to," he tells her.

"I am?"

"Sure. Think about it. You're a nonjudgmental environmentalist, and a pretty, professional woman who respects men who do simple labor and harass women on the corner."

"You're hardly a typical laborer, though."

His face grows serious now. "I'd like to be," he says. "I need to build stuff. I . . . I have some amends to make."

For what, she wants to ask, but doesn't know how. Some sort of destruction, she guesses. Making up for something.

The sky opens up, and the obligatory afternoon mountain sprinkle begins. Vanessa is very curious about what this man might have done in Iraq to be so haunted, but she's not sure it would be a good idea to push him to tell her more, not after the way he re-acted to the loud noise during the barbecue.

He looks at her, and again answers her unspoken question. "Don't worry. I'll get around to it eventually."

"Around to what?" she asks, stunned once more that he seems to be reading her mind. *Eerie.*

He laughs at her. " 'Around to what,' she says. Like you don't know."

"No, really." *How does he do that?*

"Yeah. Okay. Around to the whole story. I'm just not ready to talk about it yet."

"Maybe we should turn back," she says, holding a hand out for raindrops.

"You gettin' tired of hearing me talk?" he asks, suddenly cheery again. "When that happens, just say, 'Paul, dude, shut up already.' I'm good with that."

"No! No. It's not that. I like hearing you. I'm just not sure we should make ourselves the highest things around during a potential thunderstorm."

"Not much of a risk taker."

"Never said I was."

"Where's the fun in that?"

"Never promised to be fun," she tells him. "As I recall it, I warned you I was boring, actually."

He nods in acknowledgment. "So you wanna go back?"

"Probably the wise thing to do."

"Wisdom is overrated," he says cheerily, the haunted expression disappearing from his eyes as quickly as it had appeared. He hops down off the high rock, and turns to face her. "But we'll go. Whatever my new friend—with the very nice legs—wants."

"You said you wouldn't talk about them anymore."

"I know. But they're right *there*. And so, so pretty."

She can't resist the butterflies when they come, the bubbles of expectation that boil up from the bottom, all the way to her head, as she hops down off the rock. She blushes and finds no words to say. So she goes back to the prior subject.

"Sorry to be so boring."

"Please, Vanessa. You know I'm kidding. I think you're perfect just the way you are." She turns her eyes up to his just as he teases, "You know. For a boring, risk-averse *friend* and all."

He holds out a hand to help her up a steep spot, back to the trail.

"No *all*," she reminds him, her belly ablaze from his seductive expression and the touch of his hand over hers as he makes sure she gets her footing. "Just friends."

He holds her hand, runs his thumb across the top of it, softly and slowly. His voice low, a distant rumble, seductive. Trying to prove her wrong as he asserts that she is correct. "Right. Nothing extraneous. Just friends." Lying, but in an honest way.

"Friends," she says as she withdraws her hand, the trail left on her skin by his touch still illuminating her nerves as though with glistening mercury. Vanessa puts her fingers to her lips and whistles for Red Dog.

"Show-off," says Paul.

"You really can't do that?" She whistles again.

"I'm not perfect," he teases.

"Nope," she agrees, though she doubts the truth of her words. "You're not."

"Look on the bright side," he says as they start to walk back, the rain getting heavier. "This way, as friends-only, we can have each other forever, right? No breaking up required."

"That's a very healthy way of looking at it."

"Think your sister would approve?"

"Probably."

"Well," he teases her again. "I guess that's all that matters, since, you know, she's so much smarter than you about these things. Right? I mean, that's what everyone thinks."

Vanessa's breath catches in her throat, with a little gasp that he ignores. No, he didn't just say that, did he? Funny how his walk, so graceful the rest of the afternoon, looks like a march to her now.

Interrogator. Finding his information. Feeling with his thumb for the weak spots. Slippery. Cunning. A human fugu fish. Delicious if done carefully, deadly if not.

Dangerous.

He whistles to himself as he walks ahead, nearly dances on the balls of his feet, so certain. Whistles.

"I thought you couldn't do that," she calls out.

"Guess I just learned how."

Muscular back. Broad shoulders. Perfect male body. Clear in his beliefs. Cynical. She follows him, not Paul now, not a friend, but a skilled interviewer, the interrogator, the Viking, the fish, testing her. Constantly testing.

Back to the truck, Red Dog on the leash, the doors shut in the silence. A silence that more or less endures, minus a platitude or two, and except for the music—classic rock, now, his choice, the real him perhaps—until they arrive back at the corned-beef house.

"You mad at me, Vanessa?" he asks, turning toward her, truck in the driveway, engine still running. No wall. No joke in his eyes. A man here, with stories, with pain, with need. Stares her down, not predatory, no. Knowing. Intense. Very intelligent. A little un-hinged. A look with laser precision, cuts straight through her de-fenses, past the woman she has become, the women she has been, straight down to the girl she once was, here, in this place.

"Not mad," she says, opening her door with her right hand. "Just late." He grabs her left hand.

"Hang on," he says.

Vanessa looks back at him, her heart racing. Why does she want to touch him, to smell him, to taste him? "I have to get go-ing," she tells him.

He ignores her comment, moves closer to her, still holding her hand, and she lets him. His eyes flutter and his breathing is fast. Nervous. He looks down. Swallows. Not so sure anymore. Not so brave.

"Look, I—I'm sorry," he says. "I'm all messed up right now.

It's got nothing to do with you. I've only been back a little while and I'm not right in the head. I think I'm coming across all wrong. No, I know I am."

Her gaze slips from his eyes to his lips, and her breath catches in her throat as an ache rises in her chest. "It's okay," she says.

"I really do like you, Vanessa. And I said all that, about your sister and everything, because I think they're wrong about you, and— And I know you don't need my opinion on this, or anyone's, but I think you give people too much power over you. I hope that doesn't sound presumptuous. I'm sure it does. Anyway, this whole thing with not dating because you think you can't trust yourself just rubs me the wrong way. I hope you don't mind me saying this, but I think you're throwing the babe—that's you—out with the bathwater. I don't think you should isolate yourself, because the only mistake you made with these married scumbags was trusting people who didn't deserve you."

He pauses a moment and takes in a deep breath. Exhales slowly, rubs her hand with that thumb again, like a man testing the fabric on a shirt and liking it. His touch is quietly electric. Just this, his knowing finger on her longing skin, better than much of the actual sex she's had in her life. She's heard of chemistry for years, and never really understood, until this moment, what it meant.

He turns his eyes up to hers. "Trust is in short supply in this world. I feel like it's more precious than gold." He sounds so smart, she thinks, but he's a soldier, a warmonger, military, an interrogator who is used to getting what he wants by saying the right thing. *Be smart*, she tells herself, *don't do this*.

"Or oil," she says, by way of erecting a barrier between them, ideological.

He blinks at her, squints against the pain brought by what she's said. "Oil," he repeats, spitefully. "You think we don't know that's why they sent us?"

Silence.

"You think that'll bother me, Vanessa? You telling me that all this, being messed up like this, being broken now, that it was for nothing but greed for some greedy politician? You think you'll teach me something I didn't already know? If you do, you're just like all the other liberals, arrogant."

"You *went*," she says, angry now at his derisive use of the word "liberal," as it seems he is accustomed to saying it with distaste. "I would never have gone to that war. Anyone with half a brain would have known it was a lie."

He moves in, as though to kiss her. Gets in close, and whispers, "Listen to me. Let me talk for a second."

She waits, terrified that he might actually snap her neck or something.

He goes on. "The way you trusted those guys? Right? Bryan, Derriere."

"Darrius."

"Whatever the hell his name was, I don't care. But listen to what I'm telling you. Stop correcting me for one little second, will ya?"

"Sorry."

"The way you trusted them. That's the way I trusted my government. You might say I was in love with America back then. After 9/11 it got even bigger, that thing I had for this country, that need to protect it. I believed in the dream, Vanessa, only for me it wasn't about love and marriage. It was about God and country."

"Now you have neither," she whispers back, scared of him, hurt for him, fascinated by his terrible difference from her, wanting him to kiss her. A strange combination, and certainly certifiably self-destructive.

He shakes his head. "I didn't say that. I'm not like you. I don't give up that easy. *Now* I am struggling to hold on to my *faith* in this place. In America. I am working really hard to *trust*," he says. "Because the lies were one crime, but taking my hope and love from me, taking my country from me, I can't let that happen. I won't let them take that from me, just like you shouldn't let whatshisname—"

"Bryan."

"Bryan," he repeats with disdain. "And the other two dudes, you can't let them ruin you for love, if love comes along."

"You think that's what you are? Love come along for me?"

He looks at her in a way that makes her think he does think he could love her, and she him, but he's too proud—or too scared—to say it right now. All he can say is, "You never know. Could be me. Could be someone else. The point is, you can't let them *win*. The ones who hurt you."

"Sometimes you *do* know." She says this as if to tell him he is not the one for her, and she sees the pain wash past his eyes quickly, before he pushes it away. Somewhere here, she thinks, is a boy who got rejected a lot.

"Sometimes you're *wrong*, Vanessa. I just wonder if you're ever able to think so. Or admit it."

"I have to go," she says softly.

"No, you don't." It comes out as nearly a plea.

He moves in closer, but she pushes away, moves back. It would feel good to kiss him, but it would not be wise. Too much. Then, too *late*. Vanessa scarcely has time to think "I should not kiss him" when Paul advances toward her with fighter-jet speed and plants a light, quick one on her unmoving lips (with fighter-pilot precision). His scent and warmth electrify her, but she refuses to show it. She does not move or breathe. *It's not a real kiss if you don't kiss back*, she thinks as she balls her hands into fists. She stares at the dashboard and tries to think of something clever to say. Nothing comes to her, and Paul, insightful as always, retreats.

"I'm sorry," he says as he positions himself against the driver-side door. "I bet your sister thinks I shouldn't have done that."

Vanessa turns away, face ablaze, pushes her door open wider, drops her body to its feet outside the cab, on the ground once more. Numb. Excitedly numb. Controlling herself.

She retrieves Red Dog from the back of the truck. No flying

today. No risk. She closes the door, with a wave good-bye and a weak smile.

Paul cuts the engine, and she sees him slump against the steering wheel in defeat. But just as quickly as he's gone down, he pops back up, his face a twist of confusion and hurt. Then rage in his eyes. Eyes of a man, yes, but now, too, the eyes of a lonely boy, a band geek with a bowl cut and an Easy-Bake oven.

The guy who never gets the girl, no matter how hard he tries.

OF CHILES, GEESE, AND

SAUSAGES

A significant corner of the garden, the northeast corner, is dedicated to growing New Mexico chiles on their long, lanky stalks. A person's background doesn't matter. If you grow up here in the shadow of the Sandias or the Sangre de Cristos, you eat chiles. If you eat them, you come to love the way they water the eyes and singe the throat. And if you love them the way Vanessa loves them, then you seek to grow your own, below a sky that, at this time of year, is checkmarked with flying Vs of migratory geese winging along their ancient paths above the Rio Grande.

Five feet squared, nothing but chiles, the only patch of the garden dedicated to just one delicacy, because chiles are picky, persnickety, and greedy; they need space, and all the sun they can get.

It is said in this area that you can tell by taste whether a chile was grown north or south of Interstate 40, which bisects Albuquerque through the center. Common wisdom has it that the best chiles come from the south, from the town of Hatch, but she knows that's not necessarily true. Surely Hatch has great chiles. And, yes, she can tell the difference between northern and southern chiles, but likes them both the same.

Her tiny house with the big garden is nestled two miles north of the interstate, and some of the best chiles she has ever tasted have come from family farms up north, near Chimayo. In food, as in life, she is never committed to tradition, though she is steeped in awareness of it. Like poetry or jazz, cooking requires one to learn and understand the rules before allowing for the freedom to break them.

Here she is, squatting in her chinos and long-sleeved T-shirt, her hair tied back loosely, her feet bare and cold on the slowly freezing ground. A folksinger's haunting melody in her head, going around like a carousel. She hums the strains, imagines the harmonies. Breeze comes, cold to the bone, but only for a moment and gone. Warm again.

Getting cooler now, the air, shorter days. Longer nights. Pine smoke in the air at night, people heating their homes the way they have for centuries here. And there are pockets of this valley where she lives that are ancient, where homes made of mud bricks have one or two rooms surrounded by acres of land, where horses are still the preferred mode of transport. Albuquerque, the strangest of cities. Urban one block, rural the next. Modern-art homes next door to old adobe shacks. The rich mingled with the poor. A complicated city where everything is really quite simple.

Long nights, mid-September. She dreads the nights now. More time to lie awake in the darkness, thinking about the fact that she thinks about Paul more than Bryan, though she has known him little more than a month. Larissa back in a few days, and this worries Vanessa, because she knows exactly what her sister will say about this sudden interest in Paul. At the same time, Vanessa is eager for her sister's return, because she needs to talk to someone. No, not someone. *Larissa*. She needs to tell Larissa about this man, the way he moves her and angers her, terrifies her and ignites in her a million shades of heat. Larissa will know what to do.

She checks the chiles, long, fat, green things. The red chiles and the green chiles are the same plant, harvested at different times. She has harvested some of her green chiles already, right after the last time she saw Paul on their walk (she has avoided him since then), and roasted them, and rubbed the blackened skins from their thick, slick flesh, her hands encased in plastic gloves to protect against the burn of acid. New Mexico chiles are among the hottest in the world, and that is fine with her, because bold flavors win her respect, and capture her imagination. Bold flavors on the tongue keep the mind from wandering where it should not go. Too bad she has suddenly also developed a taste for bold men. Or a bold man. One man. Paul. Gah. What must it be like to be a woman with a settled relationship, with a man who is the same man today as he was yesterday, an unmarried man all to yourself? Curses to married men. Curses to bold men. Curses to men, period.

She snaps the chiles off, and places them firm and shiny in the straw basket. She'll leave some unharvested for now, to ripen red, awed and aware as always of the enormous difference time can make to a thing—green chile being mild and reassuring, red being hot and fierce. And so it has gone with her love life, too, she thinks, always so much more palatable in the early stages, always so painfully addictive and numbing when ripe.

Today, a day off, the sky clear and cold, maybe two o'clock now, the trees just starting to hint at the yellows and reds to come. It is with a sort of madness that she stalks the garden this afternoon, the madness of creativity. Hazel will be by later to sample a few dishes Vanessa has come up with for her bachelorette party. The soup and the bread, and sometimes doesn't that just seem to be enough? When this combination is so utterly perfect, why move on to the rest? Why not linger there, in the stew and the crust? She is still working out the main course. She has been inspired to combine the flavors of Hazel's native New Mexico, Smitty's ancestral Ireland, with a touch of Thai thrown in for good measure, not such a hard feat when you think with your palate and their hearts. Potatoes, pork, chicken, stock, cream. Chiles. Broth. A touch of whiskey. She will add coconut milk to hominy, galangal to cilantro. It will be a stew both recognizable and unrecognizable on at least three continents, and that is her goal. All the world at the table, together, surprised by their differences, surprised by their similarities. If only the rest of it with the human beings and nations and wars were so simple.

Red Dog waits at the garden gate, in sphinx pose, tail wagging but with eyes worried and sad. Vanessa interprets the dog's expression as disappointment that they haven't seen Paul in a while. Maybe she's projecting. Of course she is. Red Dog is certainly more disappointed that there has been no bacon since yesterday. Vanessa will have to make more bacon for the dog, wonders if it might not be wise to conjure up a Paul for herself, too, and wonders how exactly that might be done and whether, in fact, it might be unwise to endeavor thusly.

"He's dangerous, girl," Vanessa tells the dog as she comes through the gate. Red Dog looks at her sideways, as if to say, *Who? Paul? No way!*

Vanessa shuts the gate behind her. Together, the woman and the dog enter the house, tracking in just a bit of mud that she plans to sweep later because a little dirt never killed anyone, and the phone is ringing. Basket on the counter, Vanessa picks up the cordless, looks at the caller ID. Bryan again. Is he out of his mind? Honestly. Take a hint. She has just about had enough of his daily entreaties. She presses the phone to life, ready—itching, really—for a fight. He is red chile all over, and she is in the mood for green.

"What do you want? Haven't you done enough damage? Why do you call here? You know I don't want to talk to you."

"I left her," he says, cold, factually. "I wanted you to be the first to know."

"How about Oliver? Does he know?"

"Oliver." Bryan sighs into the phone. "Poor kid. Yeah, he knows. I'm useless without you, Vanessa."

"What do you want me to do, Bryan? Congratulate you?"

A silence, as he inhales the air, then blows it out. She can almost see him doing this, the sweet face, the dark eyes, the empathic brow. Deceptive, all of it, she reminds herself. He is nowhere as gentle and kind as he comes across. A wormy apple whose wormholes are generally turned away from the light, nothing left but a pretty yellow half skin. He's a liar. She has to force her body not to react positively to the sound of him thinking, talking. *Do not take a bite*, she tells herself. *Snake charmer.*

"I want," he says slowly, "for you to invite me over so we can talk in person."

"That's not going to happen."

"Please, Vanessa. Just let me talk to you. That's all I want. I've been tempted to show up at hawk, but I didn't think that would have a good outcome."

"Bryan, we're *over*. I don't know why you don't understand that."

"Because I love you. I didn't tell you that yet, but I do. And I think you feel strongly for me. I screwed up. But I'm sorry, and I'm doing it right this time. You know you still love me. That doesn't just disappear, a love like that."

"I loved the *idea* of you, when I thought you were an honest man. I know better now. And that's that. I have to go. I'm sorry this is hard on you, but maybe next time you'll think about some-one other than yourself. Please don't call here again."

"I want to come by after work tonight. I'll drive down. Just talk to me."

"Sorry, no. Good-bye."

"Vanessa. Don't! Don't hang up!"

She presses the phone off, and settles it in an orderly fashion back into the cradle. She feels sick and triumphant in equal meas-ure, and cannot decide which emotion to settle upon. Red Dog whines at her feet, in need of a walk. They both need a walk, Vanessa decides. Nothing clears the head quite as well as a good, long stroll along the banks of the Rio Grande in the golden light of fall.

Vanessa, her feet heavy with remembered grief, her heart rac-ing with surprise at her newfound ability to resist wormy apples, walks to the coat closet, and takes Red Dog's red leash from the hook inside the door. Red Dog begins to leap and whine and twirl in circles, after her own tail.

"Calm down," Vanessa tells her, annoyed and amused at the same time by the dog's enthusiasm. What must it be like to find ec-stasy in the small things? "It's just a walk. It's not like you won the lottery. My God."

Red Dog jumps higher, smiles bigger, twirls faster, as if to say, *Who needs the lottery when there are bunnies and squirrels sprinting them-selves madly into trees and ravines out there?* Vanessa smiles, in spite of her darkened mood. Hard to stay gloomy around Red Dog. Hard to take it all so badly with her there to remind you of the things that truly matter.

"Doesn't take much to make you happy," Vanessa tells the dog. "Sit. Sit!"

Red Dog settles herself down with great effort, wriggling all over with excitement at the promise of a walk, a real live walk. She waits, with as much patience as a dog in such circumstances might muster, for Vanessa to affix the leash to her collar. Vanessa admires the animal's self-control, and pledges to become more like Red Dog in her own personal affairs. Enjoy life with an over-flow of gratitude and pleasure, but know when to sit still and wait.

"Wish I could be more like you," Vanessa tells her as she scoops her house keys up from the entry table. Red Dog drags her hard toward the front door, all wound up, smiling at the mouth and wagging at the tail.

As Vanessa opens the front door, the phone rings again. She hes-itates at the threshold, knows better than to even consider answer-ing his call, for surely it is the same lying creature she just hung up on, wanting the last word. Be like Red Dog, she tells herself— wait. But she cannot resist. She realizes she is stupid for this. But she can't help it. It's the memory of his eyes, of his hands on her skin, of his unconventional ideas about baking, his endless creativ-ity with flour, eggs, and butter, and the conversations they'd have in bed until they both simply fell asleep, dreaming of scones and sauces. She doesn't bother to check the caller ID, because she knows it will be him. Bryan does not like to be hung up on, and always calls back. She wonders if he will ever stop.

"Don't call here again," she commands into the phone. "I've made my wishes clear, and if you truly cared about me the way you say you do, you would honor them and leave me alone."

"Uhm," says a familiar voice, deep and sensuous, but not Bryan's. "Wow. That would make sense, pretty neighbor lady, if I'd ever called you here before. But I think this is my first time."

Paul.

"Oh, God. Sorry," she says, quickly. She cradles the phone to her ear with her shoulder because it takes both hands to rein Red Dog in from her vigorous strain toward the world outside. "I thought you were someone else."

"I hope so. You didn't sound very friendly."

"Sorry."

"My guess is it was either a married man or a telemarketer."

"Telemarketer," she lies.

"They're the worst." Whimsy in his voice, as though he knows she's lying. The whimsical interrogator. Of course he knows.

At her feet, Red Dog whines. *C'mon, Mommy! What're you waiting for? Quit talking to that plastic thing.*

"How are you?" she asks, embarrassed, caught, unsure. Red Dog twists on her leash, still wagging hopefully at the door, but with a hint of doubt seeping into her gaze. She has been let down before and just suddenly remembers what that was like. *Let's go, Mommy! Let's go!*

"I'm good," he says. "I was getting worried 'cuz I haven't seen you in a while."

"I've been a little busy." She addresses the dog now.

"I'm sorry. I can call you later."

"No, no. That's okay. I was just about to take Red Dog for a walk." Vanessa realizes how happy it has made her to hear Paul's voice, though she would certainly never reveal this to him. She wonders if she is drawn to him only because of the newness of him. "We can wait a minute or two. What's up?"

"I can call later. I wouldn't want to get on Red Dog's bad side."

"She has only good sides."

"Well, in that case."

"What's new?" asks Vanessa, trying to sound casual and uninterested.

"Oh, not that much. I just wanted to talk to you. I got a job in construction, so I'm not around that much in the day. Your mom said you've been by every day the past couple weeks, but that you're basically just in and out in a real rush."

"Yeah, I guess so."

"Like you might be avoiding something. Or someone."

"Oh. No. I haven't."

"Something wrong?" He sounds amused, but curious, too. Sincere and insincere at the same time.

She doesn't know what to say.

"Is it me?" he asks. "I mean, I don't presume to think I'm that important, but it seems like we went hiking, and then I said too much about your family, and now you're rushing around your mom's and dad's in a bad mood. Didn't mean to get under your skin like that."

"You're not the one who puts me in a bad mood at my mom's," she says.

"Right. But you even seem to be avoiding my mom."

"Tell her I'm sorry. And you're right. I'm rushing past your house. You lied. You said you couldn't whistle. That's why."

"I can't. Not with the fingers in the mouth. Just through the lips. That's what I meant. Is that what's got you hidin' from me?"

"No, no. It's not that. You should get used to not seeing me, anyway. My sister gets back next week. And I'm pretty sure she'll be taking over at my mom's. I'm not exactly avoiding you. I'm weaning you."

"I see," he says doubtfully—maybe even a little pained. "So it's not me, then? If you don't come around anymore. Not even a tiny bit me?"

"Not entirely."

"So it *is* me, a *little*." He sounds happier.

"A little. Yeah. Maybe." Vanessa looks at Red Dog with an apology in her eyes, for not having had the self-control to be more like Red Dog, for not having waited.

"Can we talk?" he asks. "Like, in person? I kind of miss having you around."

"Well, like I said, I'm about to go walk my dog."

"Red Dog!" he cries, with great affection. "I miss her almost as much as I miss you."

"She's really disappointed right now that I'm still on the phone. I'll be by tomorrow, maybe we can chat then."

"I work tomorrow. Road-crew stuff, between here and Santa Fe."

"Oh." Vanessa does her best not to imagine Paul sweating in the sun, with a tool in his hand. Maybe a jackhammer.

"Feels good to be out there building stuff."

"I bet." Cough.

"Okay, so how about I stop by later tonight?"

"I'm not planning to go to my mom's tonight."

"Well, that's good, because I was thinking I'd stop by there."

"My mom's?"

"No, silly. There. Your place."

"Uhm, here?"

"I have your address, remember? I love the valley but I don't get much chance to head down there because none of my friends are rich enough for that kind of real estate."

"I'm not *rich*," she says before she can stop herself. He's laughing at her as the words tumble out.

"You're funny. Humor, that's a kind of rich."

"There are some humble houses down here."

"Jeez, Vanessa. It was just a joke. You're so defensive."

"I know. No, I mean, right. I mean . . ."

Mercifully, he changes the subject. "Wouldn't you know I've got this kick-ass pumpkin ale just sitting around, and some good

British crackers and these little German sausages—what do you call them?"

"Don't mess with me again, Paul. No more tests. Remember?" Against her better judgment, Vanessa finds herself smiling, both because of the thought of beer and sausage on an evening like this, and because Paul is unlike any other man she has ever known, unselfconscious, boisterous, brash, and yet insightful. Interesting combinations are her greatest weakness.

"Yeah. You're right. I'll be direct. They're teewurst. You ever had teewurst, Chef Vanessa?"

"Not sure," she says. She has never been enamored enough of the Bavarian-sausage thing to have differentiated them all in her mind as she has done for, say, Spanish hams, though she does like sausage more than eggplant.

"Smoked soft sausage, you spread it on crackers."

"Like cheese in a bottle," she suggests.

He laughs big. Answers in cheery sarcasm. "Right. *Just* like that. Actually, I was thinking it was more like paté, but—Easy Cheese? Sure, that works."

"It's a hair spray. It's a food. It's a hair spray," she offers in a lame attempt at humor, mostly to prove that she is not quite as uptight as their prior exchange might have indicated.

"Exactly." He pauses. "Look, I just want to talk to ya. I don't care what we eat. We could eat Spam and I'd still like talking to you. So what do you say?"

"I don't know."

"Aw, c'mon. Just a couple of friends, sitting around squirtin' cheese from a can."

"With pumpkin beer," she interjects.

"Ale. But who's keeping track?"

"Ale," she corrects herself, as a V of geese wings pass overhead, all a-chatter and honking. *God, pumpkin ale and sausage sounds absolutely perfect for this day.*

"So can I stop by? As a friend? Just a friend. I'm good like that."

"I guess," she says, enjoying his humor and directness, the fact that he bothered to call, that he's thinking about her even when she avoids him. Remembering his scent, his arms, his eyes, his jaw. His brain. His mysteries. His tush.

"Eight o'clock good?" he suggests.

Say no, Vanessa. Say no.

"Seven," she says, before she can stop herself. "I have to get up early tomorrow."

Great. Nice going. Larissa would not approve. And Paul would not approve of Larissa not approving. Gah. Can't win.

"Seven," he confirms in jubilant surprise. "Even better, less wait time. I'll see you then."

"Okay."

"Don't keep that pretty little dog waiting."

Vanessa smiles. "Okay."

They hang up, and Vanessa, only moments before close to slipping into a depressive spell and memories of Bryan, feels suddenly lighter, happier, like she can do anything. The day seems clearer, the air more redolent of good things. Red Dog bangs her tail against the wall, a repetitive thump whose more salacious aural implications are not lost on Vanessa. *A distant memory now. Not the life for me anymore. Not until I'm repaired and trustworthy to my own heart.* The dog senses her owner's worry, and responds with a look of concern all her own.

Are we going or not, Mommy? Bunnies! Squirrels!

"I'm coming, I'm coming," Vanessa tells the dog.

Red Dog grins with relief, the moment of concern come and gone and now forgotten, living in the canine now; she hops up and down like a kangaroo, the wag spreading from her tail to the rest of her body.

Vanessa opens the door just as another flock of geese jabs their collective way overhead, heading south for the winter in a great, heat-seeking triangle. What, she wonders, is the outdoors—and God's ever-changing palate—trying to tell her now? Thumps, triangles, sausages. Where her mind goes she does not will it; she struggles mightily to draw it back. Shudder at the *thought*.

"Let's go," she tells Red Dog as she fights against tempting and unwholesome thoughts of moist roasted goose breast and thighs, swollen Germanic sausages, and bold, hot red chile. *Unfair.*

Red Dog prances out into the sun, oblivious to her owner's sensual, mental, and physical distress. The dog squats at the gate to relieve herself, happily at one with her body and its needs, unapologetic of the territory she inhabits and marks at will, happy to be alive, secure in her own naive, animal way that everything is going to be fine, and, Vanessa imagines, certain in the innocent way of well-loved dogs that Paul is, in fact, a great guy who just happens to be barbarically attractive and swears he wants to be nothing more than the best of friends.

VIKING TIP SAINT-GERMAIN

$\mathcal{H}\varepsilon$ *arrives* in a drum of knuckles upon the door, exactly at seven o'clock, with a six-pack of pumpkin ale in sweating brown bottles under his arm, and high-end English crackers in cellophane and soft sausage imported from Germany in a canvas shopping bag from La Montanita Food Co-op.

He wears canvas cargo shorts, leather sandals, a long-sleeved cotton shirt in gray, with a curly indecipherable design stenciled on the front, casual and comfortable. A smile like a light going on in her chest. His hair is long enough to gel now, and he has done exactly that, pushed it up off his forehead and a little bit back. Makes him look younger. His cheeks ruddy and red from his time in the sun on his new job, she assumes. A vision of strength and good health. Expectation. Impulse.

His body spice wafts to her, blended with the cool evening air, delicious, with just a hint of soap and shampoo, shaving cream. He is recently clean, and still the underlying musk of him has diminished not even a little bit. For this she is grateful. Red Dog has expected him since she heard the truck crunch up the gravel driveway, and greets him with a huge, stupid grin and a wag that threatens to topple her. *He's good, Mommy! He's good!* Mommy knows.

"Vanessa," Paul says with a big flash of slightly crooked white teeth. "Look at you! You look beautiful." He pats the dog on the head and greets her with a string of baby talk that charms the dog and disarms her owner.

Vanessa has tried, of course, to look beautiful. But no harder than she normally would. Out of pride, she tells herself. Not to seduce. Not. Still no makeup other than a smear of clear beeswax lip balm, just the dark plain jeans and the dark red organic cotton tank top she thinks shows off her neckline, a black button-down open over it. A necklace, earrings, silver and turquoise, natural and native to the area. Sandals that are very much like his own. A bit of essential oil behind each ear, sandalwood, and unscented body lotion everywhere such a balm might be needed.

She greets him with a handshake when he tries to hug her, and reminds him of their friendship pact.

"*Your* pact, my *self-control*," he says, respecting her wish for distance nonetheless. "But I'll tell ya," he wags his finger playfully and grins, "you said more with that refusal of a hug than you meant to."

"What do you mean?"

"*Real* friends hug without issue," he says, holding her hand still with his, connecting his gaze to hers.

"Whatever."

He smiles at her. "If you really felt no attraction for me, you wouldn't need to create artificial distance. We'd just hug, like friends do. Right? End of story."

She pulls her hand away with some effort, and he lets her, with a slight chuckle. Undeterred.

"That was a loaded handshake, missy," he says with a wink, "no matter how many 'whatevers' you give me."

"Yeah, okay," she says with a weak attempt at sarcasm. "Just come in already."

"Great place you got here." He changes the subject as his contented gaze sweeps across the living room and kitchen.

She puts the beer in the refrigerator and stands back to watch his face as he takes in the surroundings. He strolls from the living area to the kitchen, his substantial feet making the floorboards creak warmly, Red Dog tagging along as though he were some sort of doggie celebrity. *Can I sniff you, please? Just one more little sniff?*

Paul observes the paintings on the walls, a collection of folk art and colorful Southwestern landscapes done by friends across the state, with an approving manner. The quilts hung on the walls. The books everywhere, stacks and stacks of them. Towers. The crushed-velvet sofa. The overstuffed reading chair and lamp. The birdcages without birds. The enormous kitchen that is the heart and center of it all, the copper pots and pans that hang, the bunches of dried herbs. He seems charmed by the place. Smiles at her to let her know how much he likes it, exhales in comfort. He is at home here, and she knows it. She has worked hard to make her home a nurturing cocoon, a creative safe haven from the insanities of the world.

"It's very *you*," he says.

"You don't know me well enough to make that call, do you?" she asks, as he sits at the island across from where she now washes fresh figs in the vegetable sink.

He chuffs in disbelief. "You know what, Vanessa? You question and even reject every good thing a person says to you. But when someone insults you, you take it as the God's honest truth. What gives?"

"Whatever," she replies, again with this tired word, and tries to sound easy and light. Of course, he's right. How does he do that? How does he know her so well, without knowing her at all?

She gets a Talavera pottery plate down for the crackers and the fruit, but decides to wait a bit. Suggests they let the beer chill some more. He looks at the tangle of greens and bursts of color in the garden, past the window, over her shoulder, and asks if he can explore out there.

"You want to tour my garden," she says in disbelief. *Men don't usually want to do things like that, do they?*

He looks at her with a stifled laugh, and whatever lascivious response he wants to share, he resists. Working hard, she thinks, not to be the soldier he has been all his life.

She shows him to the back door. He slides past her on his way out, his body heat like a low-lying rainbow in his wake. Darkness coming. Crickets, and she wonders when they will die. The dying time coming. Wonders how they are reborn, where the eggs are hidden, how an animal can be born and grow without parents. She thinks she is a human cricket. Thinks all manner of things, brain moving faster than her feet, following along in his scent trail, watching him move, aware of him as a squirrel in a tree is aware of a coyote coming out for the night.

He stops, picks, tastes, sniffs, feels, breathes, pops his back, his knuckles, grins, and just *is*. A half light that pours honey across it all, slows it down, his motions smooth and strong, the man and garden warming to sepia tones. Darkness coming. Aware of the heat of his body, aware of the grace of his limbs as they move down the paths. Smooth-faced. He explores, enthralled, and asks questions. How does she water this? (It is on a timed automatic irrigator.) When does she plant that? (In the fall.) What is this herb? (Marjoram.)

They stand in the path by the area once occupied by her enormous green and red eruptions of rhubarb, and she considers the vegetable, harvested and eaten back in the spring. It is the fugu fish of the plant world. Firm red stalks like sweet celery, entirely edible, the stuff of folk legends and pies made lovingly by mothers entirely unlike her own. The leaves deadly poison. The things a person must know in this life, the things to avoid. The delicious bits are wrapped up with the dangerous ones. And Paul begins to whistle, and then there is a car.

The headlights flash across them as the vehicle turns off the dirt road into Vanessa's driveway. Because the house is nearly rural, surrounded by land and gardens on all sides, they have a view of the driveway from the backyard. Red Dog makes for the side fence at a sprint, barking before she knows what comes their way, bravery above concern for self. Alerted to danger in her cells, ready to fight it off. Wiser than her owner. Protective.

"You expecting someone, babe?" Paul asks her as he plucks a raspberry from a bush.

"I'm not your *babe*," she says.

He laughs at her. "If I might quote a wise woman, 'whatever.' "

She balks at his boldness, the green leaf of him tangled with the sweet red spine.

"What?" he asks as they both watch the approaching car. "If you could see your face when you look at me, you'd know that I know what a lie that is," he says. "You *know* you dig me."

"Aren't *you* the cocky one?" she asks, as she squints at the long driveway. Considers for a moment that it might be Hazel coming to sample the (amazing, if she can say so) Thai green chile stew, but remembers the phone call from Bryan, placed from the depths of hell. Her gut drops. The lights of the car die, and then she sees him get out of the driver's side. Tall, dark, troubled, brooding, with eyes like warm and welcoming chestnuts. Him. The thing of her nightmares.

"It's not cocky if it's *true*," says Paul.

But his voice is distant because she is not mentally there with Paul anymore. She has zoomed through space and time and is back in those brown eyes, in the dreams, her heart exploded with the weight of the thing that crushes down.

"Bryan," she states, hands to her hips, her heart leaping in two directions at once. Yanked to shreds like the tender flesh of a long-roasted suckling pig, the kind they cut with the dull edge of a plate in Spain.

"Bryan?" asks Paul. "The married jackass you told me about on the hike?"

"I *told* him not to come here," huffs Vanessa, more to herself than to Paul, and off she storms, to the fence. To see what he wants. To send him away. To fix herself. To fix him, sear him, singe him, destroy him once and for all.

She plants herself on her side of the fence, right at the driveway, where the peas grow up the wall in a tangle of vine and exuberance. So many peas. She should pick them soon, find something to do with them. In this chill, a pot pie. A soup. Something with fresh peas, potage Saint-Germain.

Then Bryan. There he is. Taller than she remembers. Healthier than she remembers, too. Simpering, head down, like a punished dog. She's never seen him do that. A plea in his eye. A fallen soufflé, a flattened cake. A wry expression, as though this might make it all better. A flinch, a bow. Deference.

"Hi," says Bryan. Simple, direct, to the point. His eyes are lopsided. How is it she never noticed that before? He looks like his face is melting.

Paul, trotting up the path behind her, answers before Vanessa has time to reply.

"Hey, what's up." He is all smiles, beaming, big, burly, a man. Suddenly, Bryan looks very much like a boy. Surprised to find a man here with her, surprised she might have known any men other than him.

Paul strolls up to the wall, with something of a gum chewer to his jaw now, something of a baseball player considering the next move. He chews no gum. He is all swagger, confident, supposed to be here.

Bryan startles, looks at Vanessa, then back at Paul with a sort of shock, unsure. Stuttering. She doesn't remember ever seeing him do *that*, either. She cannot help but notice how very weak and insubstantial Bryan seems in the presence of Paul.

"And you are?" asks Paul, territorial, as though this were his place, as though Vanessa were his girl. And she loves him for it, in this moment. Loves him for the look of misery on Bryan's falling, melting face. The look of the hypocrite fed his own medicine. With his own spoon. The gulp of a man forced to drink his own backwash.

"Bryan," he says, with a cough. Forces himself to shake Paul's hand. Paul's bigger hand. Much bigger. Bryan winces under the vise grip.

Vanessa smiles and moves closer to Paul, who, if he notices, does not indicate so. Acts natural. It's all so easy for Paul, acting, sensing, knowing. Interrogating.

"Byron, you said?" he asks, pleasant, as though he has never heard the name before. "Like the poet." Designed to wound. Disarm. Belittle.

"No, uhm, it's *Bryan*." He looks at Vanessa. Quizzical. Wondering. Wondering. Wondering in a sort of panic: Why she never told him about this man. Who this man is. Insecure. Wondering. What it all means. What secrets she's kept from him. If he was not the only player. If she, in fact, had the upper hand all along. At their feet, Red Dog growls. She has never liked Bryan.

Her heart soars with this newfound uncertainty of his. And that is the key, she realizes: the kept secret. Yes. The kept secret, always so much more damaging than a truth told. So much worse for the imagining that comes with it. The less said, the more pain inflicted. He knew this. And now he finds himself in the spotlight of not knowing.

"Bryan," says Paul, with a big, unassuming, unthreatening, affable grin. Only it is none of those things. It is high art. "I'm Paul. Nice to meet ya, man."

Paul breaks off a pod with his hands and opens it, expert with things slit down the center, uses that magical thumb of his, pops the peas into his mouth with a grin. Like a man at the state fair. Not a care in the world. Secure. Terrifyingly so.

Bryan looks from Vanessa to Paul, and then back to her, then to her house, her dog, her garden, anywhere but in their eyes.

"You know Nessa from work?" asks Paul, through his mouthful. And then he does it. Puts one big arm around her shoulders. No look to her to reassure her that it's all innocent, that they are still just friends, nothing to indicate this might be the ruse it is. And this scares her. He, Paul, is so good at this. So good at lying for dominance. Isn't she supposed to be running from this? From men good at lying? And yet he is all hot broth and she the flour dissolving into it.

"No, not exactly," says Bryan. "We, well, I don't know. How *do* we know each other, Vanessa?"

Coward. Bryan pouty, Bryan offended, Bryan acting as though his party were rained upon. Cynical, snarky, negative energy around him in frigid waves of misery. She never realized, until now, how negative his energy was. Angry, possessive, lopsided, entitled. As though he owned her still. As though he ever did. And should.

She weighs the options. Lie. Truth. Red Dog barks and barks at him. Snarls low in her throat. Hates him. Always has. Red Dog has good instincts. Red Dog is honest. Vanessa decides on truth.

"We *know* each other because we dated for four months, and you were married the whole time, and had a son, and you never bothered to share those salient facts with me. *Bryan*."

Bryan smiles awkwardly.

"Dude, that's rough," says Paul. He looks at Vanessa with shock, as though he were hearing this for the first time. As though he can't believe she would be this weak. As though he can't believe she'd give Bryan the battle victory so easily. As though he was hoping she'd play along with his victory plan. She can see Paul recalibrating the entire ordeal in his mind, quick. So very quick. Bryan is not so quick on his feet. He still staggers mentally, unsure.

"Yeah, well, I thought I might have left something here," says Bryan. Weak. A weak excuse. "But I think I just remembered where I put it."

Where the sun doesn't shine.

"Nice car, man," says Paul, gesturing to Bryan's BMW, changing the subject. "What is that? Three series?"

"Yes." No joy in sharing this, though she knows Bryan is incredibly proud of his car. Usually so, anyway. Not so now. Pouty outdoes proud at this moment.

Paul shows no weakness. Gives no hint. Just a guy admiring another guy's car, control like deep ice, though he knows well that the thing Bryan wants is in Paul's meaty umbrage. Not in the driveway.

"Sweet," says Paul, affable Paul. Chummy. Aggressively chummy. Pulls her closer. "You want to come in for a minute, Byron?"

"Bryan."

Paul laughs it off in mock self-deprecation. "Right. Sorry, man. Long day. We got beer, some snacks. Sure ya don't wanna join us?"

Vanessa stares at Paul. Did he really just invite Bryan into her *house*? No, he didn't. Did he?

"Uh, no, thanks, man." Bryan waves and backs away. Just what Paul must have known he'd do. Diplomat. Interrogator. He must, she realizes, have been very good at his job. A pro. An aggressor.

Cockier now, Paul calls out, "Cool, man. Well, if you think of that thing you came here for, you just let us know. All right?"

Bryan looks at Vanessa one last time, and backs all the way to his car, turning only at the last moment to open the door, but not waving in response to Paul's wave. Shrinking, before her very eyes. Into nothing.

"Take it easy, Byron," says Paul, in guy talk. The way guys talk to other guys. A man much practiced in the art of man talk. Gracefully and undeniably dominant.

"Yeah!" False cheer. Bravado. Bryan shrinking. A wounded man. "You too, man."

And Paul and Vanessa stand there, like an old married couple, as Bryan guns his engine and peels away, Red Dog chasing the BMW until it is off the property. Vanessa doesn't want this moment to end. Knows that it should end, must end.

She stands still. Like a squirrel in the embrace of a coyote. Plays dead. Prays he will not hear her heart beating. Hopes he cannot sense how much she enjoys the welcome heft of his capable arm on her shoulders. Wonders when he'll take it off. Hopes he won't. At all. Not tonight.

They watch Bryan drive away. Until he is gone. And then they stand there some more, Paul's arm in place, and she too comfortable that way to make it end, though end it must.

"He's not a bad-looking guy," says Paul.

"No, he's not."

"I can see why you dug him." Paul doesn't move, either, frozen. Darkness has come. And with it, a cacophony of crickets. "Not that I notice other guys."

"No, of course not."

"I'm secure in my manhood."

"*I'll* say," she says.

And then she does it. Against all better judgment, she nestles into his warm, solid flank, beneath his wing, just a tiny bit, but enough for him to notice, and turn toward her ever so slightly. She takes in a breath of Paul, and sighs it out, and tells him, at last.

"You smell so, so good, Paul. I never told you that."

He finds this hilarious. "Yeah? Wow. I don't think anyone's ever told me that, actually." Turns toward her entirely now.

"Thank you," she says, and is unable to look him in the eye for more than a second at a time.

"For what?" That grin. She can see it in the dark. She can smell him, too, and feel him. They are close, maybe six inches of air between them now, face to face, chest to chest, and his hand, the one on the arm that was around her, slides down to her own hand, takes it up. Squeezes it. His heat radiates. Big heat.

"For acting like you were my boyfriend."

He steps closer. She is frozen. Melting inside. Dizzy with want.

"It wasn't hard to pull off." He takes her other hand in his. She feels his breath on her. "The thing about Byron," he says.

"Bryan," she whispers.

Paul narrows his eyes and smiles. "No, Byron. The poet. I think he knew you pretty well. 'She walks in beauty, like the night, of cloudless climes and starry skies; and all that's best of dark and bright, meet in her aspect and her eyes.'"

Vanessa cannot speak. Paul is the last man she would expect to recite poetry to her. Again the surprise. Always something new with this man.

He touches her cheek, gently, slowly, and moves closer.

"You hardly know me," she says. "We shouldn't do this."

It is the right thing to say. She is going to be careful this time, isn't she? Wise. Smart. She is not going to trap herself again. She hardly knows this man. Casts her glance down, her head down. Looks away, knows what's coming. Resists it with whatever she has left. So little strength. No sense whatsoever.

"You're right," he says. And he lifts her head with a finger to her chin, up gently, slowly, and brushes his lips across her forehead. Tenderly, and fast. With great feeling. "I *want* to know you, though. Badly."

"Oh," she says. A gasp from the electricity in her skin.

He releases her hands. Watches her to see what she will do. She is grateful for the darkness because her face must surely be plum purple. Sweat on her brow.

He reaches to the wall, and breaks off another ripe pea pod. She watches him in the darkness, wants him. Vanessa waits inside her skin, feels herself within her own body, but not of it, as if she were wrapped all around a low, firm throb of longing at her core. Everything is heartbeat. Everything is inhale, exhale. He slits the slender pod with those large and careful fingers, slips a finger inside the opening, probes, digs out a pea with just the tip of his pointer.

"These are so good," he tells her, the pea balanced perfectly on his finger, so small, so delicate, under his control. "Here, try one."

She lets him push the tiny, ripe green ball between her lips. Lets her lips wrap around the tip of his finger just a little bit before taking the vegetable in. Then she closes her lips tight against him. Pushes him out, sensing him wanting in.

He smiles, enjoys the game. She chews, but her mind is on that brief, lingering taste of his finger, not focused whatsoever on the pea. It was salty, rough, the give of skin, the give of her lips. Magnetic, electric. All those sensations still with her, ghosts dancing shivers across her flesh in the purpling night air, in the sky coming down all around her with its hope.

"Good?" he asks, a leading question.

"Very," she says softly, and he feeds her another pea. Then another.

Each time, he keeps his finger a moment longer on her lips, then in that space between her lips, and she allows it, each time his finger venturing just a bit farther into her mouth. Another, and another, until he leaves his finger there, in between her lips, the tip just resting on her bottom front teeth.

His fingernail hard against the velvet of her tongue. She feels him enter her this way, having never kissed him, never held him, and the exquisite novelty of this perfect gourmet intimacy sends slow, liquid waves through her. As good as the act itself. Filled up, bursting, ready, blooming. She allows her tongue to explore the tip of his finger, closes her lips around it, holds it there, closes her eyes. Tastes him. The salt she'd sensed he might taste of comes at her in full force now, mingled with the earth of peas, the unnamable, fantastic essence of Paul that she has inhaled, now here in her mouth, on her tongue, umami, human and real.

"Good?" he asks again, this time in a whisper, close to her ear. She closes her eyes, and tries to name it all. Clove. Garlic. Cinnamon. He is everything, every flavor. Earth. Sky. Her match.

She pulls the finger from her lips, dries it with her own fingers. "Very good," she repeats.

Her eyes have adjusted to the dark, and his face is close, over her. He seems to be holding his breath. She can see the expression, and it is not what she expected. Paul, confident Paul, looks like a child who has found a treasure, unsure what to do with it, stunned that it came to him. His bluff called, at last. The boy with the bowl cut, amazed that the girl has noticed him there.

She reaches her hand to his face, and strokes his cheek softly, enjoys her moment of power. He leans into her movement, like Red Dog, she thinks, needy. Pain flashing in his eyes. A man in need of affection. Wounded.

And then, as quickly as the look of astonishment and grief came, it is gone, and in its place, a furious sort of hunger. And the cocky grin, as though he has just remembered who he is and what he is capable of. He pulls her toward him, and moves in, slowly, until his lips are on hers. Softly at first, and then urgent, consuming. She closes her eyes, releases herself to this kiss, presses her body against his.

The full rush of taste comes to her now. Paul. All Paul, sweet, savory, tender, bold, salty, spicy, with just a hint of garden pea. Exquisite.

And then, she comes to her senses.

Wrong.

This is all wrong.

"I can't do this," she says, pulling away, a pea yanking itself from the pod. A painful thing, forcing herself to let go of this.

He says nothing. Dumbfounded. She did not think he had it in him to be silent, or serious, and he is both. She worries she has angered him, pushed him to that *place*. He sighs.

"Let's go inside," she says, moving from him now. "I bet that beer is cold by now. We can talk more, get to know each other."

"Yeah, okay," he manages, with a hint of humor in his voice. Annoyed with her. Amused by her. His regular way with her. "Sure thing, Vanessa—*buddy*. Whatever you want."

"It's what I want," she lies.

"If you say so."

"I do say so."

"Then I will respect it."

And in they go, still just friends. But barely.

MIDNIGHT LAGNIAPPE

CONFESSION

Two weeks later, and Larissa is in Vanessa's kitchen, the warm, cottony camel scent of Morocco still lingering in her pores, wearing a thick Irish cable-knit sweater and jeans. Larissa's girls are with their dad, and Larissa's laptop computer is open on the granite island, with emotive, colorful digital photos from her trip on display. "The veils, the veils, the veils," says Vanessa. "How do they live behind veils like that?" Larissa suggests that women in the West also live behind veils, but veils they carry inside themselves. Vanessa thinks of Hawk, and his thieving. Realizes it is true. Realizes she cannot stay in her job much longer.

As Larissa tells of her travels and research, Red Dog snoozes near the warm vent at the base of the refrigerator, a sure sign that cold is coming soon.

"It's a relief to be back," says Larissa.

Vanessa, in sweats and fat, fuzzy sleep socks, busies her hands and eyes, baking. Tries to find a way to tell Larissa about Paul. Best to bake, for now, and listen. The end result will be rustic, tangy tarts with what's left of the summer garden fruit harvest. Apricot, peach, apple. That, and not having to look at her sister during the sisterly interrogation.

It is nearly midnight, and the sisters have been socializing more or less nicely since nine, with mugs of steaming, powerful Turkish coffee that will keep them up late, possibly all night. That's okay. There has been a lot to discuss, and Larissa is still getting over her jet lag a week after her return still wired with new things learned and uncertain hours.

"Mom says it went well," says Larissa, the way you might say "I don't suppose you've been in the chocolate" to a kid with chocolate all over his or her face.

"She did *not*."

Larissa sighs in resignation at having been found out. "Okay, she said it went as well as could be *expected*." A cocked brow as she waits, hopeful that Vanessa will elaborate.

"That's more like it." Vanessa, eyes focused on her hands at work.

"She's in bad shape, Vanessa."

"Yeah. It was very sad to see her like that. I'm going to make more of an effort to spend time there."

Larissa, perhaps taken aback by her sister's uncharacteristically assertive kindness regarding their mother, thoughtfully sips her coffee and watches Vanessa for a moment before saying, "Mom says you have been spending a lot of time with the guy next door. Pete? Bob? I forget his name."

And you think that's the only reason I would go there anymore. Of course that's what you think.

"His name's Paul," Vanessa corrects her. *Look at her directly and do not turn away. Face your fears and let her know you are not sorry for yourself, for your life, for the things you do and the company you keep.*

Larissa arches a brow and buries her nose in the mug, says into her coffee, "Paul, then. You've been hanging out with Paul. Why am I not exactly surprised by this?"

"Because you know I'm friendly and outgoing?" Vanessa folds her arms and tucks the hands into her armpits to keep them still. They want so terribly to fly away on some urgent, distracting task. Some show of weakness.

Larissa frowns at her. "No, I don't think that's it."

"Paul and his mother are very nice people, Larissa. You would know this if you ever slowed down enough to talk to them. They think you are this unfriendly whirlwind."

Larissa fails to take the bait and does not engage in any defensive tactic. Rather, she affects a sympathetic face and asks, "Is there something you'd like to get off your chest?"

"I beg your pardon?" replies Vanessa, turning, against her best efforts, back to the baking and dishes and whatever else there might be to keep her away from her sister's damning eyes.

"Oh, Vanessa. You know what I mean. I leave you here, and you say you're not going to chase after the first man who comes along, and then I hear from Mom that this is exactly what you've done. How could you? Why are you so self-destructive, honey?"

"I haven't done *anything*, Larissa."

"You haven't chased Paul," Larissa states doubtfully—no, more like suspiciously. Judgmentally.

"It's not like that." *And even if it were, what business is it of yours or Mom's or anyone else's, really?*

Larissa's arched brow grows higher, because she above all others is able to tell when Vanessa lies. Vanessa takes the ramekins from the oven, sets the still-bubbling tarts on the counter to cool, and plops herself into the seat next to her sister. Exhausted by it all.

Larissa turns to face her, places a supportive hand on her back, between the shoulder blades.

"He's pretty charismatic, right?" asks Larissa.

Vanessa cannot stop herself from spilling the proverbial beans about Paul now, spends the next ten minutes describing it all, from the moment she first saw him and assumed him a dolt and a Viking, to the pea-scented fingertip clamped softly between her teeth.

Larissa listens with concern deepening the lines in her face. "Okay, so, you sucked his finger, kissed him—"

"I didn't 'suck' his finger."

"Sounds like you sucked his finger."

"You make it sound so crass, Larissa! I, I—I *tasted* him. That's all. The way you check a soup to see if it needs salt."

Larissa's eyes narrow at this, patient, judgmental, but also admiring of Vanessa's predictable obsession with taste. "And did he?" she asks Vanessa.

"Did he what?"

"Need salt." Another smirk.

Vanessa grins, relieved Larissa is not angry with her. "He was perfectly seasoned, actually."

Larissa looks thoughtful for a moment. "So there was just that one kiss?"

"Yep. That's it."

"And how are you feeling about that?"

"I really don't regret it, surprisingly," she tells her sister simply. "I know you think I should, and any other time, with any other guy, I might have. But this time, this time is actually different."

"All right. So. After the kiss. You guys came back in here, and then what happened?" Larissa returns her hands to the coffee mug. A sigh released, patience begged for, impatient with Vanessa's cluelessness—but also so terribly in need of being needed this way. "No gory details. Just the basics."

"We ate the sausage and drank the beer, and talked."

"Talked." Larissa sounds dubious, as though the verb "to talk" might hold a different meaning for each sister.

"Yes, *talked*. You don't believe me?"

Larissa shrugs with pursed lips, so Vanessa looks her dead in the eye to prove herself.

"I did *not* sleep with the man, Larissa. No matter what you might think."

"So what did you 'talk' about?"

"I don't know. Lots of stuff. Growing up, our families. Music. Life. Food. I told him about Hawk. He told me a little bit about his days at the Air Force Academy, and flying a fighter jet. He didn't talk about the war, though. He's still not opening up about that."

Larissa is the one to fold her arms now, bitter for some reason and trying hard to conceal it. Disappointed, perhaps. "Probably for the best."

The sisters sit in silence for a moment or two.

"I told him I wasn't dating anyone because I'm trying to kick the husband habit," Vanessa tells her, feeling like she used to as a kid, confessing everything to her sister all the time. Hoping, she now realizes with a sort of shock, for Larissa's approval.

"Oh?" It doesn't look like Larissa thinks telling Paul so much about her reasons for dating or not dating was a good idea.

"He thinks I'm avoiding dating not because of Bryan or any of the others, but because of *you*," says Vanessa.

Larissa straightens her spine and puffs up, like a creature whose territory has been threatened.

"Oh, really? And how would this *Paul* know a thing like that, considering he's never even *talked* to me beyond a quick hello? You know, they say that the first sign of an abusive man is that he tries to distance you from your friends and family. You should probably think about that."

"So how do you know he's all wrong for me if you've never talked to him? I mean, here you are saying he doesn't know you well enough to pass judgment, but that's exactly what you've done with him, isn't it?"

Larissa, being somewhat reasonable, considers this. "Well, with some people, you can just tell."

Vanessa shakes her head in defense of Paul. "Well, maybe he's able to tell some things, too."

"About me?" huffs Larissa. "Please."

"He's got a pretty good read on people. He was an interrogator on top of everything else."

"Vanessa." Larissa says this word in admonishment, with all that might imply—*you should know better, what were you thinking, are you crazy, etc.* "You can't be serious about getting involved with this man. An *interrogator?* It's worse than I thought."

"We're just friends, Larissa. I know you mean well, but please stop worrying."

"Friends who . . . suck each other's *fingers?*"

"*Taste.* And he didn't taste mine. I tasted his. That's it."

"I can't believe you did this," says Larissa, with a disappointed expression she tries to mask as kind concern. "After all we talked about. I go away for a month, and you fall victim to another one of these guys."

Vanessa feels her own back tighten now, under attack. She considers what her sister has said, and thinks about what Paul would make of it. She compares the way she feels around Paul—strong, funny, invincible—and how she feels around Larissa: useless, dumb, inept. Both Vanessa and Paul seem to judge her, but when Paul does it, it seems designed to make her feel better about her choices and possibilities.

"He thinks I'm too quick to blame myself," she tells Larissa. "And he thinks you and Mom are too quick to *let* me."

"Let you what?" Larissa sounds impatient now, almost whiny.

"Take the blame for everything that goes wrong. He thinks that it makes me lack confidence, like that I could have my own restaurant by now, but I have these 'tapes' playing in my head, you and Mom putting me down."

"That's what he said?"

"Yeah."

Larissa gathers in a powerful breath to calm herself. Offers up a fake smile. Some quick, *too* quick, blinking of the eyes. "Think the tarts have cooled off enough? They smell *so* good."

Vanessa gets up and tests the tarts with her fingertip. Cool enough. She gets plates, serves them each two. Returns to the counter with forks and napkins.

"So what else did this Paul say?" asks Larissa.

" 'This Paul' thinks I'm subconsciously drawn to married men because deep down inside I fear commitment."

Larissa, chomping with irritation now. Focused on the tart so as to avoid being pulled back, but not so rude as to outright ignore Vanessa. "Jeez, he's an interrogator *and* a psychotherapist, huh?" Pops a crumb into her mouth, nods with pleasure at the food.

"He's a good guy. You'd like him if you gave him half a chance. Seriously."

"Maybe so. But do you think it's smart to have told this guy so much personal stuff about yourself? You hardly know him."

"Well, on my planet, telling people personal stuff about your-self is how you *get* to know them."

Larissa smirks at her. "He's an interrogator, sweetie. Men like that, they get things out of you even if you don't realize it. I wouldn't be surprised if you told him more than you should have."

"Well, I'd probably do that even if he weren't an interrogator," Vanessa jokes. She shrugs and bites into the apricot tart. Flaky crust. Filling not too sweet. Washes it down with coffee.

"Sad, but true," says Larissa.

"Well," Vanessa says, wiping her mouth. "I think he's probably right about me and the husbands and Mom and all that. I realized that after visiting Mom and Dad while you were gone. Think about it. We formed our ideas about marriage by watching them fight and drink, Larissa. From the moment we were born. It can't have been good for us. You got over it better than I did, I think."

"They're not as bad as all that," her sister says dismissively.

"Are you kidding me?" Vanessa laughs even though her pulse accelerates with her sister's blatant lie.

Larissa shrugs it off. "I think you make too big a deal out of it, honestly."

"We are talking about Mom and Dad here, Larissa! Paul tells me the whole neighborhood can hear them fighting every night. How can you just write it out of your life story like it never happened?"

"*Paul* again. Of course he says that. After you told him your version of childhood. C'mon, Vanessa. Don't you think he's going to tell you whatever he thinks you want to hear, to get in your pants? A guy like that?" Larissa laughs. "My God. You have no shield, emotional shield, against it. It's sad to watch."

"It's totally true that people can hear them yelling and carrying on, Larissa. It's embarrassing to go over there. I can't stand it."

"That's exaggeration."

Vanessa feels her head and neck growing warm and puffy from anxiety, but decides it is time to stand up to her sister.

"No, it's *not* an exaggeration. And you *know* it. Somewhere inside you, you remember how it was. Maybe *you're* the one exaggerating."

Larissa stares at her, in shock. In horror. "Nonsense."

"Maybe all these years, the way you've coped with the dysfunction is to think it was something better than it really was. I don't blame you for it. We do what we have to. Denial is a potent medicine."

Larissa looks furious. "That is *so* not true."

Vanessa's body floods with adrenaline from the confrontation, and she feels her hands begin to tremble.

"Paul makes some good points about all of us, and I think you dislike him because of it."

"I *dislike* this guy because I can see *disaster* coming."

Vanessa considers what Larissa has said, and, for the second time that evening, dares to disagree. "Yeah? Well, I like him." Paul's courage in her veins. Taken from the taste of his fingertip.

"It's your funeral," says Larissa, with a carefree shrug. "Just don't come calling me when he hurts you. I'm sick of cleaning up the mess."

"There won't be a mess. But if there is, I'll be sure to call someone else to clean it up."

"Thank you."

"He's my friend, not my boyfriend. And I think he's smart."

"He's *military*." Larissa says this as though being such negated anyone's intelligence.

"So?"

"How is that smart? Military?" Larissa taps her temple as if pointing to her brain in an effort to get Vanessa to use her own.

"That is unfair," says Vanessa. "Just because he believed something, and, by the way, he doesn't believe it anymore. And I don't think any idiot off the street can fly a plane in combat."

"He went to war under that horrible president. I just can't see how anyone can be smart and in the military under those circumstances."

"He's retired. He works in construction now."

Larissa laughs out loud. "Oh, much better."

"He's smart, Larissa. It doesn't matter what he does for a living."

"Military is not a smart move for anyone. And construction? Vanessa. Come on. A lack of good judgment in this case is at the very least *implied*."

"He speaks four languages. Including Arabic."

Larissa's brow arches ever so slightly again, this time in interest. But she quickly stifles any indication that her mind might have changed. "I'm sure that comes in handy in illegal wars for oil."

"And he cooks. Or at least he barbecues. He made this fish, Larissa. It was lovely. And he seems to know a lot more about food than your average guy."

"I'm not buying it."

"He got me a shiraz."

"Because he interrogated you and realized that was his way in. Think, Vanessa!"

"Listen. I should think you know I'm not a complete idiot, after all these years. And I agree with you about the political stuff, Larissa. You know, I felt the same way about this guy until I got to know him. You have to know someone before you make that kind of judgment call. Everyone's different."

"So you trust this man?"

"I kind of do." Vanessa feels her temples pulsating with pressure and a headache coming on. It is late.

"Kind of."

"No. I *do*. I trust him. He's a good guy."

Larissa makes a face. "A good guy who, oh, I don't know, just happens to drop bombs on kids in his spare time, and lives with his *mother*. I swear, sometimes I think you'd date Norman Bates if he walked up to you on the street and said hello."

"We're not dating. He's my friend. You're wrong about Paul, Larissa. You need to face that."

Larissa, discomfited with the challenge to her long-standing authority over her sister, sucks down the last of her coffee with a growing impatience, and takes her now-empty plate to the dish sink, sets it down with uneasy finality. *Clunk*.

"Whatever you say, Vanessa." Dismissive.

"Don't be like that."

Larissa turns to face her, cocks her head to one side in defiance, ready for a fight. "Like what? Worried about you?"

"Exactly. Stop worrying about me."

Anger on Larissa's face now. "Well, excuse me for caring."

"Is it caring, Larissa? Think about it."

Larissa's arms fold over her chest and she nearly clucks her tongue in henlike superiority and pity.

Vanessa fights for the courage to speak her thoughts.

"Have you ever stopped to consider that maybe the only thing I did wrong was trust people who didn't deserve me?" asks Vanessa, quoting Paul almost verbatim, and feeling incredibly empowered by it.

"I think you need to learn to be on your own before you can

know what to look for in a mate," says Larissa. "That's all I'm say-ing. Love yourself first."

"Is that what you did?" Vanessa asks, knowing full well that Larissa met Fergus her second year in college, just months after breaking up with her high school boyfriend. They have been together ever since.

"That's different."

"Why? Why is that different? You were single for, what, six months? C'mon."

"It's different because," sniffs Larissa, "you're a genius at what you do, but when it comes to men, you know."

"I know *what*? Say it."

Larissa stares blankly at her.

"Say it," demands Vanessa.

"Say *what*?" Larissa sniffs back.

"That it's different because you actually *believe* that you're the smart one. Right?"

The sisters stop talking and feel the weight of what has been spoken crushing down upon the room. Finally, Larissa speaks.

"I never said I was smarter than you."

Vanessa takes her own plate to the sink, rinses it, sets it in the dish rack, and turns to face Larissa with a new look of confidence on her face. It feels good there. Scary, but good.

"You didn't have to say it," she says, longing, in that moment, to see Paul again. "It was *implied*."

Larissa seems to weigh her options. There is a silence, filled in by the iPod. And then, with a great sigh that seems to come from a desert halfway around the world, Larissa says, simply, "You're right."

"Really?" Vanessa nearly bounces with the shock.

"I should meet him before passing judgment. You're a grown-up. And, well." A pause, uncharacteristic. "Maybe I am just a little bit judgmental."

"You think?" Vanessa asks, her defenses against Larissa coming down as quickly as they erected themselves. It is impossible to stay angry at her. There is too much shared history. Too much known.

"Ask him over," says Larissa. "And I'll see what I think."

"Just you and Paul and me?"

Larissa considers this and shakes her head. "How about we meet at a restaurant, all of us, so there's no pressure on anybody to cook or anything. Me, Fergus, you, and Paul."

"Like a double date?" Vanessa asks.

"Kind of. Except you're just his friend who sucks his fingers."

"It was one finger, and I did not suck it." Vanessa laughs, feels at ease with her sister once more.

Larissa perks up, too. Smiles with love in her eyes. "How about next week. Thursday."

"Sounds good," says Vanessa.

THE ROUX THICKENS

It is the day of Hazel's bachelorette dinner party. Plans made, time gone too fast. Vanessa wakes up in the high bed, warm and happy for a moment, then terrified because the alarm did not go off and she worries she is late. She wonders how life runs through her fingers like cool water. Her calves ache as she steps to the wooden floor, and she wonders if everyone goes through this, the moments of discomfort and inflexibility collecting in clumps, age coming as surely as the top of the escalator, and nothing you can do about it. Maybe by the time she's put in the old folks' home, the married man she falls for next will at least be a widower. Silver linings.

She showers, gets dressed, finishes preparing the boxes of ingredients for the dinner. Vanessa and Hazel both have the day off from work and Hawk knows about their dinner party; he thinks it is all girl stuff, frivolous feminine concerns that he cannot think about long enough to admit into the masculine reality he inhabits. Vanessa wonders what pleasure she might derive from poking this man in the eyes. With a fork. She wonders how beautiful it will be to tell him "I quit." Soon. So, so soon. But how? Gah.

Vanessa has borrowed her sister's car for the day, which made Larissa suggest Vanessa actually get a car of her own. She settles into the borrowed Subaru for the drive to the house in Santa Fe where the dinner will take place. She wonders what sort of car she might buy herself, if she were the sort to buy a car. A hybrid. Larissa is probably right about Vanessa needing a car. "Borrowing from people doesn't mean you're not driving," she'd said as she dropped the car off. "It just means your friends and family are being inconvenienced."

Then, there she is, Vanessa, in the red rolling shine of metal, amid the yellowing grasses, purpled mountains, beneath a dome of sky splashed in bright turquoise paint. Getting used to the idea of having a car, and not at all pleased with herself about it. She wonders if Paul has anything to do with her change of heart. The views are many, the places to discover seemingly infinite. The landscape now: crows, big and black, hulking into their shoulders at the roadside, simple birds made vulture by circumstance and intelligence, waiting for the errant dog, the unlucky coyote, to wander into the road, to lose so they might win. You rarely see a crushed crow in the road, and Vanessa wonders if crows are not the savviest of birds. She wonders, too, why life must be filled at all times with endless cruelties to be ignored and denied if one is to have any sort of functional journey through it at all.

Brutality and grace, locked in an endless dance. This is how it works, a vile vein woven through all this beauty, life and death tangled together and dependent as inhale to exhale, as sleep to waking, when you are brave enough to look closely and without blinking. Roadkill. Rabbits, coyotes, dogs. Do they never clean the sides of Interstate 25, the road crews? Or do things die here with such frequency that regular removal is not enough to hide the truth of the dance between the modern and the ancient? It wounds her, these dead things. Maybe it was the eyes of that one dog, still open, surprised at the blow, the head disembodied and the rest of the animal spread like paste across the roadway.

Horror, and she thinks of Red Dog locked up safe and snug in their house, and is grateful for the confinement. She wishes to hug Red Dog right this moment, and suffers the fact that there is too much suffering to do much about any of it. And so it goes, and she begins to wonder if it isn't better that she doesn't drive at all, because the very act of driving only invites introspection, and with all that comes a helplessness beyond measure. She is melancholy today, and there is irony in this as well, for it is the day of Hazel's great happiness, and maybe, thinks Vanessa, this is not a coincidence at all. To a woman never married, such as Vanessa, to a woman for whom marriage seems to be the shackle at the other end of the men she has loved and through no fault of her own, the specter of marriage and lifelong happiness with a mate for her friend, however joyous it might make her in theory, always has the unintended result of reflecting back to her her very own failings in this regard. *Always the bride's chef*, she thinks with a smirk, *and never the bride*.

Horrors, yes, and this time it is a cat. Dear God, she thinks. Don't people brake for these creatures? Does no one in New Mexico swerve against their demise? Or is it all fate? Look at the makeshift crosses standing sentry along the shoulder of this roadway. They call them *descansos* here, and their name translates to mean, roughly, "resting things." They are usually small wooden crosses erected by family members at the site of their loved ones' fatal accidents, blooming all over with glued plastic flowers, now and then lashed tight with a teddy bear, or accompanied by a metal Christmas tree. And always the name of the deceased. Is it fate? Are we all sent to our deaths unknowing? Is this freeway the Creator's shortcut to inevitable demise for the beloved fathers and darling daughters whose deaths at its hands are marked all across this state in colorful mourning? Gah.

Curses to empathy. *Empathy is overrated*, she thinks. What she would give to be able to lose it altogether, to be as steely in the face of tragedy as she is in the face of frozen waffles, resigned but not altogether concerned. Gah.

There is a certain lack of compassion from the Creator, shown in the things dashed here through no fault of their own, and in the frozen way the cows stand on the plains, awaiting their doom and all turned to face the same direction, brave and uncertain as soldiers. She considers the contradictions of a woman loving animals so desperately, but loving, too, to eat them in all their disassembled deliciousness. You cannot think too much of these things or you will end up as frozen as the cattle on the ranch, facing south, awaiting the end of hope.

She listens to a blues singer, enjoys the tight rubbery hum of the tires across the blacktop beneath. Airy speed, a skim of freedom, and there, too, another contradiction, because what sort of environmentalist loves to drive as if flying? Soul soaring in the empty spaces between cities? The same sort of woman, she supposes, who loves animals as much as she loves to cook them. The same sort of woman, she thinks with a ping of excitement, who falls for sexy soldiers even as she hates the wars they fight. And she *has* fallen for him, she thinks. She has. Part distraction, yes, from the pain of Bryan, but part real, too. No, *entirely* real. The distraction is whipped cream. Paul is the whole pie.

Soon, she has thought and hummed her way across the five dozen spectacular miles between Albuquerque and Santa Fe, and she arrives at the small dirt road up the hillside. She winds her way up and up, to where Hazel waits for her in an unassuming adobe mansion tucked tastefully into a piñon forest. Only the rich, she thinks, can afford to live among wild things anymore. This disturbs her, but then again, she is in a mood to be disturbed, a dark mood. She realizes she better shake herself out of this funk if she is to create a happy meal for her dear friend, who has suffered mightily in her days and certainly deserves the happiness now.

Hazel borrowed the house from one of Hawk's regulars. That's one thing about Hazel. She's never afraid to ask for what she wants. Vanessa wonders what it would be like to have that kind of confidence. She supposes it would also come with a much increased risk of rejection. She parks the Subaru and gets out.

It is four in the afternoon, bags of groceries and supplies in the back of the car, with three hours until the first guests are scheduled to arrive. As she unloads the car, the air feels cold, truly cold, for the first time this year. Winter pushes itself on autumn, comes earlier in Santa Fe, which is slightly higher in altitude and a bit farther north than Albuquerque.

And still, she feels Bryan on the wind. His butter, his flour, his eggy goodness. Santa Fe is a scone to Vanessa, a biscuit, because this city belongs to him. No matter how far she thinks she has come in her journey to get over Bryan, there is still something about simply being here in *his* city that makes her heart ache, her pastry glands, too. She remembers the time they spent together here, the dreams she allowed to ferment here. The city used to welcome her with possibilities. Now, it is a beautiful reminder of her failure. Except that it is his, isn't it? His failure. Not hers, and this is what she needs to remember.

This house is large and earthy, one story, the way the adobe houses of the rich tend to be in Santa Fe, all soft corners and gentle browny slopes. It has a lovely garden in the front, and she notices the cortaderia has been trimmed back for the winter, yellowing already. An art to this, the garden that appears to be natural but in truth is quite coddled. She reminds herself to plant her perennials this coming weekend, in preparation for spring, and resists as much as she can the urge to compete. It is in the dying time that you have to begin to think about what you might want to live around you in the spring. Her mind moves to the early bloomers, to crocuses and daffodils, to tiny irises and snowdrops. Such a sad time of year, hopeful if you are optimistic, promise coming, but so far off. Hibernation. Suspension. A time of waiting.

Vanessa wears a black cashmere sweater and jeans with flat black boots. She hauls her things into the elegant house, through the wooden gate carved with an image of a saint painted in many colors. She knocks three times, lightly, and lets herself in.

"Hello?" she calls out.

"In here!" comes Hazel's shouted reply.

Vanessa follows the sound of her voice and finds Hazel, in a little black dress, reading a glossy gossip magazine at the kitchen island, waiting for her. Hollywood seems so many light-years from this place with its sagebrush and endless skies, the juxtaposition of classic Santa Fe style and a photo of a cheesy celebrity is jarring. Music plays, old-school hip-hop and contemporary soul, the stuff that gets Hazel's head bobbing. Hazel was not meant for this state, thinks Vanessa. Hazel must eventually move on. To California. To New York. Somewhere where things like fashion and celebrity matter more than magpies and desert cholla.

Vanessa greets her with a hug, compliments, and small talk, and is soon preparing the evening meal, in a funk of focus, trying as hard as she possibly can to be supportive of the sought bliss that is not her own. She works tirelessly, with Hazel mysteriously giggly and secretive at her side.

"What's so funny?" asks Vanessa.

"Oh, you'll see," Hazel promises.

Hazel won't tell her who, exactly, is coming, or whether there will be games and gifts. What Hazel does say is that this night will not be exactly what Vanessa was led to expect it would be, which makes Vanessa nervous and a little sick. Vanessa likes surprises as much as the next person, just not when they are sprung on her in the midst of a creative endeavor, like this dinner.

She hopes her friend, who is nice but maybe not the most sophisticated person she has ever known, is not planning for male strippers or anything along those lines.

The doorbell rings as the first guests arrive, and Hazel hurries to usher them in. Mysteriously, she asks Vanessa to stay in the kitchen until summoned. Like a servant. *Always the bride's slave*, she thinks, *never the bride*.

Vanessa is in the middle of preparations still, and tries not to take offense. She hears, surprisingly, the tenor boom of a man's voice in the other room. Not Smitty. Someone else, sounds older, wealthier. There is a tone to the voice of a rich man that differs from that of a poor man, a certain confidence unearned, a certain aggressive entitlement. What sort of bachelorette party has *men* in it? Hopefully, they will not pop out of cakes to undress.

Vanessa waits five or ten more minutes, until the doorbell has rung five times, before venturing into the living area—unsummoned, but what the heck—with her trays of Irish-inspired hors d'oeuvres that she thinks of more like Irish tapas, served on earthenware Spanish plates. She serves them with black velvet cocktails. A mix. That is her way.

Vanessa knows, from the instant she sees the assembled guests in the vast living room with the spectacular views of the small city, that there will be no bachelorette party for Hazel this evening. This is something else. She has, in fact, been tricked.

The crowd consists mostly of men in suits, with women in showy New Mexican shawls and dainty designer cowboy boots, wealthy Santa Fe women with quirky eyeglasses and good taste in art. Vanessa recognizes many of them, because gathered in the room are about a dozen of Hawk's wealthiest regulars, including the men in charge of the Balloon Fiesta account.

No, she didn't, thinks Vanessa with a jolt of excitement and admiration for her friend.

It is all Vanessa can do not to drop the trays on the floor as everyone looks at her, smiles at her in a curious, knowing sort of way. Like she were the newborn they had all come to see. Like she were a circus show. Like she were . . . the star.

Hazel catches the bewildered expression on Vanessa's face, excuses herself to the crowd she's talking with, hurries to Vanessa's side, helps her ease the trays to the coffee table, and pulls her back to the kitchen with a strained smile.

"*What* is going *on?*" asks Vanessa, thrilled and hopeful that the answer she has guessed is the right one.

Hazel lets go of her arms, with a wicked excitement on her face. Shoulders rise like a girl ditching seventh grade with her best friend. She leans in, and whispers. "Okay, don't be mad at me."

"No promises," says Vanessa.

"You know I have a pretty good rapport with a lot of Hawk's regulars."

Vanessa smiles in spite of her effort to control herself. Excited. Can guess what's coming. Cannot believe Hazel *did* this. Death and birth in the same breath. Thinking of crows, and dogs, and highways, and the brutality of nature, and wondering if it is not, after all, an entirely natural thing Hazel has done here. Curses to Hawk. Roadkill to Hawk.

"After the balloon account thing, I just didn't feel like I could take it anymore, so I started calling them during my off-hours and telling them the truth."

"What truth? What do you mean?" A hot knot settles beneath Vanessa's sternum.

Hazel seems taken aback. "*The* truth. I told them that Hawk steals your ideas."

Vanessa feels a surge of adrenaline in her gut. "You did that for me?" she asks.

"For you, for truth. For women." Hazel with arms open at her sides, face open and honest, completely open. Hiding nothing. Sincere, and supportive, and furious, and stronger than Vanessa has been in her own defense.

Vanessa hugs her friend. "I appreciate this more than you realize," she says. "It took balls, woman."

"It took *ovaries*," corrects Hazel. "Let Hawk keep the testicles."

Vanessa laughs. Then she panics. "What if I'm not ready, though? I would have done a different menu if I'd known."

"I realized that," says Hazel. "I wanted you to cook with love, so I lied to you. I'm sorry. But I bet the menu you made for me will be better than anything you'd do to be a show-off."

Vanessa stands there, looking at her best friend, holding her hands.

"You are one crazy broad, you know that?" she asks Hazel. "You're going to get both of us *fired*!"

"That's the idea! Now, get back in there and cook, Vanessa!"

"What if I can't pull it off, though?" asks Vanessa with a look of worry on her face.

Hazel's eyes grow wet with frustration. Her lower lip trembles. "Please don't talk like that. I used all my savings for this," Hazel tells her. Vanessa had not thought of this. Of course she did. The decorations. The valet parking attendants. "This house, I rented it off Craigslist for this."

"I though you borrowed it from Hawk's friend?"

Hazel shakes her head. "No. I couldn't do that. I didn't want him knowing anything about it. And I don't . . . I don't actually have friends with houses like this."

"Oh my God," says Vanessa. "You really believe in me this much?"

"Yes."

The friends embrace. "You're crazy," Vanessa says again.

"I know."

They release each other and Vanessa thinks. Worries. "What do you think they'll say, Hazel? They love Hawk. It's like I'm betraying their god."

"They love what they *think* is Hawk's food. But it's your food. When they realize that, you'll get your money for your restaurant. See? You never needed that stupid guy in Philadelphia. All you needed was me."

Vanessa's eyes flood with tears. Of course, she thinks. Everything she needed was right there in front of her.

"But Hawk's a celebrity. People are loyal to him. This could end very badly."

"It could end really well, too. Just be confident."

"Hazel. You know how this business is toward women."

"Yes," says Hazel, eyes stony and strong. "And I'm sick of it. Now get out there and prove them all wrong."

Vanessa stands there, grinning like an idiot, in a wave of panic.

"Deep breath. You can do it." Hazel gives her hand another squeeze. "I believe in you. I always have."

"Okay," says Vanessa. The thought of her own restaurant burning in her mind. The thrill of it all almost too much to take.

"I'm putting my job on the line, too," Hazel reminds her. "I'm not exactly an heiress over here. I need that job. The way I see it, if we raise money to get you a restaurant of your own tonight, I get first dibs on being your manager. Or at least your headwaiter."

Vanessa holds her arms open to hug her friend again, and fights back the tears. "Thank you, Hazel. I love you."

"I love you, too. Now, enough of that, ya big sap. If you don't mind, I have some hungry, very rich guests waiting to see how you measure up."

"To *Hawk*," says Vanessa, nervous.

"Technically, yes. To *Hawk*. But to Hawk as he *pretends* to be. In fact, you are only measuring up to yourself. I'll be waiting with the others."

And with that, Hazel turns on her fancy heel and sweeps out of the room with the flourish of a fairy godmother.

OF PIGS, ROOTS, AND
CABBAGE

She brined the pork loin over the past two days, seared and slow-broiled it halfway through, in her own house, partly because such an activity brings certain warmth and stability to a home, but also so that it would not take too long in the oven here. Now it crackles and roasts beautifully in the good oven of the rented kitchen, scent and sound entwined, and the high desert cold all around beyond the walls. Perfection.

As the fatty, succulent aroma of the roast fills the air, Vanessa stands at the sink peeling carrots and washing Asian cabbage for the rest of the simple, savory main dish, a mix of Thai, Irish, and New Mexican influence. She spies a few snow flurries drifting past the kitchen window. She could not have asked for a more perfect marriage of weather and menu. There is something instinctive stirred in humans, she believes, with the onset of autumn, desires for rich, stewed foods, something handed down to us from ancestors, if not the need to hibernate, at least the need for calories and heat. Safety of the roast. The satisfaction she feels at this moment is supreme and difficult to name. Garlic in the nose, and thyme, and butter, an Octoberish aroma rising from the bubbling browning of the apple cider marinade.

She checks the roast. Nearly done. Decadence, the meat glistening in its Irish butter, a cut the Irish call bacon, she has learned, and that is how it is with words. A good Irish bacon not the same as a good American bacon, and so it is that Hazel has chosen Smitty, a man Vanessa would never have given a second look, and the two of them are happy and Vanessa is alone again. Perhaps there is something to be learned there. Perhaps not; maybe Vanessa is just unlucky. One thing for sure, however. The same words—bacon, man, love, forever—can mean different things to different people. Maybe it is not her destiny to have a man at all, but rather just excellent friends and a sister and nieces.

In the end, the meat will be all that matters to Vanessa tonight, and it will come out more like the fabled Christmas pork roasts of Puerto Rico, falling apart to the touch of a fork; it will melt buttery in the mouth. Delicious in any language or dialect. There is constancy to food. You can count on it.

An hour later, the guests sit around the large table in the formal dining room in apparently good cheer, judging from the explosions of laughter that come to Vanessa's ears every few minutes. Hazel returns to the kitchen—pinkened in the cheeks from a cocktail or two, maybe, too, from anticipation and her apparent sense of fairy-godmother-like power—to take up the tray and do what she does so well, deliver deliciousness to the people, hoisting its leaden weight as though she did not feel it, like an ant with a pebble twice its size.

Hazel whisks out the Irish green chile stew, first, and then a tart, earthy beet salad, and then, the main dish. Hazel stares in open admiration at the plates as Vanessa prepares them.

"Oh, Vanessa," she says in an airy way, her eyes growing misty.

"It is you, and Smitty," Vanessa explains. "In food."

Hazel hugs Vanessa. "Thank you for this. It's perfect."

Vanessa focuses on the task, arranging the tender flakes of pork lightly on the plate with a cubed potato stuffing to which she has added just a touch of green chile, all of it edged in with delicately steamed Asian cabbage laced with shredded carrots, sort of a steamed slaw with a dash of cumin and spicy mustard. Thai, Irish, New Mexican threads running through it all. A thin and subtle gravy, a garnish.

Hazel runs the plates out as Vanessa takes the piñon soda-bread biscuits from the oven. Hazel delivers this, too, and returns for the wines and the ice water.

And it is done.

Vanessa stands and surveys the mess, tries to still her racing heart. Right now, she thinks, there are investors, wealthy people, eating her meal, deciding with every bite whether or not to—to what? To give her the life she has always wanted and deserved. The fall from the cliff begins.

Soon, she busies herself with setting up the Irish whiskey and Mexican chocolate cake, already baked this morning, but heated in the oven now, preparing the warm *horchata* pine-nut coffee, nervous at Hazel's long absence. Is it bad? Are they finding problems? Should Vanessa go to the dining room herself and try to charm the diners as Hawk might do? That feels unnatural, shameful. Better to stand back and wait.

Vanessa does not wait much longer. Soon, Hazel appears, carting in the cleaned dinner plates, flushed and excited, the pink having advanced to red. If she weren't smiling so massively, Vanessa might have thought her embarrassed. Nodding. Vanessa cannot speak. She just waits, and Hazel responds with only one word, giddy and gushing: "Yes."

"Yes?" asks Vanessa.

"Yes!" Hazel gestures to the empty plates, does a little dance.

"What do you mean, yes?" Vanessa's heart races.

Hazel sets the used plates down and grabs Vanessa's hands. "Yes, they loved it."

"They did?"

"And yes, they now see that you are the force behind hawk."

"Seriously?" A heart that flies on a million tiny wings.

"You should come talk to them."

"I should?"

Hazel washes her hands and begins to load the cake plates onto her tray. "Come join us," she says. "Everyone has lots of questions for you. You can't stay back here in the kitchen all night."

Vanessa smooths her hair back, takes a few deep breaths, realizes how hungry she is. She has not eaten practically all day. Nerves. She follows her friend from the kitchen to the dining room, wondering what will come of it all. She does not wait long for an answer.

At the first sight of her, the assembled guests follow the lead of the incredibly wealthy John Randolph, the confident cowboy at the head of the table, and they begin to clap. He smiles at her, and winks in a fatherly way. When he pushes away from the table to stand, the others join him in the ovation.

"Bravo!" someone shouts.

"To the new kid in town," someone else says.

John Randolph raises his wineglass in Vanessa's direction, and says over the din, "Miss Duran, you're a sneaky woman, hiding behind Hawk's skirts all these years, but we'll forgive ya 'cuz you're one hell of a cook." He is grinning.

Dizzy, dizzy, where is the floor? Hands shaken, her back patted and slapped, and business cards fluttering toward her like snow, like money from the sky. Promises of money, suggestions for a name for her restaurant, ideas flowing like wine, excitement, and Vanessa slips into all of it as though it were a hot bath.

Dinner eaten, dessert waiting on the table. Day ended beyond the bank of windows, purple-black night begun. The way of things. Nature. Endings and beginnings, all tied together, crows waiting by the side of the road for a thing to die, and now, too, maybe a Hawk that can go back to hunting for himself.

DASHING ABOUT DASHI

A minimall mere meters from the interstate. It is not the type of place you'd expect to find excellent food, generally. And yet that is exactly what Vanessa and Larissa discovered here, off Interstate 25, one afternoon a couple of years ago, when they had come out of the movie theater into a snowstorm, and lucked into the small Japanese restaurant tucked between a chain ice cream store and a subpar Brazilian restaurant. Vanessa had been reluctant to eat there at first, but Larissa, the globe-trotting sister, had reminded her then that you just never know, and so they went.

Now, the sisters reunite at the Japanese restaurant again, this time for dinner with Fergus, Larissa's doting and darling professorial

husband, and Paul, who is not making the job of selling him any easier for Vanessa, as he is now ten minutes tardy.

"I thought these military types were punctual, at least," muses
Larissa as she looks over the sushi menu. Eyebrow cocked, incrim-
inating.

"Give the man a chance," says Fergus. He does not like war or
soldiers any more than his wife, but, as a man, seems to feel the
need to defend all of his gender against her heartless judgment.

"He'll be here," says Vanessa. "Don't worry." She changes the
subject to the menu, and asks them what they plan to have.

"Is this weird for you?" asks Fergus, not at all the response Vanessa
anticipated.

"What? Having you guys hang out with Paul?"

Fergus grins and chuckles. "No, that's weird, obviously. It's
weird for all of us. But I meant eating at restaurants. Sorry. I should
have been more specific. I'll try it again. Is eating at restaurants
weird for you, as a chef?"

Vanessa feels her face brighten to a shade of mild humiliation.
Tries to shrug it off and continues to look over the offerings. "No,
not really."

Fergus persists. "I mean, aren't you always dissecting every
little thing? Like this," he points to the listing for carne asada sushi
roll, "doesn't that kind of thing just piss you off? Being a foodie and
all that?"

Vanessa shakes her head and shrugs again. "Hey, I'm the last person in the world who's going to get upset with a chef for being creative or innovative."

"Yeah, but would you *eat* it?"

"I'd eat just about anything. That's how you know what's out there."

Vanessa considers ordering this exact item, just to show her annoyance.

Fergus is a nice man, she thinks, a good father, and he has never given Larissa any reason to doubt him, but he is, at heart, an elitist with a sense of entitlement. Plus, there is this way that he and Larissa, when they're together, seem to forget that anyone else exists, other than their children, about whom they gush and ramble endlessly. That they are a happy couple, no one disputes. But this happiness too often spills out as annoying public displays of affection, little pet names uttered across tables in a way that makes you want to jump out the nearest window just to save yourself from the corniness. When you are with these two, thinks Vanessa, you are constantly reminded of just how alone you are, and just how dependent upon each other they are.

"What about you, snookums?" Fergus asks Larissa. "Would you ever eat a carne asada sushi roll?" He speaks in baby talk.

Larissa responds with a kiss, and they canoodle.

"I bet it's good," says Vanessa, keeping her eyes politely on her menu. "What's not to like? Roasted beef, rice, seaweed."

Fergus extracts himself from the clutches of Larissa, laughs, assuming her to have been sarcastic, and this exhausts her. He is not too bright, for a smart guy.

Happily for them all, Paul comes crashing through the door at this moment, quite literally because his entrance has caused the skinny person leaving through the same door at the same second to drop his take-out bag. It explodes in a mess of udon and broth upon the floor. Paul, ever Paul, sets out immediately to right the situation, cleaning up the mess with napkins, offering to pay for a new order for the man whose dinner he ruined.

"Oh, God," says Vanessa.

"And here's our boy," says Larissa, doubtfully watching the scene unfold.

"Yeah."

"A real charmer," jokes Fergus.

"That could have happened to anyone," Vanessa insists. "God, you guys, you aren't going to make this easy, are you? You *want* to hate him, so you're going to hate him no matter what he does. I don't know why I agreed to this."

"We're sorry, aren't we, pookie?" Larissa leans into her husband and pecks him on the cheek. He kisses back, and Vanessa gets up from the table, bored by them and angry at them in equal measure, goes to the front of the place to greet Paul and offer to help him herself.

Paul, red in the face, stressed from being late and clumsy. His eyes tell Vanessa he knows how much it meant for her that he be there on time and be impressive.

"Guess I blew it," he suggests. He smells of an autumn night, and pheromones. And Paul.

"You okay?" she asks.

He smiles warmly at her and she knows he has found her charming for caring. She wonders if many people have cared about him at all for him to be so impressed by so little.

"I'm fine. Not sure about the dude whose dinner I ruined. Man, how's that for grace, Vanessa? Jeez."

Vanessa sees the man in question, at the bar now, waiting for his order to be renewed. "He'll live," she says. "Don't stress."

"I'm so sorry," he says. Dumps the soiled napkins in the trash bin behind the counter with the cash register on it. Makes a small bow to the Buddha on the counter, with the red and white mints in the bowl next to him. The Buddha of fresh breath, thinks Vanessa.

"Everything all right?" she asks him.

"Fine, just got a flat on the way over here, and I've been crazy." He takes a deep breath. "But enough of that. How are you? How's your sister? Jazzed to hang with me and be awed by my grace?"

Vanessa laughs, for even under these tense circumstances he has still found a way to make it easier to have him around than to not have him around. "They're ready to play Twenty Questions with you, I'm sure," she tells him.

Paul claps his hands together and says, sarcastically, "Awesome."

"Awesome," she parrots, mockingly.

"My favorite word."

"The most awesome word."

He laughs. "Lead the way. Can't wait to see your sister try to take my balls off with chopsticks."

Vanessa grins at him, and feels strong and confident in his presence. Together they walk back to the table. The space is narrow and loftlike, with high ceilings, and practically empty. There are only two other tables with people at them.

"Paul, you remember my beloved sister, Larissa. And this is her always-charming husband, Fergus."

Fergus stands to shake Paul's hand, perhaps a little harder than necessary. Larissa blinks up at them with wide eyes that Vanessa instantly recognizes have been set on fully open so as to mask her obvious approval of Paul's looks. Vanessa *knew* it. She knew Larissa was into Paul. That's what this whole stupid thing has been about. Her sister's sexual frustration, in spite of her obviously cuddly relationship with Fergus.

Paul does not look anything like a soldier this evening, his hair now long enough to fall over his eyes, his facial hair sculpted into a goatee and mustache. He wears jeans and trendy flat sneakers, a sweater that might have come from one of the Nob Hill shops aimed at men decades younger than him. It works for him, shows off his strong, solid chest, and the overall effect is one of youth, energy, and a calm, compassionate intelligence. Gone, thinks Vanessa, is the Viking.

"Please sit down," Paul tells Fergus. "I'm not important enough to stand up for."

Larissa shoots Vanessa a look of surprise at Paul's self-deprecating comment. *Yeah, I know*, thinks Vanessa. *I was constantly surprised by him, too.*

Fergus puffs up a bit, as men often do in the company of men they do not know, and Larissa folds her hands on the table in front of her, staring Paul down with an intensity she probably thinks looks more like curiosity and friendliness.

"Sorry to keep you all waiting," says Paul, depositing his canvas jacket on the back of his chair. He does not explain the flat tire, or go into detail, or make excuses. "I hope it hasn't inconvenienced you too much."

"He got a flat tire," says Vanessa, feeling the need to explain.

"Flat tire," says Larissa, clearly suspicious.

"We were just discussing the menu," says Fergus. "No big deal. Tell me, Paul. What do you make of a carne asada sushi roll?"

"Sounds good. Rice, meat, seaweed. What's not to love?"

Fergus and Larissa stare dumbfounded at each other. Fergus says to Larissa, "That's what she just," and Larissa interrupts him to say, "I know."

Paul uses the opportunity of taking his seat to look more closely at the surroundings. "Nice place. I didn't even know this was here. You go away from New Mexico for a few years, and everything changes. It's pretty incredible."

Nervous, Vanessa explains how she and Larissa found the restaurant. Larissa smiles tightly and does not support Vanessa with the usual help in storytelling. On the defensive.

Paul listens well to the story, with steady eye contact and head motions to indicate comprehension, with an occasional question requesting clarification or more information, friendly, leans back in his chair and waits until she is finished talking to pick up the menu and look for himself.

"Sometimes you find the best things completely by coincidence," he says, shooting Vanessa a secret wink from behind his menu.

"When you least expect it," adds Vanessa, hoping the blush in her cheeks is not too obvious to the others.

"How true is that," says Larissa, distracted by her own menu. "Sweetie," she adds, to Fergus, leaning in and rubbing her cheek against his, "anything look good to you, pookie?"

Vanessa, amazed that Paul has put everyone at ease just by being at ease himself, tunes out the conversation between Larissa and Fergus, their kiss-filled discussion of prawns versus shrimp, something she normally might weigh in on, except that right now she can't stop thinking about the scent coming off of Paul. Lemons. Fresh things, green things, a scent of promise. When he notices her looking at him, Paul slips his foot next to hers under the table, and presses against it. Vanessa meets the pressure with a caress of her own.

The waitress comes to take their drink orders. Larissa and Fergus will share an order of sake. Vanessa asks for green tea. Paul says that sounds good, and orders a pot of his own. Still playing footsie, and it is so juvenile Vanessa has to work overtime to stop herself from giggling.

"Can you tell me," he asks, stopping the waitress as she turns to

walk away, "how is your dashi made, for the udon pots? The traditional way, or with the powder?"

Vanessa looks at Larissa, finds her sister watching Paul closely,
as a cat might observe a rodent in a cage, waiting for an opening to
pounce. She is trying, Vanessa believes, to figure out whether Paul
is doing this questioning as a ploy to control Vanessa by wowing
her with his culinary prowess.

"I'm not sure," says the waitress. "I can have the cook tell you?
You want him to come out here?"

"No," says Paul. "That's okay. I just thought that if you knew
it'd be interesting."

"Okay, you sure?" asks the waitress.

"Completely sure. Sorry to have bothered you about it."

Larissa shoots her sister a look of annoyance and protection.
Mother hen. Ah, yes. Of course. Vanessa is certain Larissa believes Paul is putting on a show to control her.

"What is this interest you have in how they prepare the food
here?" asks Larissa, thinking she is slick. Fergus looks down at the
tabletop, trying not to show that he knows the conversation has already slipped from pleasantries to graceless interrogation. Vanessa
senses he is uncomfortable about his wife's behavior, but cannot
be sure because he has never said anything to that effect.

Paul shrugs and gives off a harmless vibe. "No big deal. It's just
that I've traveled a little bit in my career, and I like food, so I wonder about how certain things translate when you bring them back
to the States."

"Like dashi," says Larissa.

"Right."

"What is dashi, anyway, snookums?" Fergus asks Larissa. "I think I'm the only person here who isn't a food expert." Larissa kisses Fergus in reply and tells him not to worry. .

Vanessa might think they were playing good cop/bad cop, if she was not aware that Fergus, in fact, knows very little about food.

"It's the broth starter for a lot of these Japanese soups," says Paul. Vanessa feels her heart soar at these words. How many men who are not officially in the food business know a thing like this, she wonders. How many men who even *are* in the food business know about dashi? Not many, *that's* how many.

"What's the big deal with dashi?" asks Larissa, smug in her certainty that Paul won't have an answer for this. She is wrong, of course.

"When I lived in Japan, I got spoiled," he says. "There, they make the dashi with actual kelp, seaweed—dried, simmered in water, and strained out. Here in the States, they usually take the easy way out and use granules or a powder dashi." He shrugs modestly. "You can't blame 'em. The traditional way takes a lot more time and ingredients that are pretty hard to find in a landlocked place like New Mexico. Most people wouldn't know the difference. Heck, I wouldn't have known the difference most of my life, but once you've had the real deal you can't help hoping you'll find a place that does it right home-side."

Vanessa feels the way a girl might feel upon hearing that she was elected prom queen. Or like someone who has won the lottery. A layman, a nonchef, who thinks about things like dashi preparation.

Larissa glares her sister's way as a warning against getting too enthusiastic about Paul's apparent interest in food, as if to tell her it is false.

"I bet Vanessa finds it pretty interesting that you are so knowledgeable about food," says Larissa. As if any man would go so far out of his way to impress a woman as to pretend to have lived in Japan and developed an appreciation of excellent broth.

"I don't know," says Paul, with a disinterested shrug. He turns to Vanessa. "*Do* you find it interesting? Most women I've known find me tedious and boring."

"Yes, I find it interesting, but not as interesting as this line of questioning from my sister," Vanessa says, her eyes connected to Larissa's.

"Vanessa and I don't know each other all that well yet," says Paul to Fergus and Larissa, with a humble shrug. "So I'm sure you'd know a lot better than I would just what might impress her or not."

"True," warns Larissa.

He jerks his thumb toward the front door of the restaurant, and leans in a little closer to the table, as though sharing a secret. "Honestly? I'd say that any chance I had at impressing anyone was pretty much dashed at the door. How was that for being an idiot? Right?"

Fergus laughs, in spite of Larissa's admonishing look to stop him. "It was a pretty grand entrance," he says.

"Dude," says Paul, breaking into an embarrassed yet joyous grin, a man entirely comfortable with admitting when he has been a fool. "Any grander and I'd be in the hospital right now."

The men chuckle, and Vanessa smiles. Larissa is the only one who stews. Silence now, as they look over the menus. The waitress returns, they place their orders, and Larissa begins again, asking the sorts of questions Vanessa finds annoying. What does he do for a living, which she already knows. How did he decide to go into the Air Force.

"Okay," says Paul, boisterous and measured at the same time. "I'm going to be totally honest about that, because I don't really know you guys and I know you aren't going to rat me out to anyone in the service." He waits, a secret grin playing on his face. "*Top Gun*," he says with a defeated shrug. He falls against the back of his chair, point having been made. Done.

"*Top Gun?*" repeats Vanessa.

"The movie?" asks Fergus.

"The movie," says Paul. "I know, pretty sad. But it's the God's honest truth. I mean, my dad always wanted us boys to go into the military, because he never did anything that manly, you know. He wished he had, but his feet were flat. They didn't want him. Right? Okay. So Dad thought it would give us discipline, especially me, because I was the hell-raiser and the back-talker. My brother was a good kid.

"I didn't want to do something just because my dad said so, right? But then I saw *Top Gun* and it was all over. Oh, man. I loved that movie. I was just out of high school, and I didn't know what I wanted to do with my life, all I knew was I didn't want to end up a scientist like my dad because that was too boring, being in an office all day. And then my buddies and I saw *Top Gun* at this dollar theater that shows movies a couple years out of date, with Tom Cruise, and I was all, 'Dude, he's badass,' you know? I was hyped up on it." Paul starts to pantomime whatever memory he has of the movie, like he's flying a little jet. "Tom was all, 'Yo, I'm king of the sky and the chicks dig me.' It was the ultimate geek's wet dream. I thought about going into the Navy, like Tom in the movie, but it seemed like I'd have more flying time if I was straight Air Force. And here I am. Thanks to everyone's favorite neighborhood Scientologist."

"How charming," says Larissa with thick sarcasm.

"Paul was a total geek, according to his friends," offers Vanessa.

Larissa looks doubtful.

"He had a bowl cut and an Easy-Bake oven," Vanessa says to augment her point.

"You just *had* to go there, didn't you?" Paul teases Vanessa.

Larissa stares at him, dumbfounded and, Vanessa figures, completely missing the self-deprecating humor of what Paul says.

"So have you ever killed anyone?" Larissa asks Paul.

The table falls silent, and Paul's easy smile fades to a blank expression.

"You know what?" Paul finally says to Larissa, a look of barely concealed insult in his eyes. "There's this thing called *war*. Sometimes, countries have to go to war, and usually, people get killed. It sucks, but that's the way it is. Most of the time, that's so that people like you can be safe here, and have the freedom of speech that lets you ask complete strangers questions they might not be entirely comfortable discussing with someone they just met."

"So the answer is yes," Larissa says.

"Paul," says Vanessa. "You don't have to answer her."

Paul smiles at Vanessa, with something else in his expression, something she interprets as a controlled rage. "I realize that."

He looks at Larissa now. "Look, Larissa. I like you, so far, and I really like your sister, and if the time ever comes that me and you get to be friends, I'll tell both of you all about my experience in the war zone. But for now, if you don't mind, I'd rather not discuss it, any more than, say, the two of you," he points to Fergus and Larissa, "might want to regale us with the details of your conjugal relations."

"Don't tempt them," says Vanessa.

"Sounds fair," says Fergus. "Right, Lar?" He elbows his wife.

"Sure, Paul, no problem," says Larissa. "Let's talk about how you decided your career because of a Hollywood movie again." Unimpressed. "Do you think that's wise, Paul?"

"Larissa." Vanessa tries to catch her sister's eyes to stop her. "C'mon."

Paul speaks. "Nope. I don't think it was wise at all. I don't know many eighteen-year-old boys who make wise decisions. It was dumb. I'm not proud of it, either. But, in self-defense, I will say that it was more than twenty years ago, and I think I made the most of it." Paul looks from Larissa to Vanessa, a gleam in his eye, and asks, "Didn't you warn your sister about what a complete dork I was, pretty neighbor lady?"

"I tried," says Vanessa. "She insisted on seeing you as Satan."

"Actually, my sister speaks very highly of you," says Larissa, as though she cannot for the life of her figure out why.

Paul matches her disdain for him with good humor, and, Vanessa realizes, no small degree of control over the situation. He does not care what Larissa thinks of him, Vanessa understands. He really and truly doesn't. "Why would you do that, Vanessa? Speak highly of me? Crazy girl."

"Because you deserve it," she answers, her anger at Larissa growing. "Because I see you as you are, rather than as I'd like you to be to fulfill my preconceptions."

Paul's face betrays—though only for a split second—his disappointment in Vanessa's apparent lack of self-control in this interrogation. As though she has taken all the fun away from the game. He quickly covers his emotions with a smile, and turns to the television on the wall behind the bar. The drinks have come to the table now, and he pours himself a small pottery cup of tea and points it, as he lifts it to his mouth, toward the football game on the screen.

"You follow the Broncos, man?" he asks Fergus.

Larissa bristles instantly at Paul's attempt at traditional American-style male-bonding in her presence. That simply isn't *done* in her universe, where men and women must always meet on equal foot-ing, and inclusivity is a given at the table in mixed company. Finally, her expression seems to tell Vanessa, a real reason, an obvious rea-son, to hate this man.

Fergus is, of course, made uncomfortable by the football ques-tion, because he is an academic in an overblown social-sciences field where men do not follow football, at least not in any open sort of way that might, say, draw the disdain of the feminists in his department or classes, or the mockery of the other men. No, Vanessa thinks, Fergus is too neutered by his profession, mar-riage, and politics for anything like that—and surely Paul must recognize this. She has no doubt Paul *knew* Fergus was not the sports type from the second he met him. She has even less doubt that the question was designed to irk Larissa, not Fergus.

"Not that much," says Fergus, with an awkward shrug.

Fergus's discomfort makes Larissa uncomfortable for him, and puts her, previously on the offensive, instantly on the defensive—the furious kind of defensive unique to female animals, who are wired to protect their broods at all cost. *Brilliant move*, thinks Vanessa.

"We don't watch TV much." Larissa blinks obnoxiously at Paul, not hiding her displeasure with the notion of football.

"That's not exactly true," says Vanessa. "You guys watch TV."

"Well, we don't watch the things regular people watch," Larissa amends.

Vanessa rolls her eyes at Paul. "Right, Larissa's too good for that."

"Huh? Oh, hey, hang on a second, okay? Sorry." Paul pretends he has not heard. They all nod, and he gets up to go to the bar, comes back with the day's newspaper. Opens it quietly in his lap, and runs his finger down the columns.

"Shoot," he says, with a goofy grin. "My team lost. I mean, I know a lot of people out here follow the Broncos, but me, I'm a Seahawks guy ever since I lived in Seattle. Not doing too well. Ah, well, I don't mean to bore you guys with trivial stuff. It's just, I've been so busy all day I haven't had a chance to see how they did. Anyway, let's talk about something important. Enough of that. My apologies. What were you talking about? TV or something?"

Brilliant, thinks Vanessa. *You don't have to watch TV to follow football.* Larissa. He's toying with Larissa. And Larissa has no idea.

Paul folds the paper up, drops it on the floor underneath his seat, sips his tea, and smiles at Larissa with his eyes fixed steadily on hers. "So I hear you're an anthropologist. Just back from the Kingdom of Morocco? The first country to recognize our country as a free nation, as I recall."

Larissa frowns. Paul has used the full official name of that country, and an arcane fact, revealing a level of education that Larissa did not expect, and especially not on her own turf. Not so strong now, *is* she? Not the one in control.

Paul asks about her trip, and she, so as not to be rude, answers, but soon finds his remarkably informed and well-formulated questions leading her off into the direction of her deepest passions. Before long, Larissa is speaking animatedly with Paul as though they were old friends, about the anthropological significance of butane camping stoves for nomadic women in the desert.

By the time the food arrives, Larissa and Paul are laughing at shared jokes, and even Fergus seems taken aback by the sudden chumminess, a friendliness Larissa seems to realize only once the spell is broken by her chicken teriyaki bento box being placed in front of her, and silence where her excited expounding upon her own interests once lay. Guilt floods her eyes, and embarrassment, as she looks up to find Vanessa smiling at her.

"Told ya," says Vanessa. Paul chucks her a look of appreciation, knowing precisely what it is that Vanessa must have told Larissa.

"Ooh. This looks good," Larissa says to her bento box.

"Yes," Paul concurs, looking straight at Vanessa. "It does."

Quickly, he moves his glance to Larissa, with an aw-shucks sort of smile. And before they realize what's going on, Paul, in his boy-ish way, has turned the conversation to Fergus's work next, and gets Fergus to open up to him in a way Vanessa has never seen him do. Uncanny, Paul's talent with people.

Vanessa settles into her dinner. She has ordered her usual here— an udon and tempura pot in a dark and oniony mushroom broth, woven through with fresh vegetables. All umami pluck and tang. The delightful slippery solid feel of the thick white noodles against her teeth. It is the perfect soup for a cool evening. She thinks about the dinner in Santa Fe, and the investors, and the exciting news she has yet to share with anyone other than Hazel.

When she looks up, Paul is watching her sip from her large spoon, almost as if he has been able to read her mind.

"How about you, Vanessa? How's work going these days? Any news on the hawk front?"

Uncanny.

Vanessa looks around the table, sees that everyone is comfortable. Maybe it's the sake, she thinks, but it seems that Larissa and Fergus appear to actually like Paul. That means it is probably safe to tell everyone about the John Randolph dinner.

"Well," says Vanessa. She wipes her mouth to make sure there's nothing on it. Runs her tongue over her front teeth with her mouth closed, probing for any errant strand of seaweed. Nothing. Safe to continue. "I have sort of big news."

"*Sort of* big news?" asks Paul.

"Okay, big news. No sort of." She shrugs like a giddy girl. "It's pretty big."

"Out with it, then!" says Paul.

Larissa slows her chewing and waits to hear the rest, dread in her eyes, and why is it that her mind has somehow already gone to the negative? Fergus follows his wife's lead, as he will, and seems braced for a painful blow.

Vanessa tells them everything, about the dinner, Hazel's role in it, the investors. Though Larissa and Fergus are aware of Hawk stealing Vanessa's ideas, she recaps the details of it for Paul. Then, she delivers the biggest news of all.

"The investors want to give me money to start my own restaurant," she says, giddy. "As much as I need."

Paul's face bursts into a massive smile and he rips one hand through the air in front of him to punctuate his excitement. "I *knew* it!" he cries. "I knew you had it in you to stop letting people push you around. You're a superstar. I told you that."

Larissa, though, is more reserved. In fact, she seems confused. Fergus, initially happy for Vanessa but following his wife's lead, seems not to know how to react.

"I know you've worked really hard for Hawk," Larissa says, measuring her words. Vanessa can feel Paul tense at her side as Larissa speaks. "But are you sure you're ready for this? I mean, it's a huge responsibility, running your own restaurant. There's a lot more to it than just being a good cook."

Vanessa feels her heart squeeze in her chest, almost the same feeling as having the wind knocked out of you.

Paul scoots closer to Vanessa now, and puts a supportive hand on her shoulder.

"Hey, easy now. I'm sure Vanessa understands the complexity of running a restaurant," he suggests.

"Yeah?" answers Larissa, haughty. "And this is because you've known her for exactly how long now? A couple of *months*?"

Vanessa is speechless, looks at Paul, and is both relieved and scared to see that the polite smile from earlier is now completely gone as he sets Larissa squarely in his sights.

"With all due respect, Larissa—and Fergus, I hope you don't

mind that I'm about to be completely honest with your wife, and I mean no disrespect to either of you with it."

Fergus moves closer to Larissa now, in much the same way Paul just moved to Vanessa—in imitation of him, Vanessa thinks. Fergus, for all he does, really has never had to be a man about anything.

"It's pretty clear to me that you want your sister to fail," Paul tells Larissa, who gets furious and as such begins to laugh at him. "No, no," he says. "Hang on, let me finish. It's okay to want that, right? Maybe, when you guys were little girls, you got something out of coming to your little sister's rescue, Larissa. Both of you probably benefited in some way from it, or you both wouldn't still be trying to do that dance."

Larissa rolls her eyes, but it is clear from her wounded expression that Paul has struck a nerve. Vanessa does not sense in him any desire for power in this, just for communication.

"I wasn't there when you girls were growing up," he says.

"We're women, Paul. Not girls."

"True. Now you are women. Then, you were girls. I wasn't there *when you were girls*, so I don't know how it went down, but I do live next door to your parents, and a couple of things are pretty obvious to me about them, and how they roll. Without mentioning exactly what I think of your parents' habits, because I think you both know, I'd just say I think you guys had a rough ride."

"Oh, please," says Larissa. She shoots a look at Vanessa. "Have you been feeding him this garbage?"

"No," says Vanessa.

"Any ideas I have about your parents I have because of my own personal interactions with them," says Paul. "And all I can imagine is that it was hard for a big sister to see a little sister going through all that, and you got used to distracting Vanessa, and taking care of her, pretending things were okay for her sake, and that was your role. I would imagine, and there's no way I know this for sure, but I'd bet you two were all you guys had to hold on to. I admire you for doing it back then, and you're probably a big part of the reason Vanessa's as great as she is now. But it's not the role you need to play anymore."

Vanessa does not want to cry, but the tears come. Paul puts his arm around her now.

"You see what he's doing?" cries Larissa. Fergus quiets her, reminds her they're in public, and she continues in a fierce whisper. "He's *manipulating* you, Vanessa. That's what he was trained to do. The government spends billions of dollars trying to figure out how to break people down. He's trying to control your relationship with me. It's sick."

"No," says Paul. "What is *sick* is that you can't see how talented and cool your sister is now, and you can't be happy for her as the biggest dream she's ever had is starting to come true. *That's* sick."

Larissa says nothing, and Fergus moves away from her. She glares at him. And then Fergus surprises everyone.

"I've been trying to tell her the same thing," he says, meekly.

Larissa slugs him on the arm. "What?" he asks. "I have. You should let go of this need to control her, snookums."

Vanessa stares at her brother-in-law. "Really?"

"What is *wrong* with you!" cries Larissa to her husband. "I can't believe this."

"What?" he tells her.

"You turning on me like this. Just because we disagreed about the dishwashing liquid this morning."

Fergus rolls his eyes. "That's not why."

"I don't want to use the kind that pollutes, but that natural kind you keep bringing home doesn't *work*, Fergus." Larissa sounds crazy now.

"We're not talking about dish soap right now," Fergus reminds her. "Listen, Lar. You sort of do have this need to control everyone all the time, and I've told you I don't think you have to do it with Vanessa, she's a grown-up."

"Fine, everyone gang up on me," says Larissa, trembling. "Unbelievable." She shoots Paul a nasty look. "You're good. You're really good, you know that? You got them both to turn against me. I just hope you don't end up breaking her heart, because she's been through a lot of that lately and you're the last thing she needs. But then, you probably know that already, which is why you picked her."

"I would never want to hurt Vanessa," says Paul. "And with all due respect, you don't *know* me." His face grows red with stifled anger.

Larissa's tantrum continues, the few people in the restaurant watching uncomfortably now. She tells Paul, "You should get a medal for it, whatever it is that you do. I'm trying to help, and you made them turn on me. That's good."

"Nobody's turned against you," says Paul.

"Yeah, okay, welcome to opposite world."

Vanessa tries to calm her down. "It's not that. C'mon."

"Sometimes the truth hurts," offers Paul, the veins in his neck bulging with emotion, too much emotion, thinks Vanessa. "But that doesn't make it untrue. And it doesn't mean the people who say it don't care about you anymore."

Larissa can't take it any longer, and storms away from the table, tears in her eyes, toward the bathroom. With her gone, the three who are left seem to relax, but only a little. Fergus comes to Vanessa and gives her an awkward hug.

"Congratulations on the restaurant, Vanessa," he tells her. "You deserve this. I'm sure it'll be great."

Paul pats Fergus on the back. "Attaboy, pookie," he says, causing Fergus to first stare, then ignore the comment.

Vanessa fights the urge to run to the bathroom to make sure Larissa still loves her. Resists. Just as she resists the urge to cry. Paul places a hand on her back, reassuring, but does not keep it there too long for comfort. Fergus takes his seat and smiles at them in a strange way.

"I'm sure she meant to congratulate you," he tells Vanessa.

"Yeah."

"You want to get out of here?" Paul asks Vanessa, under his breath.

"What about Larissa?" she asks, terrified to leave her sister with this rift between them, terrified Larissa will never forgive her, and she will lose her best friend.

"She'll come around," says Fergus.

"You think?" asks Vanessa.

"I know she will. Just give her some time."

Paul gives Fergus a thumbs-up and tells him he's a good man. "You mind if we take off?" he asks.

"It's probably for the best," says Fergus. "I'll deal with her."

Paul, still seeming a bit peeved, jokes that he needs some fresh air to clear his head. He peels a couple of twenties from his wallet, and pops them down on the table. Tells Fergus it was nice to meet him.

And with that, Vanessa, who came to the restaurant with her sister and Fergus, leaves with Paul.

THE LAUGH OF RISTRAS

"*So,*" *says* Paul as he pulls the truck onto the frontage road, heading south because that is the only direction you can go here. "Where to?"

He is cheerful again, too cheerful, too loud, trying hard to cover whatever sharp feeling the exchange with Larissa placed in him.

Vanessa doesn't know what to say. Her tongue lies heavy in her mouth. Her guilt, a rock at the bottom of her liver. For a moment, she imagines herself like the character Kim—"the poorest of the poor"—in Kipling's novel by the same name, and Paul as her Tibetan lama Teshoo, each of them lost and clueless in their

own way, each trying to free themselves of something, and clinging to each other in the subconscious hope of finding salvation.

"Oh, c'mon now," says Paul after sneaking a look at her pouting in the passenger seat. "You're not still worrying about Larissa,
are you?"

"She didn't look well, running off to the bathroom all upset. I
don't think I've ever seen her like that."

"She's an adult. You're an adult. You two really ought to stop
being so enmeshed."

"Enmeshed. Big word."

"Vanessa, Vanessa, Vanessa." Paul is laughing, and it is not entirely innocent.

"Don't do that."

"Which? Patronize you, or laugh at you?"

"Both. Neither. Either. Just stop." She can't stop herself from
smiling in spite of the circumstance. This man, at times scary, at
times funny, at times tender. Not sure what to make of him and his
large hands on the steering wheel, capable as hands ever have been.

He chuckles for a moment longer, and then gathers himself.
"Sorry. You're right. I'm not being nice. Your sister put me in a foul
mood."

"It went badly, didn't it?"

"What did, babe?"

"The dinner."

"I've had more fun in a war zone." He does not seem to be kidding.

"I'm sorry she pushed you about that. About Iraq. It's really none of her business."

"She's got balls."

"Poor Larissa."

"Vanessa." Paul turns his head to look at her for a moment. Too long a moment.

"Watch the road, please," she says.

He does what she says, but with another chuckle, as though she is foolish for not believing in his supreme power behind the wheel. Drives with the ease most people have walking. Graceful. She considers the sort of expertise he must have to pilot a fighter jet. Driving a truck must be nothing to him now.

"I really, really like you," he says. "In case you haven't noticed."

"Oh."

"As a friend," he offers, hopeful, it seems, that he might elicit from her a change of heart.

"Friends are important," she says, generically. The twist of his mouth indicates that he agrees, but still wishes for more.

"Hey," he says, with the enthusiasm of those who consciously change the subject. "The night is young. We can get a drink. We could catch a movie. Or I could take you home. I promise to be a gentleman and a friend, and leave you alone. If that's what you want from me."

"I don't feel like going home." *Because that's not what I want from you and you know it, because at home I would be vulnerable to your scent, because at home you would know exactly where in the garden to take me to feed me from the tip of your finger, because the thought of you in my bed has come to me more than a hundred times since this night began and that is truly the last place I need to go.*

"Hey!" Paul brightens as he eases the truck to a stop at a red light. He gestures to the downtown skyline, minuscule as it is. Lately, the powers that be have taken to illuminating the few skyscrapers that exist there with blue and green lights in a flaccid attempt at urban chic. Albuquerque tries.

"Hey, what?"

"I meant to ask you something—where do you plan to open up your restaurant? What are you going to call it?"

"That's two somethings you asked." It is so easy to banter with this man, to tease him. To make him smile. To make him brood. He is all over the map, and it excites her. And that scares her.

"Don't get bratty with me, missy," he says, a little more than half teasing. "Just because Larissa treated you badly does not give you the right to do the same thing to the people you actually *like*."

"I like my sister."

A face of being impressed and annoyed at the same time. "Your generosity of spirit continues to amaze me."

"Ris," she says.

"What?"

"Ris. I want to call my restaurant Ris. R-I-S."

"Ris." He considers it, then says, "French for 'laugh,' right?"

Vanessa stares in astonishment.

"I told you. The language thing. It comes easy. Too easy."

"Must be nice."

"It's a great name, Vanessa. It has that hint at *ristra* to it, so it's got the local New Mexico chile thing, too."

"I know! Right?" She actually had not thought of that angle, but it works.

"Well, let's drive around looking at empty buildings," he suggests. "Let's pick a couple of neighborhoods, and just cruise around and see what's out there."

Exactly what she would have wanted to do, if she had been cognizant of wanting anything but Larissa's happiness. Larissa's *ris*.

"Have you thought of possible locations?"

"In general terms. Nothing specific yet. It's all so new."

"Let me guess. Downtown, and Nob Hill."

"Yep. And yep. How do you do that?"

"Do what?"

"Know exactly what I'm thinking all the time. Job training, I guess."

He laughs this off. "Vanessa. This is a small city. There aren't all that many places you could open a restaurant and have it do great."

"There are some good restaurants in places other than downtown and Nob Hill."

"There are?"

Vanessa lists four or five decent restaurants in various minimalls or developments in different parts of the city.

"Yeah," he says. "I haven't tried any of those. You'll have to show me."

"Okay."

"But I still think you're more of a downtown or Nob Hill girl."

"Probably."

"On our way."

Paul guns the engine and pulls them onto the interstate. A squeak of moderate fear escapes Vanessa because of the speed of the truck, and how quickly said speed is achieved.

"Don't worry," he tells her. "I know what I'm doing."

"That," she tells him with a fragile smile, "is exactly *why* I worry."

ÉCLAIR YOUR INDEPENDENCE

Because it is Albuquerque, and Albuquerque is not all that big, and because there are few people on the interstate, and because Paul drives like he is in the Indy 500, within moments they are downtown.

This part of town is a marriage of decay and urban revitalization. Old dusty shops selling Indian trinkets and cowboy hats nestle next to edgy new tattoo parlors, which lean up against high-end shoe boutiques and gourmet chocolate makers. There is a comforting schizophrenia to downtown Albuquerque, evidence of a city that, in spite of all efforts to make it like other places, refuses to be anything other than what it is and always has been.

At this hour, most of the old shops are boarded up. Only night-clubs open now. Some innocent, with students from the univer-sity. Some full of Harley types. Some, like the hot-pink strip club, with greasy losers slipping in and out. Police pry sleeping men from the benches outside the bus and train depot, right across from the shiny Brazilian restaurant everyone crows about, but which Vanessa finds gummy and excessive with its endless buffet. She is a fan of slow food and not of the American obsession with eating more than necessary.

The truck stops at a red light just in time for a couple of sad-looking older men, likely homeless, to stop at the curb near them. One of the men vomits into the gutter, the other comforts him with a hand on the back, just as Paul did for her earlier. This ges-ture and scene make Vanessa unspeakably sad. *These men*, she thinks, *are someone's sons*.

"Maybe Nob Hill," says Paul, eyeing the men warily.

"Poor guys."

"It's their choice," says Paul. "It's all about personal responsi-bility, Vanessa."

"You don't know what they've been through in life."

"That's true. But I do know that plenty of people have hard lives and come out of it okay. Some of them even end up talented chefs with their own restaurants."

She looks at him, and his proud, understanding smile melts her.

"Let's check out Nob Hill," he suggests. Without waiting for her to agree, he turns the steering wheel, to drive east up Central, the fabled Route 66, until they hit the area between Girard and Carlisle, just past the university. If she did not agree with his judgment, she might find his control of the situation uncomfortable. But she does agree with his judgment. So far, on most things.

Nob Hill. Here, the young and fashionable fill the restaurants, cafés, and shops. It is what those who revitalized downtown had hoped downtown might become. Oh, well.

"No pukers," he says cheerily.

"I'm sure there are pukers."

"Yes, but they're college students and they're doing it in the bathrooms."

She laughs. He's probably right.

"This is the place," says Paul.

"You think?"

"It's you. This is where you belong."

They cruise around, looking for FOR LEASE and FOR SALE signs. There are some empty spaces, in modern new buildings. There are empty houses in the area, too, that might be zoned for business. Whenever they come upon a promising property, they get out to inspect it.

The next two hours are spent creeping around and looking in windows of empty spaces in the chill of night, with Paul spooking her at random and laughing crazily. She feels guilty for not fixing things with Larissa, but the feeling is overridden by the easy pleasure of this man's company.

Paul asks questions, lots of questions, about her plans, her future, her past, and Vanessa, so used to men who mostly talk about themselves, savors the opportunity to tell one of them about herself. And then, as they round a corner from an alley onto Central once more, the realization, he has not told her anything about him. Again. Silence toward her, a wall, even as he has expressed such animated interest in talking, for all the talk has been about her.

Vanessa stands with Paul in the orange cast of a streetlight near the Flying Star Cafe, near Carlisle and Central.

"You cold?" he asks, shivering. He juts his jaw toward the café. "How about dessert?"

Vanessa wrinkles her nose at the restaurant, mostly because everyone in town in the restaurant industry harbors a jealous snobbery toward the pedestrian Flying Star, a local chain that continues to swell in popularity, mostly because of its fattening desserts and excellent coffee.

"I don't know," she says.

"Oh, c'mon. You're not too good for the Flying *Star*, are you?" he asks her, understanding instantly her reticence.

She bites her lip, and he takes her gently by the arm to lead her into the café. "What?" he asks, sarcastic and compassionate at the same time. "Is it the foot-long éclairs? The massive portions? The pancakes that overhang the plates? Or the fact that everyone in town loves this place?"

"No one needs that much éclair," she states. "It's obscene."

"That's why we're going to *share* one," he tells her.

She sighs as they enter the café, which is literally spilling over with fashionable people and intellectuals—not that the two groups are mutually exclusive, but inferences could be made. It has been years since she set foot in a Flying Star.

"You'll like it, I promise," he says. "You can't hate a thing just because it's popular. Sometimes, the unwashed masses get something right. Besides, where else can you get a ten-pound éclair at ten at night?"

"Dante's inferno?" she suggests.

"You surprise me, Vanessa. I didn't take you for a snob."

"Okay, okay, you've made your point. Let's just get the éclair."

They take their place at the back of the ordering line. He looks around with boyish enthusiasm, happy to be here, happy to be alive. So mercurial. One mood to the next. She looks at him, wonders about him, and the war, and his past. The things he's done. Things he does not offer up. Whether he *has*, in fact, killed people, and what that must have looked like and felt like, and how he could have done it, because she does not think she would ever be able to kill another human being, for any cause. For any war.

"See something you like?" he asks, catching her staring.

"I think so."

He grabs her, and hugs her. Just a quick, big bear hug. "You rock, friend," he tells her. Grinning, but distant in his own guarded way.

"Why do you insist on remaining such a mystery?" she asks. "When you pry to know so much about me?"

He pretends to read the menu board on the wall behind the counter. "What do you want to know, pretty neighbor lady?"

"Everything."

"That will take years, Which is good, because I hope to be your friend for years."

The line inches forward. Noise, talking, laughter. A happy place, not nearly as pretentious as hawk, and maybe that's why people like it. Ris, she thinks, manning two lines of thought at once, will be as earthbound as the Flying Star.

"I need to know what happened there," she says, close to his ear. Somehow, the noise and activity of this place, the clang of plates, the drone of dozens of conversations, give her cover, make it safe to ask him.

"Where's that, babe?"

"In Iraq."

His eyes roll as if to say *not again*. Paul sighs as though she makes him very tired. "Look, Vanessa. Why does it matter? I just want to move on from that part of my life. I just want us to get a nice big éclair, a freakin' thirteen-pound éclair, and some coffee that could take the paint off a car, and I want us to sit down and talk about normal things. As friends."

The line moves forward. She tells Paul, "It matters because no matter how much I like you, and I like you a lot, I really do, but no matter how much I like you I think I'd have a real problem being with someone who believed in that war, Paul. I think I'd have a real problem with it."

"Are you saying you want to be with me, Vanessa?" He takes

her hand up in his and squeezes it. "Because that would be going back on your 'just friends' clause, and I'm not sure I can handle that kind of inconsistency in the woman I want to be with."

Vanessa takes her hand from his. "I'm not inconsistent."

"So you won't be taking me home with you?"

"Absolutely not."

Paul grins. "Good. Because I was planning, and I'm still planning, to drop you off at your house, make sure you get in safe and sound, and then I am planning to go back home and take a very cold shower. One thing about the military is it teaches a man self-control and respect, and I have plenty of both."

"I appreciate that," she says.

The line crawls forward again. The clerk behind the big shiny glass counter full of decadent desserts asks them if she can help them. Paul asks her how she's doing tonight, charms her in his big boomy voice. Eventually, he orders a giant éclair and two cups of coffee, and they move on to the cash-register area to pay.

"I'm sorry," she tells him as they wait for the order to be rung up. "I shouldn't have brought it up. It's just, we're sort of a political family, and I was raised a certain way. We have never dated military guys."

"We?"

"Me and Larissa."

He rolls his eyes again. "Vanessa, Vanessa, Vanessa." He is still pleasant, but beneath it is something angry, and his anger frightens her. More frightening still is the excitement she feels at her fear of his anger. Not exactly healthy, this. His mood changes quickly. Many flavors.

"Please don't do that," she says.

He pays, takes the red tray with their enormous pastry, two forks, and cups of coffee on it, and walks toward an empty table at the back of the main room, with a look of controlled fury and frustration on his face. She follows, and sits, and he sits, and they look at each other.

He breaks a piece of the éclair off with his fork, and feeds it to her, telling her it's okay to eat the food of the masses, the fury still there, but also a great affection.

"Just because a thing is popular doesn't always mean it's bad," he reminds her.

"Just bad *for* you," she suggests.

He shakes his head affectionately. "Now, now, Miss Vanessa. Maybe you should be open to being wrong about something now and then." He airplanes the fork in the air like a parent might for a reticent child.

"Maybe." She accepts the morsel. It's not as flaky or delicate as the incredible things Bryan made, and the thick, dry chocolate glaze feels more like frosting straight out of a can on her tongue than a homemade éclair, but the company is certainly better than Bryan's. She chews, and the éclair ignites her brain. It is satisfying, rich, reminds her of things she would have enjoyed as a kid, a solid, proletarian dessert.

"Good, right?" he asks.

She reluctantly admits that it is, and his face lights up.

"Can't go wrong with an éclair," he says, taking a bite of his own.

"That's not quite true," she reminds him.

"Well, to an unsophisticated palate like mine, this éclair? It's awesome." He speaks with his mouth full, but in a subtle, elegant way that makes him seem delicious rather than disgusting.

"Awesome." She grins at him, hoping to tease her way back into his good graces. The last thing she wants to do is offend someone's taste in food. She knows how that feels, unfortunately.

He looks at her as though she has not said it, his mind elsewhere, and he says, point-blank and shockingly, "I do want you, Vanessa."

He stares at her directly.

"More than you know. And I'll tell you what you need to know about my politics one of these days, so you can figure out if you want me back."

He puts another piece of the pastry into his own mouth now.

"God," she says. "It makes me sound like kind of a jerk when you put it that way. I don't care about your politics."

"Yeah, okay." He laughs.

"But I'm happy to hear what you have to say," she says.

His expression does not falter. Still staring her down. "I'll tell you everything. But you have to do it on my terms."

"What does that mean?" she asks.

"It means that your next day off, you're mine, and we're doing some things my way. Now, don't look at me like that. I'm not going to touch you unless you ask me to. It's innocent. You see, I'm not all that good at talking, so I have another way to tell you what you need to know about me. Kind of a nonverbal way."

"Oh. I had no idea you were into interpretive dance."

He grins but doesn't laugh because his mouth is again filled with éclair. Snakes his arms in the air like a freak-show act. "You feel me now?" he asks.

"I feel like I should call security," she deadpans.

He smiles, stops the arms, and says, "But seriously, I'm more of a tactile person. A kinetic energy kind of thing."

"I thought you were a linguist."

"That, too."

"Linguists are good with words," she reminds him. "Linguists do not need to be Lord of the Dance."

"Ha! Okay, smarty-pants. I'll give you extra credit for tryin' a *Riverdance* reference. But you miss the point. See, Vanessa, I'm okay with words, it's true. As puzzles to be solved, yeah. I'm good with words. What I'm not good at is using them to tell you what I think or feel."

"I see."

"So when is your next day off?"

"I have tomorrow off," she says.

"Then we'll do it tomorrow. I've got work, but I'll call in sick."

"Sick man dancing," she muses. "Sounds horrific."

"I'll let you be the judge."

Vanessa agrees, and instantly wonders if she will live to regret it as much as she is already regretting giving in to the populist seduction of a gargantuan éclair.

DOUBLE ESPRESSO

Morning, the next day. Paul has called nearly before dawn, to tell her to wear jeans and a comfortable shirt, with sneakers, for their outing. She jokes, asks if he's planning to chase her through the forest in the East Mountains or something, but he doesn't seem to find it funny. He laughs politely, and says she has to wait and see.

She chooses a pair of old and faded Levis, her gardening and housecleaning jeans, because they are soft and loose and don't look like she is trying too hard to look good. She pairs them with a soft gray T-shirt with a Mickey Mouse logo on it, from her college years. Gift from an old dorm-mate. Larissa despises this shirt, and maybe that's why she's picked it.

Larissa has not called, and Vanessa has not called her. She will. Eventually. Maybe tomorrow.

She's worn her hair down, but not in any particular style, because even though she would like to make an effort to look pretty to Paul, she realizes that doing so will undermine her ultimate objective to remain just friends with him. On her feet, ASICS running shoes, with thick, squishy sports socks. She feels good, and capable, and strong. Able to run fast, if need be.

At eight o'clock, Red Dog begins to howl at the front door, having heard the truck crunching up the gravel driveway before Vanessa has. And then, moments later, there he stands, in his own version of her outfit, though his jeans look newer and the red T-shirt has no logo on it at all and certainly not a cartoon character. His sneakers look well-loved, and are gray. The man himself is looking very good, like he slept well and had a nutritious breakfast.

His smile almost blinds her, as they say their hellos and he pulls her in for a friendly hug. He smells of laundry soap and shampoo again, very clean, but also very male in a way that melts her right at her center. She wants to bite his shoulder, like a teething baby.

He tells her it's good to see her, and also tells her she looks good.

"Very naturally beautiful." Those are his exact words.

She thanks him, but wishes he hadn't mentioned her appearance at all. Again, she holds her tongue about complimenting him, even though she can say with almost complete certainty that she has never been embraced by a man this solid. Vanessa wishes Red Dog farewell, tries not to feel the crushing weight of the creature's obvious disappointment in not being included in the day's outing.

"I'll be back soon," Vanessa tells Red Dog. Then, to Paul: "Right? We *are* coming back soon?"

He shakes his head doubtfully, lips pursed. "You might want to leave the dog door open, and some food out."

"How long are we going to be gone?"

He shrugs, and she gives him a look of horror.

"Quit worrying," he says.

"Anyone in their right mind worries when faced with the possibility of an inarticulate war veteran doing *Riverdance* for days on end," she snaps, as she pours kibble into Red Dog's bowl by the refrigerator.

"Touché," says Paul. "But you won't even notice time passing, I'm that beautiful to watch."

"Whatever," says Vanessa.

"C'mon, punk," he says back, mussing her hair.

"Stop it," she says, mussing his back.

"Do it again," he says. "I like it when you touch me."

It continues in high spirits like this, until Red Dog is situated for at least a full day. Off they go in the truck, and he's got a mischievous expression on his face as he looks back over his shoulder to back out of the driveway onto the street.

"You ready for the big day, pretty neighbor lady?" he asks her.

"When are you going to stop calling me that?"

"When your parents aren't my neighbors anymore. Then I'll just call you *pretty lady*."

"Big improvement."

"You didn't answer the question. Are you ready for today, or what?"

She asks him what he's got planned and he insists that it is a secret, and turns on the stereo. A female country singer's voice comes through, and to her—okay, she's not going to admit surprise. Let her think of another word. To her *delight*, she finds herself actually really liking the song. It is bluesy, and genuine-sounding, and the lyrics are extremely feminist.

"Who is this?"

"Miranda Lambert," he tells her. "Gotta love her."

"She sounds great."

"She reminds me of all my ex-girlfriends," he tells her. She listens again to the song, only to discover that it is actually called "Crazy Ex-Girlfriend," and it's about a woman who tracks her ex down at a bar with his new woman, and beats the woman up.

"Sounds like you dated some real winners," she tells him.

This makes Paul laugh to himself. "I'm a sucker for a smart girl with bad manners," he tells her, and she does not know whether to be flattered, insulted, or neither.

"How come a guy like you is still single, anyway?" she asks him. "Seems like there'd be no shortage of women throwing themselves at you."

"I could say the same of you," he says.

"Not many women throwing themselves at me," she answers. "The occasional lesbian wearing beer goggles, mistaking me for Rosie O'Donnell, but that's about it."

"If you ever took one of 'em up on it, I wouldn't mind watching," he jokes.

"What is *up* with that?" she asks him. "Why do men always say they want to watch two women get it on?" Vanessa astounds herself, speaking so freely with this man. In the past, she was always somewhat more reserved with the men she dated. More grown-up. Paul brings out the childish, stupid side of her, which, considering how seriously she takes most everything else in her life, isn't that bad a thing.

"It's the ultimate fantasy."

"But why? I mean, if it's two lesbians, they're not going to care one way or another if you're there."

"We don't see it that way. We see it as, like, we've turned the chicks on so much they can't keep their hands off each other, like they're just doing each other until we get there."

"Lovely. Lesbians just love being called chicks, I bet."

"Someone's ornery today," he says, though not displeased as such.

They zip through the city, and she means *zip*. This man drives fast, with his music loud, and he plays drums on the steering wheel as he drives, and he looks very impressed with himself, and happy, and full of energy.

Unlike some people who drive too fast, Paul can handle it. At first, she is terrified and asks him to slow down, which he does, but only exactly one mile per hour. He seems to enjoy her discomfort terribly.

When he takes the Gibson Boulevard exit off of Interstate 25, a part of town she never visits unless she has missed the exit for the airport, she asks him again where he's taking her. There's not a whole lot in this neighborhood, except the sports arena for the university, and an old cemetery.

"We're not going to play flag football, are we?" she asks him. "I think I'd lose pretty badly."

"You can keep trying, Vanessa," Paul answers, cocky and, she hates to say it, more tempting than a triple fudge cake with rasp-berry sorbet and a dollop of whipped cream. "But I'm not going to tell you. Even if you get it right, which you won't."

He hands her a laminated card. Pink. She looks closer, and it says PRESS PASS and has her name on it, as well as the name of a newspaper that, to her knowledge, doesn't exist.

"What is this?"

"Credentials."

"Credentials." She looks at him in disbelief.

"You can't get on base without them, or you can, but you couldn't get in the plane."

"Did you just say 'the plane'?"

"Yup. Just like Tattoo from *Fantasy Island*."

"I don't understand," she says.

"Cheesy, stupid show from the seventies," he explains. "Little midget who used to point up in the sky and say 'De plane! De plane!'"

"No, genius," she says. "I understood that part. The part I do not understand is why you would channel Tattoo at all. What airplane? Are we going on a trip? Because I didn't pack anything."

He just grins at her.

"Stop that."

He keeps grinning.

"I am starting to regret agreeing to this," she says.

"Nah. You'll be glad we did it. Just promise you won't be all honest when the people ask you about working for the press."

"I don't understand."

He grins some more. "I know. I love it."

"Paul."

"Just go along with it. I promise it's all gonna be fine."

"Says you."

"Today, we're in Paul's world, and what Paul says goes."

"Why did I agree to this?"

"Because you dig me."

"Whatever."

He is chuckling again, as he turns the truck into the parking lot of a minimall that is essentially abandoned except for a Chinese grocery store and a decrepit-looking Starbucks with a drive-through window. He parks the car.

"You comin'?" he asks. When she doesn't answer, he says, "Don't tell me you object to Starbucks, too?"

"I had coffee already." *Real Italian espresso, thank you.*

"Yeah? Well, you're going to need more. In Paul's world, it's all about the adrenaline. And when you don't have enough of your own, you fake it with espresso. Come on."

"Can't we use the drive-through?" she asks. "It's easier."

Paul shakes his head vigorously. "No, no! You can't go through life using the drive-through. You have to get out and talk to real people, or you miss the whole point."

He waits a moment before asking her, again, if she is coming in with him. After the last proclamation he's made, she doesn't really see that she has a choice.

"Good girl," he says, as she opens the door. "You want to get to know Paul today, you do things Paul's way. Tomorrow, you go back to doing it V's way."

"V?"

He opens the door to the coffee chain for her. "Everyone should have a nickname," he says.

"I thought mine was 'pretty neighbor lady.'"

He follows her into the warm, caffeinated air of the place, answering her last statement with something about how everyone needs a long nickname and a short nickname, but she's not hearing it all because she has just spotted a disconcertingly familiar face in the line ahead of them.

Hawk is here. With a woman who looks like a model.

Oh, God, she thinks. She can't just run out of the café. That would be weird. And it's inevitable that her boss is going to see her in a place that both of them pretend to despise in each other's presence.

"Something wrong?" Paul asks her.

"Huh? Oh, uhm, no." She tries not to talk too loud, so that Hawk won't hear her, and of course all of this is incredibly silly because even if he sees them, so what? She is planning to give notice tomorrow, and break the news to him that the investors are on her side now. So why does she feel *caught*? Because she is no good at confrontation, never has been.

Now it is Vanessa who pretends to be studying the menu boards, and Paul lets her be. She focuses obliquely on Hawk, and hears him place his order.

"A double venti caramel macchiato, please," he says. *Excuse* her? Isn't this the same man who lectured her and everyone on the kitchen staff on the evils of big coffee, sold by big corporations? She gasps.

"What's wrong?" asks Paul.

"Hold on," she tells him.

At this moment, Hawk turns around and spots her. She smiles as falsely as possible at him, and blinks quickly with her head cocked to one side. He smiles back awkwardly, and looks as if he wants to hide.

"Vanessa," he says, his pomposity only slightly derailed. "My favorite little assistant. What a pleasant surprise."

"Hawk," she says. "How nice to see you, here at the Starbucks, ordering a double venti caramel macchiato."

"She got me hooked," he says, shrugging, gesturing to his model, who, it must be noted, sips a bottle of water. Ah, yes, thinks Vanessa, blame the woman when a thing goes wrong, take credit for her success when a thing goes right.

"You want anything in particular, babe?" Paul asks her, already at the counter.

Hawk takes this opportunity to say good-bye, without waiting to meet Vanessa's obvious friend, and leaves. Well, then, she thinks. That just makes things all that much easier for later this week, doesn't it? As in tomorrow, when she is set to quit her job, and tell him why, and tell him about her investors.

When Vanessa doesn't answer his question, Paul orders her a double shot of espresso.

"You're going to need it," he tells her.

Back in the truck, she explains that the bald man with the model accessory is her boss.

"Rude dude. I don't like him," says Paul.

"How could you not like Hawk? Everyone usually loves Hawk. He's a celebrity."

"Okay, number one, I'm not everyone. Number two, celebrity doesn't impress me. Especially not after what you told me about him stealing your recipes. Wish I'd known it was him. I woulda decked him."

"I can't believe he didn't even wait to meet you."

"His loss."

"Definitely right about that."

Paul laughs. "Yeah, okay. Drink your coffee."

He starts up the truck, and pulls out with his usual velocity.

"I can't really drink it if you're driving like that," she says. "I'm gonna burn my tongue."

"Okay." He slows down. "Better?"

"Thank you."

Paul continues to drive east, past the airport, and into a bland, industrial part of town that Vanessa never visits—the part occupied by Kirtland Air Force Base. So he's not taking her to the airport for a trip to somewhere fun. Nope. He's taking her to the base. She is starting to get a sinking feeling in her belly, confirmed as a solid rock when Paul pulls his truck off Gibson onto the lane leading to the checkpoint that lets people on the base.

"What are you doing?" she asks, downing her coffee in two very hot gulps now.

"Just relax," he says, as his window whirs down and the guard steps forward.

"How can I relax when you just gave me liquid speed and you're taking me into enemy territory?"

"Not funny," he says. "Can it with the political jokes for a minute here, so we don't end up in prison."

"Sorry."

Paul ignores her in favor of the guard, speaking to him in "yes, sirs" and "no, sirs" and handing him some kind of pink piece of paper that makes the guard behave instantly respectful of him. Within seconds, they are waved onto the base and told that "they're expecting you."

"What was that?" Vanessa asks.

"What? That guard?"

"No. The pink slip of paper."

"Military papers. Officer stuff."

"Pink?" she asks, incredulously, suppressing a giggle.

"You got a problem with pink?" He grins at her.

"Well, I just figured that with the connotations—gay, Communist, girly—you guys might have picked something else. Aquamarine, tangerine. Anything other than pink."

"You're a funny, funny girl," he says, eyes dancing with pleasure. And then he pulls into a parking lot near a hangar, as in an airplane hangar, and they get out.

And then her life changes forever.

THE SCENT OF GASOLINE

Fifteen minutes later, after Paul has done all the talking and
Vanessa has done little but smile, try to seem harmless, and show
various people her fake press pass when asked—oh, and signed a
waiver for her life when she found out that Paul had cleared her, as
"a news reporter," to go up on a media flight with him piloting the
plane—Paul and Vanessa stand in a little room inside the hangar
and he watches enraptured as a couple of female Air Force cadets
help her into something called a "G suit."

Paul tells Vanessa a G is a measurement having to do with grav-
itational force on your body. From this she deduces that they are
going to be going very fast, fast enough to warrant a G suit. Faster
than possible in the meager truck on the measly freeway.

Vanessa's G suit is army green, which she finds ironic considering that this is the Air Force, but she holds her tongue, realizes her obnoxious attitude at the moment is little more than defensiveness in an unfamiliar situation. The suit is not fancy-looking; honestly, it looks a lot like a jumpsuit that a grease monkey might wear at an auto-body shop. The big difference, she discovers, is that *her* grease-monkey suit is filled with "bladders" that inflate and deflate with air, once she's hooked inside the cockpit of something Paul tells her is an F-16.

"Is that an airplane?" she asks him.

The women who are helping her get the suit over her clothes grin at each other as if they would very much like to laugh at her. Air Force women, with Air Force humor. She will never be able to relate to these people.

"It's like a cross between an airplane and a Harley," says Paul.

"Yay," she says, sarcastically, even though her pulse is racing and the adrenaline is flooding her once again. Or is it the double espresso? She feels light-headed.

"You said you weren't afraid of speed," he reminds her. "But I witnessed the lie of that on the freeway today. You can handle more than you let on. Now, we get a chance to see if you were telling the truth about being afraid of heights."

"You are *not* taking me up in a plane," she whispers to him, thrilled to her bones that he is. She finds this to be the single most exciting nondate date she has ever been on, but she is not about to give Paul the satisfaction of telling him so.

"Up in a *jet*," he corrects her.

"Cross between a Harley and something," she says.

"Quick learner." He winks at her.

"So what are the bladders for?" she asks them all. "Why the air compression?"

"It keeps you from passing out, basically," says one of the young women.

Vanessa glares at Paul, half jokingly. "Why would there be any reason for me to pass out?" she demands. *Other than you yourself.*

"You'll see," he tells her, and, after being handed their helmets, out the door they go, with the two young women giggling at Vanessa behind her back.

Paul strides across the tarmac as if he belonged there, greeting people as they go, and she follows along behind him, in a state of panic as she sees the planes all lined up out there. They are not planes as she knows them. They are needle-nosed things, with wings like arrows, sharp missiles everywhere, and faces that look, incongruously, like Chihuahuas.

"I can't do this," she says.

"Sure you can." Paul just grins, puts on his mirrored sunglasses, and grins some more, in his element, and thrilled to have her right where he wants her—squirming and at his mercy. She thinks this quality of his, this confident, edgy caretaking role, would make him a very good lover. Not that she'll ever find out. It is just a thought.

They get to one of the planes, and it looks very small, with only enough room for two people in the cockpit. He shows her how to climb up a ladder, stand on the wing of the plane, but only in a certain spot, in preparation of entering the thing.

The top of the small cockpit, like a skylight or a long oval plastic bubble, is lifted in the front, hinged at the back, with the seats beneath it. Paul helps to lower her into the cockpit, and settles her into the tiny backseat. Why this turns her on, she cannot say for sure, but she does know that time has slowed down the way it does when something really exciting is happening, and she is seeing colors brighter than they usually are, and hearing things more acutely, and the smells! Grease, oil, gasoline, desert wind, and Paul.

He slips her into the seat, tightens the belts all around her with his big, capable hands, an old pro at this to be sure, and then he gives her a set of white plastic earbuds, the kind you wear with an iPod.

"Put these in your ears before you put the helmet on," he tells her.

"Why?"

"I have my iPod programmed for the flight," he tells her, as he shows her the device, fitted with a dual jack for two sets of earbuds, hers and his. "You wanted to know about me, so I came up with a few songs that say it better than I could. There's a speaker inside the helmet, too, so you'll be able to hear me talking to you from up front. You've also got a little microphone in your helmet, so I can hear you if you have something to say. Only put one ear-bud in, so the other ear hears the speaker. *Capiche?*"

She does as he says, and watches as he gracefully gets himself into position and makes hand signals that mean nothing to her at the men and women on the ground. Then, the top of the plane comes down, slowly, and they are sealed inside. Vanessa hears the speaker inside the helmet crackle to life, and then comes Paul's voice, through the static.

"You ready, pretty neighbor lady?"

"Should I say 'roger'?" she quips, trying to be cute in a defensive sort of way. But, of course, he's quick on his feet and has an even better comeback for her.

"No, baby. I wanna hear you scream *Paul*."

And under his command, the engines fire up—vibrations running through the body of the jet, in a hot blast of raw, masculine power.

A BLOODY BEAUTIFUL

MERINGUE

The plane pushes back and taxis toward the runway. Paul starts up the iPod, and the first song to come piping into Vanessa's ears is none other than "Danger Zone," by Kenny Loggins—aka, the theme song from the movie *Top Gun*.

She is about to insult him for this choice, when the song abruptly ends with the sound of a scratched record, and his voice comes through the helmet speaker.

"I caught you underestimating me again," he says, and she can almost *hear* the man winking. Against her nerves and thrill of terror, she laughs. How does he do this, make her laugh at moments like this?

And then, the real music begins, and to tell you that her jaw drops (once again in astonishment) is an understatement. To say it is an understatement is *itself* an understatement.

The first song is a new version of a song she recognizes as being by Black Sabbath, recorded by someone else now, she is not sure who. It begins with a small voice, almost a baby's voice, asking "Why?" over and over, and then come the staccato electric guitars, as they round the corner of the runway. They idle there, waiting first for another plane to land, and then for Paul, apparently, to decide that it is time to go. They sit still as the first lyrics come, just the voice, the tapping high-hat drum, and the guitar:

Generals gathered in their masses
Just like witches at black masses . . .

And then come the drums, the incredibly loud, strong, metal drums, and the little plane darts fast as a mouse down the runway, just a short blast of a drive, and before Vanessa can understand what's happening, they're already off the ground in a thunderous roar.

This is not your usual flight, because there is no moment to gather her thoughts. Within seconds of having lifted off, the nose of the plane is pointed directly toward the sky, and they rocket up, her face pushing back, her body pressed with enormous force against the back of her seat. The suit squeezes her legs, and it occurs to her that this is the part where she would have otherwise passed out. Without the G suit and the bladders and so on.

Vanessa screams and realizes only after the sound comes to her ears that it has come from her. She has never felt such unbridled power, such intense excitement, such danger, and such confusion in her life. She hears herself screaming again. *A roller coaster on steroids*, she thinks.

They rotate in the sky, like a corkscrew, as they ascend at a speed that seems impossible to her brain. And the song goes on, a blast of metal and fury, an antiwar song.

An antiwar song.

What does he mean by this? All that saluting and whatnot on the ground, all that "yes, sir" and "no, sir" militaristic banter, and yet here they are, in the fighter plane, and there's a blatant antiwar song blasting in her ears as they rocket to the sky. What does it mean?

"Fourteen thousand feet," he tells her in the speaker. "In ten seconds."

Treating people just like pawns in chess
Wait till their judgment day comes . . . war pigs

"Who are the pigs?" she screams. "Them, or us?"

He doesn't answer. Instead, he levels the jet out of the climb, and they are flying, the way planes are supposed to fly, parallel to the ground, only much, much faster, and there is no wall next to Vanessa, no ceiling over her head, just a tiny little piece of metal beneath her, tight as the jumpsuit on her body, and the thin layer of clouds directly next to her head, and Paul, magnificent, powerful, brutal, obviously skilled and intelligent Paul, right in front of her, taking them wherever he wants them to go.

Vanessa looks to the side, and sees the city of Albuquerque slip past as if it were a leaf in a fast-moving stream. The music changes to match the softer feel of what the plane does, to a ballad that is unmistakably sung by the Cranberries, a strummed acoustic guitar with a trumpet in the background, and Dolores O'Riordan's distinctive voice:

> At times of war, we're all the losers, there's no victory
> We shoot to kill and kill your lover, fine by me

"How fast are we going?" Vanessa cries out.

"Little more than seven hundred miles an hour," he answers. "But she can do almost double that. I'm goin' easy on ya."

"Dear God," she breathes. She can't stop looking around her, a child in this new world, awed.

It belies the sense of serenity and peace up here, this speed, because it feels as though they are suspended in space, floating over nothingness, just the blue, blue sky above their heads, to the front, to the sides, and the mellow, sad, terribly, terribly sad song, a lullaby, really, of the most profoundly tragic nature.

"Five minutes to Santa Fe," he says, and sure enough, she looks down and sees that city fast approaching beneath them, the mountains on her right, and sky, endless sky above.

A cloud bank clings to the Sangre de Cristos, the "blood of Christ" mountains, called such by the Spanish settlers to this land for the range's propensity to turn red at sunset. Cumulus clouds, firm and lofty, and to her they resemble nothing so much as the whipped lightness of a good meringue. Meringue kisses, she thinks, nearly tasting the confection in her mouth. War, fighter jet, meringue, mountains, peaks, valleys.

She finds inspiration for her menus in the strangest of places, and at the moment, she is overcome with the idea to head home and make pink meringue kisses, in honor of this day and this moment and this man, bloody meringue, the light puffiness of the clouds, the pain of the war and the blood of all martyrs, the mountains named for this, too, and then the pedestrian nature of the giant éclair conjured for the sweetness. A recipe, even here, even now, and this is proof, if ever there needed to be, that she is a chef through and through.

The song changes again, as Paul speeds up and the idea for the recipe dissolves like sugar in hot water. Unlike commercial jets, where you don't feel the speed change, this sense of increasing velocity is intense, and now she understands why Paul compared it to a motorcycle before. That's exactly what it feels like, except that they hang thousands of feet above the earth, tenuous, suspended on a spider's web. She listens as the unmistakable syncopation of a reggae song comes next. Bob Marley's voice now, and he's singing: *War . . .*

Paul moves the plane in time to the music, a drummer at the wheel, or whatever the control thing is for this plane. Joystick? She doesn't know. The plane dips, left, right, left, right, with the groove, and then, when the chorus comes, the plane rolls upside down, and keeps going until it's upright again, with Vanessa shrieking the whole time.

"You like that?" he asks.

"No!" she screams, laughing, and he does it again.

"Stop it!"

He turns them upside down again, and leaves them that way this time, dangling from their seatbelts, and making her scream louder than she has ever screamed before. He does this for a bit, uprights them, and dips the plane in time to the music again. Vanessa is laughing, crying, confused, because this song, like the others, is a protest against war, though it's about the war of race in the world, and about the necessity for all people to be equal, regardless of their skin tone.

Dear God, she thinks. He's *not* a right-wing nutjob, after all. Why did she think he was? Oh, that's right. Crew cut, military, big truck, obnoxious demeanor, yellow ribbon magnet. All that talk about sacrifice and country. It all feels upside down, her world. Her life. Her judgments.

The song ends, and there is a brief silence, and he says, "I can't see your face, V, but I'd bet all my money that you've got that surprised look on it again."

She says nothing, and another song comes on. As soon as she

hears its recognizable disco beat, she begins to laugh, with tears in her eyes. It is Diana Ross, singing:

Upside down boy, you turn me

Inside out and round and round . . .

Paul speeds up again, and takes them into another roll upside down, only this time, to get out of it, he points the nose directly at the ground. Vanessa shrieks in a way she has never shrieked, a life-or-death kind of screaming.

She hears him laughing and whooping, as they careen toward the earth, fast, too fast, and terror grips her as she realizes she doesn't know which way is up, literally. Nor does she know this man well enough to know whether he might be *suicidal*.

Vanessa closes her eyes and holds her breath, preparing for her own death, and then, just like that, it is over, and the machine is upright, and they are slowing down, and she is sick to her stomach, with the bladders on her legs filled and emptying and Vanessa herself none too certain that her very own bladder is not about to do the same.

"What is *wrong* with you?" she demands.

He answers by singing along: " 'Instinctively, you give to me, the love that I need, I cherish the moment with you, respectfully, I say to thee, I'm aware that you're cheatin', when no one makes me feel like you do.' "

"No fair!" she screams, with the realization of the double meaning in the song choice. It is about a woman who is the other woman, her apparent fate over all these past failed relationships. The husband habit. He's teasing her again, even now, even here. "You're so mean! What is *wrong* with you?"

He's laughing again, and gunning his little plane all over the sky, with Vanessa helplessly in it.

"That's Taos," he says, of the little city that is now below them. "You ready to head back for the rest of our day together?"

"You mean there's more?" she asks, trying her hardest to sound disappointed.

"I'm sorry," he says, when the song ends. "I hope I didn't take it too far with that one." As if he has read her mind. Again.

He turns the plane into a bank toward the west, easing them back around to head home. Vanessa doesn't answer him, primarily because she is pouting and sick to her stomach—and, in spite of all that, falling in love with this man.

No matter how ridiculous Larissa would find such sentiment, Vanessa knows her feelings, and this is real.

"C'mon, pretty neighbor lady. Say *something*, so I know you didn't pass out on me back there"

"What do you want me to say? Oh, wait, I remember. *Paul*." She makes a fake orgasm voice: "Paul, oh, *Paul!*"

"Mmm," he says. "Do that again."

"Shut up."

"Hey, V. You know I'm just messin' with you. That I'm teasing, right?"

"I am aware."

"Good," he says. He sounds suddenly very serious, and earnest. "Because the next song is for you, and it's no joke. Okay? No laughing back there. I'm putting my heart out there for you."

Trapped in Paul's world, in Paul's angry, troubled, strange, funny, complicated world, she listens, nervously, to what comes next. It sounds hokey, and country, and a little lame, to be honest, but she tries to keep an open mind, as she thinks Paul himself would, if it were her telling him how she really felt about him. Which she could never do.

She holds her breath as the twangy male voice sings out.

Honey, why don't we get drunk and screw . . .
I just bought a waterbed filled up for me and you

If Vanessa could slap him, she would. She really would. He lowers the volume slowly, and the song fades away so that all she can hear is Paul laughing like the frat boy he is. She feels so foolish. What was she thinking? That he'd confess a romantic love for her up here, after all these aerial gymnastics?

"You're an idiot!" she cries.

"I know! Ain't it great? Anyway, that's it for the songs, V. Thanks for listening. We'll be back on the ground in a few minutes."

Just when she thinks the fun and games are coming to a close, another song comes on, without an introduction from Captain Idiot the Viking. She sits behind him as he moves the little jet gently through the sky now, softly, almost lovingly, if that were possible considering its sheer destructive force, and neither one of them speaks as the song guides them back to earth.

Aaron Neville, singing his heart out, and it goes a little something like this:

Ain't no sunshine when she's gone
Only darkness every day

A person cannot will themselves to get them, goose bumps. Impossible. Equally impossible is it to will them *away*, once they sprout up from the depths of your emotional center. But, thank God, you *can* wear a G suit, that at the very least can press them down, as if they were not there at all.

I know, I know, I know, I know, I know, I know . . .

And she does.

She *knows*.

CHILI AND BEER

Back on the ground, and she cannot make eye contact with the women, who help her remove the G suit as cleverly as they helped her put it on.

It's not that there's something wrong with them, or that she doesn't like them. It's that she wonders, now, if they have secrets like Paul did. Like Paul does. She wonders whether they will turn him in to someone if they were to find out his secret, namely, that Paul is not in favor of the very war he fought in.

The clouds moving in now, storm coming, and her own heart clearer than she imagined it might be. She cannot make eye contact with the women because of the terrible fear that they, being women, might read in her own eyes the secret she now keeps locked close to her spine. She is falling. No, not falling. She has fallen for Paul. To hell with Larissa's warnings. Larissa doesn't know everything.

"How did she do?" one of the women asks Paul.

"Oh," he says. "You know how reporters are."

"Dishonest?" offers the other woman.

Paul laughs, as if he finds the woman very funny, and he seems sincere enough, but now Vanessa understands more what that wall is she has so often found behind his eyes. He is lying.

He catches her eye, and does a brief impression of the Lord of the Dance. She laughs.

Vanessa, her eyes acting now on their own will, against her heart's, looks at him, brow knit, want filling her every cell. *You have hidden yourself so well from me. How did you do it?*

Him, looking back, with a twitch of a grin at the furthest edge of his lip, to tell her he knows that she knows him now, he knows that knowing him makes him irresistible to her now. Savors the fact that he kept it from her this long.

Another test.

Grins a bit toward her because he knows now, and she knows now, and there is nothing left in between them, no more barriers. He has peeled a bit of the bandage off the wound he carries like a child carries a blanket, and shown her a corner of his soul she did not know she would ever find.

"Surprise," he tells her, his voice low and soft, his body close to hers and moving past it.

"It's better than the whoopee cushion I was expecting," she tells him, still defensive, still not quite sure what to do with the big, spilling-over thing in her hands. The savory thing, the sweet thing, all of it together in one place.

The women look puzzled, and that's okay, because the suit is off and the lights are too fluorescent and demanding, the space here too small. Paul has held out his elbow to her, ever the gentleman, or not, and she has taken it, and they are leaving, she knows not to where, and she is okay with that.

She does not speak as they walk back through the base, back to the truck, just watches this man in his former element. There is something more relaxed to him now, not exactly drained, but at peace. She imagines he must have wanted to tell her for a long time.

Once in the truck she still cannot speak, and he does not seem to have much to say, either, except that they're about to "take a little drive." More than an hour later, she finds herself in the high plains beyond Las Vegas, New Mexico, a small college town to the east of Santa Fe.

Small dirt road, a ranch of some kind, with a sign that you drive beneath, an entry gate with a wagon wheel on it, and then a cabin, a small but new square wooden structure, in a stand of trees like an oasis. A windmill. Horses in the distance.

He parks, and they go to the cabin, and there is a porch swing covered by an itchy blanket, the kind you use on a horse, in reds and dark blues and grays. He gestures for her to sit. She complies, gasps at the view from that spot, a land that goes on forever, a sky that is so high the clouds seem to rest directly on the horizon. He joins her on the swing. A cold wind blows. Farther north than Albuquerque. Clean air stings her face. Wakes her up. Alerts her, to what she is not yet sure.

"Welcome to our ranch," he says. "It was my dad's dad's dad's. Been in the family for a long time. Now it's mine. My dad used to bring me and my brother here when we were kids."

"That must have been nice," she says. *You own a ranch like this, but live with your mother?* She cannot ask this question, not yet. Nor can she ask how his dad died, or if he liked his dad. She senses this is all coming. He's revealing so much as it is, no need to push the wrong buttons.

Paul shrugs. "There were nice things about it. Like the horses. I loved riding the horses. I liked brushing them and talking to them. You ever gotten to know a horse, Vanessa?"

"Can't say I have."

"You'd like horses. They're a lot like dogs. They're as smart as dogs. I'm pretty sure about that. When I was a kid I pretty much believed they could talk to me. I still believe it."

"Huh." She does not know where this conversation is leading, or what to even say. Which is fine, because he keeps talking.

"Nice. You think it must have been nice to come here. Yeah, well, not always. I liked being out in the open. But there was something I hated about coming here, Vanessa, and that's why I brought you here. I thought you should know what that thing was. And why I hate it."

"That sounds a little scary," she says.

"Nah. Don't let it."

She waits for him to tell her what that thing is, but he doesn't. He looks out at the land, his eyes narrowing with memories.

"Lunch is waiting for us inside," he says. "Let's get grub."

Inside, the cabin is toasty warm and cozy, with pale wooden floors, and the kind of leather sofa and chairs with metal studs in them. There is one large main room, with high ceilings and Western art on the walls. It serves as a living room and kitchen and dining room, with a fireplace, and modern kitchen appliances, nearly gourmet, actually. Tasteful, in a bachelor kind of way. Manly, but clean and beautiful, too. An expensive cabin. There's a loft above, that looks to be a bedroom of some kind.

Paul asks her to sit and relax on the sofa, while he gets lunch ready. He goes to the fridge and takes out a pot with a lid on it. He tells her it is homemade chili, with an "i," low-fat, made with ground turkey, places this on the gas range to warm.

"I called up here last night and had Margaret take this out of the freezer for us," he tells her.

"Margaret?"

"A friend," he says. She tries not to feel jealous.

Next, he produces a loaf of French bread. He sets the oven to warm, and places the bread on a baking sheet.

"This is all new," he explains, about the little house. "I had it re-done. We used to have a trailer out here when I was a kid, and then, later, the main house, which is still around, but I like this better."

"Where's the main house?"

"About twenty acres from here. You'll see it later and you'll know why I like this place better."

"How big is your ranch?"

"Fifty acres, just about."

"Wow."

He smiles at her, winks. "I'm fulla surprises, pretty neighbor lady."

"I realize that."

"You want a beer?" he asks, popping the cap on a bottle of amber ale for himself.

"Sure."

He brings her a beer, returns to the stove to check the progress of the chili. Deems it just about warm enough, pops the bread in the oven, sets the rustic farmhouse table with bowls, spoons, butter, napkins.

"Can I help you with any of that?" she asks.

"Nah, just relax. I know that ride must've taken a lot out of you." He grins at her.

"You're a good pilot."

"Duh," he says.

Vanessa watches as he readies their lunch, admiring the ease with which he does this. Most of her friends are too intimidated to attempt to cook in front of her. Paul doesn't seem to place her on a pedestal just because she is a chef. She asks him about this now, and he laughs at her.

"Hey, I don't think I'm a great cook or something," he says. "I just figure you're human, and you can eat the regular stuff, too."

As it turns out, he is a good cook, as good with the chili as he was with the grilled fish at the first barbecue months ago. She compliments him, and he accepts it graciously. *Months ago*, she thinks. It has passed quickly.

As they eat, Vanessa asks him about flying. Was it hard to learn to do? Does he miss doing it all the time? Was he ever afraid he'd crash? He answers her, and shares a little bit about his journey in the Air Force, the difficulties of rising through the ranks as he did, without having had a dad or grandfather in the force. He talks to her about guys he knew who rose in the ranks because of connections, and how much he resented that, how he had to work twice as hard for the same thing. He tells her how it works, the education and the training, the dues you have to pay, and how he shot up in the ranks pretty rapidly once they figured his language skills were useful. How he's been all over the world. How hard it was to keep a girlfriend under those circumstances of constantly moving, how hard it is to date women in the force because of the tension and sexism, the lying and backstabbing that goes both ways.

She asks if he's ever had a serious girlfriend, and he says he did. Katie. He tells her about wanting to marry Katie, and finding out, days after he'd proposed, that she was cheating on him. With his best friend.

"They'd been seeing each other behind my back for more than a year. That pretty much did me in for women for a while," he says. "Which is why I totally understood you when you told me that you were taking a break from guys. Been there, done that."

"Taken a break from guys?"

"Yeah, real funny, V," he says. "Homophobia. The comedic staple of the unimaginative."

"I didn't mean it that way," she says. "And I can't even believe I'm defending myself to you about being open-minded."

He looks at her for a long moment, takes a long draw on his beer, and leans back, hands behind his head. He stares long enough, and smiles hard enough, to make her uncomfortable.

"What?" she asks. "Why are you looking at me like that?"

"You're just so damn pretty, Vanessa," he says.

"I'm really not," she insists. "It's not something I really even think about. I'm not, like, the kind of woman who's running out to get her nails done or her brows waxed or anything like that."

Paul screws up his face and chuckles. "Oh, c'mon. Is that what you think I want from you? That you're out getting manicures? Sheesh."

"I don't know. It's just, you know, when men talk about attractive women, that's usually what comes to mind."

"Not for me."

"Apparently."

"You are beautiful inside and out, and you don't need any of that other crap to make you any more beautiful."

Vanessa feels herself starting to blush.

"Seriously," he says. "That first day I saw you, when you were rude to me . . ."

"I'm sorry about that," she says. "I figured you were some kind of a meathead."

He laughs. "I know you did. I know it. And I *am* some kind of a meathead, just not the kind you assumed I was. You're funny. But that first time I saw you I thought you were totally hot, Vanessa, and then when you talked, and you were smart, and funny, and then when you knew about food, and turned out to be a chef, no less." He whistles. "I knew it was over."

"What was over?"

"Paul's worldwide search for the perfect woman."

"That's sort of dramatic, don't you think? You don't really know me that well."

He laughs. "That doesn't hold water anymore, pretty neighbor lady. You're gonna have to come up with some other reason to keep me at arm's length."

"You're probably right."

"I'm always right. I tried to tell you that."

Now it's Vanessa's turn to laugh. The beer has started to go to her head, probably because the massive doses of caffeine and adrenaline, and the change in altitude, have done something to her capillaries.

"Say it. I just want to hear you say it," he says. "Say, 'Paul's always right.' "

Vanessa finishes off the last of her chili, and laughs some more. "No way," she says. "I'll never say that. You can be right all you want, but I will never cede my throne as the one who is actually *always* right."

Paul clears the dishes and washes them, and the easy banter continues, until he asks her if she's ever ridden a horse.

"Actually, no," she says.

"First time for everything," he tells her.

He opens a closet near the front door, and produces two over-coats. "I've got someone I want you to meet," he says. "Her name is Rosie."

HONEST VENISON

Rosie is a caramel horse with dark, enormous eyes framed with long lashes. She lives with five other horses in a stable on the ranch, accessible from Paul's cabin via a walk of about a quarter mile down a second dirt road. The stable is painted pale yellow, and smells of straw and spiderwebs. It all makes Vanessa think of fresh butter, though this, she realizes, is absurd, given the lack of cows. But then, that's just how her mind works. Positive associations.

Paul kisses Rosie on the soft pink nose, and the horse appears to kiss him back. He tells Vanessa that Rosie has been his horse for twelve years, and that every free moment he gets, he comes to spend with her here. When Vanessa asks him how he has been able to care for Rosie, being away in Iraq, and living in Seattle and all over the world, he laughs at her naïveté and explains that a couple named Margaret and Jared live on the ranch and take care of things in his absence. Margaret, she thinks. The woman who thawed the chili for them.

"Oh. Like feudal serfs?" she suggests. It comes out too quickly for her to stop herself. He takes it in stride. Used to her now. Unfettered.

"They get free rent, and can pretty much live for free in Second House for the rest of their lives if they want to. I don't hear them complaining."

"Second House?"

Paul starts to saddle Rosie, and continues to talk. "The main house I told you about, the one my dad built, that's First House. Second House is for the ranch help."

"How nice that you give them the leftovers," she says, unable to contain her discomfort with the idea of live-in servants.

"Hey," he says. "Second House is a lot nicer than First House. You'll see."

"Oh," she says. "I think I should shut up now."

"Nah, speak your mind. You'll just end up being wrong about me as usual. It's okay. You'll like Margaret and Jared. They've been with us for the past thirty years. They raised their kids here. One of 'em just graduated from Georgetown Law. We helped pay his way, not that he needed much help. Dude's smart as hell."

"And your little house, that's Third House?"

"Nah, that's just Paul's cabin." He grins at her.

"Ah," she says.

He finishes with Rosie, and leads the horse from the stable out into a pen. Vanessa follows. Paul opens a gate, leads the horse out, waits for Vanessa to come through, closes it behind her. Then, he tells Vanessa how to mount the horse, and helps her get up into the saddle.

"I'll get up after you," he says.

"We're riding Rosie together?"

"That's right."

"Can she support all that weight?"

Paul laughs again. "Rosie's a strong old girl, aren't ya, Rosie?"

And then he is up, behind her. She feels his arms wrap around her waist as his hands take the reins. The horse does not seem much bothered by any of it, and is soon off and walking across a field, and into a stand of trees, and up a hill, and on they go, for a good half hour, through the beautiful countryside, with Vanessa puzzled as to what could possibly exist out here for Paul to hate. And that is the exact word he used, *hate*.

When they get to the next stand of trees, running alongside a small creek at the base of a hill, Paul dismounts, helps Vanessa down, and tethers Rosie to a post that seems to have been placed here for just that purpose. He gives the horse a handful of apple pieces from a sack, a saddlebag most likely, and the horse snuffles her big warm lips around the treats.

Suddenly, Paul whispers. "This way," he tells Vanessa. "We'll leave Rosie to graze here awhile."

She follows him as he steps lightly through the trees, up a hill, and when he finally stops, she comes to his side.

"There," he whispers, pointing down at the valley that unfolds in front of them.

Vanessa spots a herd of animals in the distance, on the plain, assumes them at first to be horses, but when he hands her the binoculars, she realizes they are something else altogether. They are delicate, brown, with white and black stripes, and some of them have antlers. They graze together, heads zooming up at the slightest sound on the wind. She opens her eyes wide to Paul, as if to ask him what they are.

"Elk," he says softly. "Lots of elk up this way."

"Wow," she says back. Her mind goes to venison, and other wild game.

"We got deer up this way, too," he says. "Dad was big on hunting."

"Wow," she says again, not sure how to react. She could never hunt. She is more than happy to eat nearly every animal on earth, but could never take one's life.

They stand silently, watching the animals. Finally, Paul speaks.

"This is what I hated about coming here," he tells her.

"The elk?" she whispers back.

He shakes his head. "*Killing* 'em. That's what I hated. My dad was a big hunter. I was probably five or six the first time he took me. I liked animals, Vanessa. Always have. I still do. I love 'em. I'll never forget it. I was a little kid, and he took me out here, and he downed a doe, and took me with him to get it. She wasn't dead yet, just there bleeding, you know? She looked right at me. And her baby, that fawn, was standing there, not knowing where to go or what to do. I was sickened by it. I hated it, but you know how it is. You have to suck it up, when you're a boy, right? You gotta play soldiers and cowboys and Indians, you gotta like to shoot stuff, and you gotta play sports, right, or you're not a real boy. And my dad wanted me to learn to hunt, to do this thing that his dad taught him, and that his dad's dad had taught his dad, and so that's what it was like. Like my legacy, and I hated every minute of it, but when you're a kid you don't have the guts or the power to stand up to your dad about something like that, and you think there's something wrong with you."

"I'm sorry," she tells him.

"Hey, I'm not saying I'm a vegan or anything like that. But I thought you should know that no matter what you think of me, and the job I picked, that the way I came into the world, you know, it wasn't the way you think. I got made into what I was, by my upbringing, you know? Deep down, the real Paul, though? I'm just a big wuss."

"No," she says. "You're not."

"Nah, I know. But I wanted to show you this place, and these animals. Everybody knows now, if you're up on the Stebbit ranch, you better not shoot anything. That's what it's like. I'm not real big on shooting. I'm big on watching wildlife, and trying to keep their habitat in place. The way I see it, that's the right kind of power to have over the animal kingdom, right, to steward it."

Vanessa considers this, and what the implications might be. "Did they know that about you in the Air Force? I'd think being able to shoot stuff is pretty important for a soldier."

"Airman. But close enough. Nah, you know. They never knew much about me, and that's how I liked it," he says. "If you're going to go military, and you don't want to see combat, your best bet is the Air Force."

"Do you hate that I love to eat animals?" she asks him.

"No, babe. I don't. I like 'em on my plate, too. I just don't like to see anything die because of me."

She slips her hand into his, and squeezes it. "We have a lot in common," she says.

He squeezes back, and turns to her, and kisses her, softly, gently, a small kiss, and smiles. She sees the glisten of a tear in his eye as he smiles at her. "*Yeah*, we do. You're just figuring that out, pretty neighbor lady?"

"I guess I'm a little slow," she jokes.

The wind gusts cold all around them, and he pulls her in, wraps her in his big, solid arms.

"It's good to take some things slow," he says. "But I'm a speed demon. You know that now. And I've been thinking. You know? Maybe it's time me and you, we sped things up a little."

He kisses her again, deeper this time, and longer, and more

passionate. She loses herself to sensation, and taste, and smell, and he is, quite simply, perfect. She presses into him, and he presses back, and it is warm, and safe, and strong, and delicious. The scent of grass and water, the scent of cold, clear wind.

"You ready to move this forward?" he asks, pulling out of the kiss and dragging her by the hand back to Rosie. The horse looks up from nuzzling the grass, seeming to sense the pheromones between them, and whinnies her approval.

"I'm ready," says Vanessa.

Her only regret is that Paul's little house is at least twenty minutes away. They return Rosie to the stables, and hurry back to the cabin. There, they draw the shades and speed things up just fine—mixing, blending, whipping, grinding, tasting, spooning, smoothing, kneading, rolling, sizzling, drizzling, combining.

And, as with any other magical, sensory undertaking in Vanessa's sensual life, the end result of their creative, patient attention to detail is nothing short of miraculous.

Afterward, they lie side by side, and Paul talks. He tells her everything she wanted to know.

He tells her that he served his country because he was raised to think that was the right thing to do, but his country lied to him, and to the rest of us, in this last war. He participated in bombing raids upon sites he was led to believe were strategic targets, weapons caches and terrorist hideouts, only to later discover that those sites were filled with innocent civilians. He cries quietly as he remembers it, just the wetness on his cheeks and no other indication that his mood has changed, and he tells of the shame they are made to feel about this sort of reaction. They are not supposed to cry, or feel, because in the military that is interpreted as weakness. He tells her that he sees no amount of fairness in bombing people with high-tech weapons from the sky, while those same people do their best to defend themselves with sticks and rocks on the ground.

"There was a time," he tells her, "when I didn't want to live any-more, knowing what I'd done to those poor people. Most of the people over in Iraq, Vanessa? They're just kids. Kids. Illiterate kids, with no access to world news. They don't know what's going on, why their cities are blowing up, and all they know is that they're scared and they're dying. It's not right. The people in charge over there use religion to keep everybody under control, it's no differ-ent than here, really."

He tells her how he held his tongue until he was able to finish his retirement paperwork, how he feels lucky he was old enough to get out without having to be a conscientious objector, which he would have done if he'd been younger. Tells her how his mom saved his life.

"I got out, moved in with my mom to try to help me get my head straight. Without her, I would have probably offed myself right after I came back."

"You wanted to kill yourself."

"Hell, yeah. It seemed like the only just thing to do, Vanessa."

"Why? If you were only doing what you thought was right?"

"Because it *wasn't* right. That's why. Okay. Listen to me. After the raids, I heard about what people on the ground were saying, and I went down there myself to find out. I wasn't supposed to do it, but I went out on my own in those places, to ask people there what had happened. They're the ones who told me, 'there used to be a village here,' or, 'this used to be a school.' Things I destroyed, Vanessa. I saw the scraps that were left, parts of things, children's bloody shoes and toys. Baby shoes, Vanessa, little tiny feet, blown off, and I did that. Do you understand? You don't want to live after you've seen that. This wasn't what I went in there for. I'm the kid who couldn't even shoot an elk, and here I am walking around in the rubble of all that, where I thought I'd taken out some weapons for the bad guys, and it turns out it was just these people who had nothing to do with anything."

"My God," she says. "I am so sorry."

"Mom helped me see that there wasn't anything I could have done to stop it. That I made these mistakes in good faith. It didn't make it all that much easier, because I know what I have done, but I was following orders, and I have to remember that."

"That's why I've never been big on following orders."

"I admire people like you," he says. "I don't know what that's like, to be like you. I was raised different, Vanessa. For people like me, following orders is the top way you should love and respect."

"I know."

"I have to be honest with you. A big part of the reason I like you is that you're exactly the kind of woman I would have steered clear of before all this."

"Gee, thanks."

He smiles a little bit. "I mean, being so liberal. I like smart girls, bad girls, and you're all that, but usually they were more like Ann Coulter."

"Great."

"No, you're way better. Trust me. It's just, okay, listen. My dad taught me that our country is the biggest and the best, and he made me proud to be a free American. All that got reinforced in the Air Force, because it's all the same thing. It took a lot for me to understand that maybe it was a story we told ourselves. When I saw how big the world really is, you know? It was a real awakening for me. We're not the center of the world, you know."

"I know."

"Yeah, of course you do. But I didn't."

"That's not your fault. How could you have known?"

"I don't know. I guess I realized that instead of killing myself to avenge the lives of all those people, those innocent people, Vanessa, I needed to spend the rest of my life building things and helping people, to set my life right."

"Thus, the construction job," she says. "Even though you own a ranch."

"I have a house in Seattle, too."

"You do?"

"A nice little house I built with my buddies, overlooks a lake. You'll like it. I have a good pension, too. Just as much as I made as a top officer in the force. I don't have to do a damn thing for the rest of my life if I don't want to."

"I had no idea."

"I bet Larissa thinks I was a total loser because I live with my mom and work in construction."

"Pretty much. But I bet you wanted her to think that. Right? You were testing her."

He grins. "Yeah, well you can tell her I'm trying to build things because of all the things I destroyed. That's the whole point. And you tell her that I'm at my mom's because sometimes, the silence in the middle of the night, living by myself, sounds like it needs the perfect gunshot to make it complete."

"That's scary, Paul."

"I realize that. I'm getting help."

"Good."

"And you tell your sister about how I'm volunteering to help kids in the South Valley, and the food bank." He's quiet, and thoughtful. "There's a lot I've done. I can't tell you all of it, not yet. A lot I've done to help people, but that will come in time."

"Tell me when you're ready," she says. And then, before she can stop herself, she tells him, "I want you to know, I think I love you."

He tightens his hold on her, and she can feel his body tremble with the sobs he's holding down. He kisses the top of her head, and then he lets himself cry.

"I love you, too, Vanessa. And I want you to let me love you big, okay? I need to love big now. Because that's the only thing that's ever gonna stop any of this craziness, is love."

Vanessa feels her eyes well with tears, for the pain he's in, for the pain he caused, for the confusion of it all, for the cruelty of humanity against itself, for the lies men tell to women, yes, for her hurt, but now, maybe worse than that, she is sad for the lies men tell to other men.

And especially sad, she realizes, are the lies men in every culture seem to tell little boys.

A SPILL OF NOBLE ROT

It is a new year, past Christmas and not yet quite to Valentine's Day. Months have passed since that first night together at the ranch, when Vanessa returned home to a Red Dog worried and shivery with relief that she had not been left alone for all eternity.

It should be a happy time, one week removed from the opening of Ris on a busy corner of Nob Hill, the menu written, the simple black-and-white uniforms home with the waitstaff. More than half of Hawk's employees defected with her, and Hazel is her manager. The cozy restaurant space has been designed and put in motion, homey, whimsical, and sophisticated all at once, a colorful place best described as southwestern folk funk. Perhaps she has created a signature look for the city. Perhaps her life is ending. Really, at this point it could go either way. Of course she should be happy. The local press, to the extent that this city *has* a local press, has gone crazy over the story of her Cyrano relationship to Hawk. Both the conservative daily broadsheet and the juvenile alternative weekly have painted her as a poetic backstage hero, and promised to be at her coming-out party with bells and whistles on.

In spite of all this, Vanessa sits at the desk in the little back office of Ris, with her sister seated opposite and looking solemnly on. Vanessa drinks herself into a semistupor with sweet dessert wine. The vile document in question, the source of today's misery, lies facedown on the desktop, as does the framed photo of Vanessa and Paul, taken by Hazel, atop Sandia Crest the day the three of them plus Smitty had taken the Tramway up. Curses to official documents from Washington State, curses to photos of herself happy with unwarranted trust.

"You're reminding me of Mom," says Larissa, the way some people might say a toupee reminds them of coyote vomit.

"Please don't make this any worse than it already is," wails Vanessa.

"Can I see it?" Larissa points to the piece of paper.

Vanessa frowns at her sister before reluctantly handing her the document. Larissa holds it out far, then brings it in close, examines it in every light available to her, and says, "Well, I'll be damned. He *is* married."

"Please don't say 'I told you so,'" says Vanessa.

"I'm not sure I can say anything right now," says Larissa.

Vanessa drops her head into her hands and remembers.

The first kiss. The taste of summer peas. The flight, and the meringue clouds. The eyes of the horse. The herd of elk. The stories. And all those afternoons walking together after that, in the foothills, at the river, talking. The nights spent making love and talking until the sun came up. Her stories and pains and joys held out for him, like porcelain antique dolls, and he taking them in his hands with the care of a collector. The concerts, how she had a real reason to dress up, and how her friends and his friends slowly seemed to become friends with one another, on their own merits, until it was one close group of people. A community. A family.

And those nights. What can she say about them, without resorting in the end to clichés? That he was a concerned lover, and a ferocious lover, that all those parts of his personality that she had seen outside of the bedroom became magnified and intensified within it. The tears come and cloud her view of Larissa, who is up off her seat now, and rushing over.

"I am so stupid. I really am," says Vanessa.

Larissa does not argue, even as she wraps her capable arms around her miserable sister. "How did you find out? Where did you find this?"

Vanessa tells Larissa how she found the paper. She'd spent the night at Paul's last night, his mother having been out of town for a conference, and he went jogging this morning. Nothing unusual there.

Curious, Vanessa began to snoop around in his closet, mostly hoping to find old photos and things like that. Maybe a picture of an old girlfriend, something to tease him about. Katie. She was terribly curious to know what Katie looked like.

She picked a box with band trophies, and some old random things. A harmless-looking box, that turned out not to be harmless at all. At first, she did find some funny things, the bowl-cut photos and the chubby kid that he once, unbelievably, was.

She found documents and letters, old mail and things that did not interest her much, and then she found it: the marriage license. It is dated nine months ago, from the state of Washington. The groom is listed as Paul Kyle Stebbit, and the bride, a mysterious woman named Faizah Abdul-Qadar.

"I knew he was no good," Larissa says. "I warned you."

Vanessa shakes her head. "I know."

Larissa scowls at the paper some more. "I'm very curious to know what he has to say for himself. He even had me fooled there for a while, Vanessa, but you know what? I think my first impression of him was dead-on now."

"I asked you not to say that," says Vanessa.

"I did not say 'I told you so.'"

"Yes, you did."

"Look, let's not fight right now, okay?"

Vanessa blows her nose in a tissue. "Who is this woman? Where is she?"

"Didn't you say he has a house in Seattle?" asks Larissa. "Doesn't he fly out there sometimes?"

Vanessa nods. "He says he's going to take care of some business."

"Yeah, business," says Larissa. "I'd bet you anything that Faizah Whatsherface here, she lives out there."

"What do I do, Larissa?" she asks, crying.

"I don't know, Vanessa. This time, I'm at a complete loss for words."

Of course, this loss does not last long, for Larissa is Larissa, and always has a prescription at the ready.

"Okay," she says after a moment's thought. "First, you need to let me take you home, because you're drinking, and we both know that's not a good way to handle a thing like this. You need to get busy, make something, cook something, get this out of your system, re-member who you are and what you're brilliant at, and most of all, remember that this is not your fault."

Vanessa blows her nose, and stares up at her sister. In awe. "I have never heard you say that," she says.

"Well, I guess I'm sorry about that, then. But it's absolutely true. Of all the lies that bastard might have told you to get you right where he wanted to, there were a couple of things he said that made sense, and the biggie for me was that you're a great person, Vanessa, and anyone who really loves you needs to let you know that."

Vanessa falls against her sister now, and the two of them stay that way for a long moment. It is how things have always been, the two girls who protected each other over the years from pains real, imagined, and worse.

"I love you, Vanessa," Larissa tells her. "And you deserve to be happy. You deserve the best. If it didn't work out with this one, well, there's always a reason, and sometimes we don't know that reason until later."

"Do you really believe that?"

"Sure I do. You'll see." Larissa smiles and dabs Vanessa's tears away with a tissue. "There's a great guy out there just for you. You had to get rid of Paul before you'd have room for the good one."

"Who are you?" asks Vanessa. "And what have you done with my sister? She's about yay high, looks like a hippie, she's sort of mean to me when I mess up with men."

"Okay, okay. Come on, ya lush. Now, let's get you home, and into a nice, hot bath, and I'll make you a nice pot of coffee, and then how about we read something fun and inspiring for a while, together, the way we used to do when we were kids?"

"If you really are my sister, your coffee sucks."

"I'll do my best."

"She is a good reader, though," says Vanessa. "My sister? Me and her? We love books."

"I know," says Larissa, slipping Vanessa's jacket over her shoulders and easing her toward the door. "We'll find a nice story, one of our favorites from way back. How's that sound, honey?"

"Nothing romantic, though," says Vanessa.

"Sherlock Holmes?" suggests Larissa.

Vanessa stumbles as Larissa guides her out the door to the back parking lot, toward the red Subaru, and she says, "Dear Watson, I think that's just what I need."

MILK BUBBLES POPPED

Hours later, Vanessa has sobered up slightly. She reclines in a steaming bubble bath, Red Dog sorrowful on the bath mat because she has detected the mood, and absorbed it to her very marrow, as all good dogs will.

Larissa sits on the closed toilet seat, her knees pressed close together so she can balance the book on her knees. She's reading aloud a passage from "The Adventure of the Priory School," in her best British accent, which is paltry at best yet still much better than her coffee. Vanessa sips it intermittently, because she is impressed with Larissa's transformation and seeks to return the generosity in kind.

The phone ringer is off, and they are focused entirely upon

regaining equilibrium and strength for Vanessa, and this is supposed by both to be best achieved through literature, food, and laughter.

Quickly, however, her narration is broken by the agitated baying of the depressed creature on the mat.

"*Aroooo*," wails Red Dog, laboring to her feet, tail wagging meagerly, ears perked.

"Oh, God," says Vanessa, as the knock comes loud from the front door. Red Dog paws at the bathroom door for escape, so she might eviscerate whatever has come to visit them, or at the very least lick it to death.

"You think it's him?" asks Larissa.

"Unless it's FedEx, I don't know who else it could be."

Larissa offers to deal with it, and Vanessa, still a tiny bit dizzy, happily accepts, sliding down lower into the thick foam of scented bubbles and hot water. From beneath the milky suds, she can hear the low tenor of Paul's voice booming through, and getting louder, and then Larissa's own. Bickering. Discussion. It goes on and on, too long, Vanessa thinks. She wants it all to be over. She just wants to disappear for a while, not inhabit this bruised spirit anymore.

Then, Larissa's voice so loud she cannot help but hear it. Right outside the door.

"Paul! You can't go in there. Get out of here!"

Then the knock, and his voice.

"Vanessa. I'm coming in." Then, to Larissa, "Get off me, will ya? Jesus, woman. I'm not going to hurt anybody."

"You already hurt somebody, and that somebody is my sister."

"It's all a misunderstanding. There's a good reason for all of this, if you'd just give me a chance to explain it."

Vanessa sits up a bit, ears out of the water. She says nothing, and before too long, the door opens, and in walk Paul and Larissa, both red in the face, looking like two kids who've been scrapping in the school yard and just got caught by the teacher.

"Well, hello, everyone," says Vanessa with sarcasm. "Why don't we just invite the whole neighborhood over for a show."

Paul is still in his dark green jogging pants and long-sleeved black T-shirt. He says he's been trying to reach her, that he saw the box on the floor of the bedroom, that he figures she's found something that he ought to have told her about a long time ago.

"Gee, ya think?" she asks. Whatever she does, she tells herself she will not cry in front of him. Not again. She is cold to him, dead to him, it's over, she will never let another man into her heart. One good thing about repeated brutalization of the heart is that you get mean.

"Vanessa," says Larissa. "I can call the cops."

Paul looks at Larissa the way the mean girl in school looks at the nerd. Pleads with Vanessa. "Just give me five minutes to explain this. Then I'll go."

"Five minutes," says Vanessa.

"Alone," he says to Larissa.

"No," says Vanessa. "She stays. This woman who is so very like my sister, but somehow completely someone else. She can stay."

Paul does not try to hide his annoyance, but relents to the demand.

"Fine," he says. A patter comes to the roof, and Vanessa realizes it has begun to rain outside.

"Faizah Abdul-Qadar," he begins, "is a friend."

Vanessa laughs bitterly, numb now but sure she will cry this out later. "I figured that much. You're real big on being friends with the women you screw."

"I have never screwed her," he says, as though Vanessa has suggested the man sleeps with his own mother. "I have never touched her, nor would I want to."

"What is she then, some kind of a mail-order bride? Will she be delivered soon?"

Paul struggles to hold a deep breath, ready to explode. He lets his breath out slowly, in a controlled way, so that he can speak. "Vanessa, would you mind just holding off on the accusations until I'm finished, so we can talk about this like civilized people?"

"Please! You're one to talk about civilized! You're married, and you know I have this history of accidentally ending up with married men? You're the uncivilized one here. You're a damn sadist!"

"Please let me finish," he says.

"Talk," she commands, slipping down a bit to hide in the bubbles.

"Okay. Will you listen to what I'm about to tell you?"

"She's listening," says Larissa. Paul snaps his head to Larissa, looks as though he wants to say something off-color to her, but controls himself.

Paul folds his legs beneath him to sit on the white tile floor near Vanessa's bathtub, like a man trying to close in on a rabid animal, close, but careful, and not close enough for her to, say, kick him, or hit him, or bite him. She can't bring herself to look at him, because if she did she would probably start to cry and show weakness, so she looks at the wall in the corner instead, feeling very sorry for herself. The tears come even though she commands them not to. Tears are quite disobedient.

"Listen to me. Okay, Vanessa? Just listen. I told you about that kid, the one I translated for in Iraq," he reminds her. "Remember that? The boy?"

"I don't remember any boy."

"When I bombed that village, and I found out later that the people on the ground were saying it wasn't a munitions-storage facility like they told me. I found out about all this by chance, Vanessa, when they used me to translate this kid's testimony, they were trying to peg him as a terrorist, and he was telling me this story about this place that got bombed, and it was the place I had been sent to, so I went and checked it out and realized I had destroyed a village. I told you about this."

"He destroyed a village?" says Larissa miserably.

"You," Paul tells Larissa. "Could you just can it for a minute until I'm done here?"

"How could you bomb a village?" Larissa asks Paul.

"I didn't know it was a village. I thought it was a munitions-storage facility."

"My God," says Larissa.

Paul turns his attention back to Vanessa. "Do you remember any of this, Vanessa?"

"Yes," she says. "You told me about the village, but I don't remember you telling me about any boy."

"Well, okay. There was a kid, this boy."

Vanessa doesn't move a muscle except to heave through her sobs. Larissa fetches her a washcloth and moves to stand between them, her face interested, but defensive.

Paul continues. "When I went with him to the town I bombed, he took me to meet some of the survivors. Faizah was one of them, Vanessa."

Vanessa glares at him as she imagines him hitting on a woman in a town he bombed. "That's so disgusting," she spits. "Get out of my house."

"It's not what you think. Just listen to me. You can't even imagine, being here, you have no idea what's going on over there, okay?" Paul's own eyes spill with tears now, though none of the rest of his face, body, or voice betray that he is crying.

He says, "Parents abandoning their kids because the kids are full of shrapnel and no one can help them, there's no doctors left in the whole country, Vanessa. Larissa. Both of you. You can't even *begin* to understand what that was like, seeing all these kids just left to die by their families. You see that, and these fuckers over here say 'collateral damage' in their press conferences, and I swear to God, Vanessa, if I didn't do something about it, if I didn't help *one person*, after what they made me do, after what I did, Jesus Christ. Okay?"

Vanessa and Larissa look at each other, the weight of what he has begun to tell them sinking in.

He takes a deep breath, and when Vanessa peeks up at him she sees that his face is red with anger. He keeps talking.

"Faizah had been married, before the bombing, and she had three children, twin baby girls, and an older boy. Her parents were dead, and her husband's parents were dead. When I met her, she was sitting along what was left of the one little road into their village, with her two babies, and whatever she had been able to salvage from their little house, a picture of her husband and another of her boy, and she was lost, Vanessa. She didn't have anything. Her husband and her son were both killed in the bombing. I killed them."

He stops speaking, his voice cracked through with emotion now.

"My God," says Larissa. Vanessa sees on her face that Larissa is seeing Paul differently than she has ever seen him before, because of all this.

Paul takes a moment to compose himself, and continues. "He was a good man, she told me. He was a teacher in the school where her son went. I bombed that school, Vanessa. They told me it was a weapons cache. The intelligence they use, Jesus. I don't know anymore. I don't know if they just didn't know what they were doing, if we were that bad, or if they knew exactly what they were doing and this was Cheney's idea of terrorizing a nation into submission. You stay over there long enough, you see enough of it, you just don't know anymore. It's good those guys are gone."

Now Larissa can't hold back anymore, and they are all three of them crying. Paul keeps talking through his tears, his eyes distant with the horrible memory.

"She was so young, and so resigned to dying. She didn't want to live. I sat with her, and listened to what she had to say, and she told me that there was nothing for her in Iraq now. She was a widow, with twin girls, and even though under Saddam Hussein women had been able to work, she told me that now that the Americans had come to 'liberate' them, the extremists were taking over and would forbid it.

"She was a teacher, too, like her husband, but the new leaders in the town, leaders our own government supported, okay? They told her she had to stop working. She was all alone, with nothing, with her best friend and the love of her life gone, like that, in an instant, and her little boy.

"He was eight, her boy. She was dirty, and her face was streaked with tears, and her shoes were torn up, and she struggled to keep her hair and face covered as much as she could, even though it was a million degrees out, and dusty, and her babies looked lifeless in her lap. I honestly thought they were dead, that she was there holding these dead babies, clinging to life with her little daughters, and thank God that wasn't true. They were alive, but just barely. And I did this to them."

He stops talking again, distant, furious, a boy and a man, a monster and a saint, all in one person, one horribly, terribly tormented person.

"She told me they were hungry, and thirsty, and that they relied on the kindness of strangers to give them food and water, but that now there was no kindness left in the village, where everyone was lost and desperate. She looked at me, and asked me why my country did it, Vanessa.

"She didn't know I was the one who followed the orders to bomb her village. She just asked me why America was doing this to them. She asked me what they had ever done to us, and I couldn't think of an answer. She told me that she would die there, on that road, and I asked her if there was anyone she could call, or find, and she insisted that there was no one, only one relative, a distant cousin, her mother's cousin, who lived in Chicago.

"I came to see her again the next day, and her babies looked worse than before, so I asked her to come with me to the military hospital, and I got her food and clean clothes, and the babies had some milk there.

"She was so forlorn, Vanessa. I already knew by then that I would be leaving active duty in a matter of days. I didn't want to be there anymore, and when I felt like we had a moment without anyone else listening, I told her that I wanted to bring her with me.

"She's a Muslim, and it was hard for her to understand that I wasn't trying to shame her, or to ruin her reputation or her life. Muslims over there, it's nothing like they tell you here. People here have it all wrong about them. They are people, Vanessa, like any other people, and I'm sick and tired of the way we tried to make this some kind of holy war against them. So many of the guys I worked with in that damn war told me they were doing it for Christ or something stupid like that. Sometimes, I swear we'd all just be better off without religion.

"Anyway, I explained to her that it was the only thing I could do, the only way to get her out of that hell, I could marry her in paper only, to get her here, and I would help her find her uncle, and I would find a place where she would be able to work as a teacher or whatever else she wanted to do. It was the least I could do, I told her, and I confessed to her that it was me who bombed her village, and I swore to her that it was the worst thing I had ever done, that I was following orders, but that I could not do it anymore, that they were lying to me as surely as they were lying to her.

"She thought about this for a number of days, while she gathered her strength, and I know that she did not want to do it, that there was a part of her that felt this was the ultimate betrayal of her husband, but she also knew that there was nothing left for her daughters in Iraq anymore, and that the only thing she could do as a mother was to take this path I offered her, out of there.

"I found her a place to rent, and paid for it, and we set about creating an illusion that she lived with me in my house out there, with kids rooms and the whole deal, Vanessa, that we were a couple, but we never were.

"And we were married, in the Green Zone, by an American imam, and then a priest, and I was granted permission to bring her back with me. She did not say a single word on the flight back. She just stared out the window with those babies in her lap, and she was watching the world leave her, and she cried without making a noise. She had to leave her son's body there, without her to care for his spirit, she told me later. She felt that was the worst thing a mother could do, leave her child's spirit to wander the earth alone. I had to tell her he had his father, and that his spirit would find her no matter where she was."

Vanessa looks at him now, and tries to discern whether he is making all of this up. He looks sincere. In fact, he appears to be devastated.

"How can we be sure what you're telling us is true?" asks Larissa.

"She's in Seattle still," he says. "She has to stay there, in my house, for at least a year, so that we don't raise suspicions. That's another reason I'm living with my mom here. So I can still convince people I'm living out there with Faizah. If I bought another house, in my own name, out here, right now, there might be suspicion."

"So that's why you keep going back there."

"No. I really *am* a reservist, and I have to go back to do training flights. But it's good that I go back so that I can take her with me to the base and we can try to convince people. Keep up the illusion."

"And you didn't think to *tell* me any of this?" Vanessa rages.

"I know. I should have. But, it's just—Vanessa. I love you. And I've loved you since the first time you insulted me outside your mom's. I've never known a woman like you. When you told me about your pattern, the thing with the married men, I just didn't want to risk messing things up by telling you about Faizah and her girls.

"I wanted us to get to that naturally, when it felt right. I also— you have to understand that this isn't something we can just go around telling people, you know? If word got out that it was a sham marriage, it could be really bad for them. They'd send Faizah back, and that would be the end of her because she had married me. They'd kill her there, for marrying me.

"We have to be married at least two years for her to get her citizenship. After that, she's golden, and we divorce and she goes to Chicago to be with her relative, and we're on our way. And, hopefully, those kids grow up without a need or a want in the rest of their lives. I'm going to make sure they have everything their father would have wanted for them, Vanessa."

Larissa dabs her eyes, and slowly backs toward the door, and steps out to leave them alone, probably as humiliated by her assumptions about Paul as Vanessa is right now.

"I'll call you later," she says before she leaves. "I think you've got this under control here."

"Bye, Larissa," says Paul sarcastically. "Always a pleasure to see you."

"Likewise, Paul," she jabs back, and then is gone.

"Great," Vanessa says. "This is just great."

She dissolves again in tears, imagining Paul playing husband with some unknown woman. "I'm in love with an unavailable man. Even if your intentions were good."

"Vanessa, please be reasonable. It's not a real marriage. It's the only way I could think of to rescue someone whose entire life I destroyed. Can't you understand that?"

"If it's true, it's very gallant of you. But if it's not true—"

"Tell me what I need to do to convince you," he says. "You think I could make something like this up, right here on the spot? Jesus, V!"

"Take me to meet her," she says, drying her eyes with the washcloth. "I want to talk to her. I want to hear you tell this woman, in front of me, that you love me, and I want to hear her side of the story, without any coaching from you."

Paul claps his hands together with finality and says, "Done. Easy. The restaurant opening is this weekend, right?"

"Yeah."

"So we have to go tomorrow."

"Yes."

Paul stands up, and asks if he can use her computer. She says yes.

"Awesome," Paul says. "I'll get the tickets right now. We'll go tomorrow. Pack your stuff, pretty neighbor lady. I'm taking you to meet my wife."

LAMB OF PEACE

They fly on Southwest Airlines, which is a relief because you get to pick your own seat. Vanessa is still angry enough with Paul that she chooses a seat far from him, in the back of the plane. He thinks she is being unreasonable, but is patient with her anyway. He tells her that if she's still acting like this after he proves her wrong, she will deserve a spanking. He promises to spank her regardless. She does not respond to this.

The flight takes a little more than three hours, and once they've landed in the unfathomably green and blue place that is Seattle, on an unusually sunny winter day, Paul drags her through the airport and gets them a rental car, a Hyundai Sonata. Vanessa continues to pout. He thinks she is pouting because she has low blood sugar, but she knows better. She is pouting because he is Paul, and Paul is married. Even if it is not a real marriage, it is still a real marriage. He suggests she find some humor in it, but as yet she can find no such thing.

He takes Vanessa to a French restaurant in a funky part of town, hoping to calm her down, or lighten her up, or any combination of those two things, telling her that it is his favorite place for salad, which inspires her to avoid the salad in principle.

Instead, Vanessa orders confit of Muscovy duck leg. Paul laughs at her with sorrowful eyes, his patience wearing thin, as he digs into his salad with walnuts and goat cheese.

"You're going to regret treating me like this," he assures her. "It might not be in the next few minutes, but it will happen today."

"You're so sure of that."

"Yes, I am."

They don't talk much, or at all really, for the rest of the meal. And then, they leave.

It turns out that Paul's house in Seattle is actually quite a bit farther north of the city, in a town called Anacortes. Two hours later, after Paul makes a call on his cell phone to tell Faizah that they are gong to be there shortly, they pull into the driveway of a spectacular modern-style wooden home, with a wall of windows overlooking a large and beautiful lake.

"This is your little house in Seattle?" she asks.

"The one and only."

"It's not little, and it's not in Seattle."

He laughs.

"You should start being more honest with me."

"I'll try," he assures her. "Let's go in."

By now, Paul is just as happy to not talk to her as she has been miserably silent with him. He's had enough, and this makes Vanessa start to believe that what he has told her is true. This marriage of his must be exactly as he has described it. *Either that*, she thinks as they walk up the stairs to the front door, past potted flowers along the hillside, *or he's brought me here to kill me.*

Paul is all business. He stomps up the wooden steps first. He has not opened her door for her, as is his usual way. He's pissed, and if what he has told her is true, she does not exactly blame him.

Though he owns the house, he knocks on the front door three times, without looking at Vanessa, his head tilted down and his heels lifting up and down with nerves and anxiousness and, she assumes, infuriation.

Moments later, a young woman with sad, dark eyes opens the door, a black scarf over her hair. She wears jeans, with a black top and a scarf wrapped around her shoulders, and she holds a baby. She is short, and pale, and thin, not all that pretty, but not unattractive, either.

Vanessa knows, the moment that she sees this woman and the way she greets Paul—with a mixture of dread and gratitude—that what he has told Vanessa about Faizah is true.

Paul ushers Vanessa in, and closes the door before any words are exchanged. Then, after a brief polite greeting is exchanged, he gets right to the point.

"Faizah," he says matter-of-factly, "this is my girlfriend, Vanessa."

Faizah smiles uncomfortably at Vanessa, and invites them to sit on the sofa in the living room. Vanessa is awed by the grandeur and beauty of this spectacular home, similar in some respects to the cabin in New Mexico. It is a house you might see in an architectural magazine.

The room smells of rice cooking, and some sort of spices, tea maybe. Lamb? That's what it is. Lamb stewing. Another baby sleeps in a little swing that moves back and forth with the help of a small, quiet motor. Toys are scattered around.

They sit, and Paul begins to speak to Faizah in Arabic. Vanessa has never heard him speak the language, and his fluency astonishes her. It's like seeing him for the first time, again.

Faizah listens to whatever he says, and her eyes flash over to look at Vanessa every now and then, to let her know that they are discussing her. Vanessa can tell by the way Paul and Faizah talk to one another, by their body language, that there is nothing between them. She had thought to ask Paul to leave the room, so that she could speak to Faizah alone, but doesn't feel this necessary now.

When he's done, Paul turns to Vanessa, and tells her that he has explained the whole situation to his "wife."

"How do I know you're telling me the truth? I don't speak Arabic."

"He tells truth," the woman tells Vanessa. "I speak a little bit English. Paul and me, we married only for paper to get me here. We tell not anybody this. I cannot return to Iraq. Please you to understand."

Vanessa looks at Faizah's eyes. There is nothing deceptive about them. There is nothing loving in the way of a man and a woman between these two. What is there? Anguish deeper than anything Vanessa has ever known.

Faizah goes to another room and returns with the photos of her husband and her son that Paul had told Vanessa about, and she weeps as she shows them to Vanessa, and tells her how much she misses them.

The man in the photos is happy, young, smiling, and the boy is sparkly, with crooked teeth and spiky hair.

Paul changes the subject and asks her how she is doing. She says she is fine, and tells them that she is taking English classes twice a week, and that she has made some friends, other women who speak Arabic, and that they have begun to get together once a week with their children and families.

She tells Paul that life is good here, and she thanks him again for what he has done, but he does not want thanks. He tells her it is not enough, that what he does will never be enough because he can never give back what he took from her, and she tells him that she has forgiven him because forgiveness is the only way any of us move on.

She takes a book from the side table and gives it to Paul, says it is for him, that she has been reading it. It is a book about forgiveness, by Desmond Tutu, in Arabic translation.

Faizah tells Paul in her halting English, for Vanessa's benefit, that he was only doing what his country told him to do, and that she understands he did not know when he did it that he was killing civilians. There is no way he could have known, she says. Paul tells her in slow English she is an incredible woman, and stronger than anyone he has ever known. And he begins to cry again.

"I'm sorry," Vanessa tells him, and in it, in her voice, in her facial expression, is the clear message that she knows he has been honest with her.

"I told you you'd feel bad about treating me bad," he jokes.

Vanessa looks at Faizah, and tells her that her secret is safe with them. Faizah thanks Vanessa, and the baby she holds, who is awake, looks at Vanessa with her big, dark eyes, and she smiles, healthy, happy, blissfully unaware of the origins of her life, of the sacrifices her mother has made to bring her here.

"Faizah," says Paul, in slow English so that she and Vanessa both understand what he is saying. "I came here today to tell you that I love this woman, Vanessa, and that, if she will have me, I want to marry her."

Vanessa gasps. This was not planned for. She certainly did not expect it.

Faizah watches Vanessa gasping like a fish out of water, and a smile crosses her face, a smile of understanding and womanly kinship. She covers her mouth with her hand, and she giggles.

Paul produces a ring from his pocket, and gets on his knee, holds it out to Vanessa. He laughs at himself, and then he says, "This is so weird, right? I'm here with my wife, proposing to another woman."

"You'd think we were in Utah," says Vanessa.

Faizah does not seem to understand, and looks to Paul in confusion. "I'll explain it to you later," he tells her.

Turning his attention back to Vanessa, he says, "I know this sounds crazy. I know it's probably the single worst proposal of all time. But I want to know. If you can wait another thirty months or so, until Faizah and I get divorced, will you be willing to marry me then?"

Vanessa looks at Faizah, and she has tears in her eyes. She nods at her, as if giving her blessing, and tells Vanessa it would be a relief to her to know that this man who has suffered so much for his sins would have some comfort and companionship in his life.

"We all deserve to be happy," says Faizah.

Astonished, Vanessa struggles for a moment to find words, but when she does find them, they are very straightforward and easy to understand.

"You," she says to the woman, "are the most remarkable woman I have ever met. And your 'husband' here is the most remarkable man. So, yes, I would be happy to marry him."

Paul laughs his usual Paul laugh. "Man, that sounds weird," he says.

Faizah asks them to stay for dinner, and serves the lamb with eggplant on a table overlooking the lake at sunset. Vanessa is amazed to discover she likes the dish very much, amazed that the vegetable so long considered an enemy actually feels and tastes just right upon her tongue. She asks for the recipe, and realizes it's all in the preparation of a thing, in the reaction under duress.

At last, she thinks, she has found a reason to love the unlikable thing she has long overlooked in the garden, the thing she had tolerated, but written off, the excellent, unusual thing, with great potential that she had never taken the time to get to know well enough to allow it into her life. She looks across the table at Paul, and smiles. The one. There is no question left in her mind.

A man like a good bacon? Not so, after all. Turns out it has been a man like a well-handled eggplant she's been after all along.